The Wild Card

The Wild Card

Beth Elliott

ROBERT HALE · LONDON

ISBN 978-0-7090-8524-9

Robert Hale Limited
Clerkenwell House
Clerkenwell Green
London EC1R 0HT

www.halebooks.com

2 4 6 8 10 9 7 5 3 1

Typeset in 11½/14pt Palatino
by Derek Doyle & Associates, Shaw Heath
Printed and bound in Great Britain
by Biddles Limited, King's Lynn

For Marion and Seyda,
my research companions

CHAPTER ONE

It was so hard, thought Kitty as she sped down the gravel drive towards the side door of the Rectory, running to do the thing she absolutely did not want to do. She pressed a hand to her side to ease the stitch. She had hurried all the way from the hospital, but even so she was late and her mother would be displeased. She dived through the door and pushed it to behind her. It slammed and she bit her lip, rushing on to the small parlour where her mother would be sewing.

'Kitty, I have been waiting for you for over an hour! And just look at you – bursting into the room like a hoyden.' Mrs Towers folded up the shirt she was hemming and rose. 'No doubt it was you who slammed the door just now.'

Kitty was too breathless to reply. She tried to smile at her mother but saw with a pang of dismay that Mrs Towers was frowning at the tangle of chestnut curls as her daughter pushed back her hood.

'I am truly sorry, Mama,' panted Kitty at last, pulling off her wet boots. 'I did intend to get back on time, but just as I was leaving the hospital a wretchedly sick girl was brought in, so Papa needed my help with her.'

'It is too bad of him to use you so,' frowned Mrs Towers.

'Oh, no, you know how much I enjoy the work. So many poor and needy folk. And now we are getting more and more crippled soldiers. They are destitute, starving – after all their bravery fighting in this dreadful war. . . .'

'Your kindness and courage do you credit, my dear,' said her mother, 'but there will always be crippled soldiers, needy people. You cannot help them all. Indeed, Kitty, you must think of your own prospects in life.'

Kitty was arranging her dripping cloak over the back of a chair near the fire, but at these words she looked up in alarm. 'I cannot believe how quickly this moment has come. I really am not ready for it,' she protested, 'it feels as if you are sending me into the lion's den.'

Her mother shook her head in reproof. 'My dear, we have discussed all this. It is very unkind to describe Great-aunt Picton as a lion. And Grosvenor Square is hardly the lion's den! You are nineteen years of age and it is high time you were established.' She held up a hand to check the hot reply that Kitty was about to make. 'You will soon forget your nerves when you go into society, I assure you. Come now, we must make haste.' She led the way upstairs to Kitty's bedroom.

Here a trunk lay open in the middle of the floor. Kitty's eyes were still smouldering as she surveyed the dresses, linen and scarves laid out on the bed and chairs.

'Quickly, my dear, I cannot spare much time.' Mrs Towers at once began folding and packing the freshly laundered gowns. Kitty watched her for a minute. Was her mother so eager to get rid of her? Reluctantly, she set to work as well. How quickly her possessions were piling up in the trunk. It felt as if she was being turned out of her home. Her heart swelled with anger. The work she did in the hospital was so much more worthwhile than an idle society life in London.

And it was quite in vain to send her! She had long ago made up her mind never to marry unless she fell deeply in love with a young man who loved her equally in return. The dress she was folding slipped out of her fingers. With an impatient sigh she snatched it up and shook it before starting to fold it again. She grimaced. Of course, eligible and wealthy men never were young and handsome. And she would not sell herself just to gain a home. This was all a complete waste of time and money.

She shook back her chestnut curls and looked up. 'Did your mother send you up to London for a season to catch a husband?'

Her mother frowned. 'What a vulgar expression! No, she did not – you know very well that your father and I became acquainted at the assemblies in Chester. And even though he was a younger son, my parents could see he was the perfect husband for me.'

'So why must I go to London, to a great-aunt I do not even know? You of all people know, Mama, that I do not yearn for balls and expensive gowns – just a decent life with time to help those who need it.' There was a distinct tremor in Kitty's voice. Mrs Towers laid down the dress she was folding and came to take both her daughter's hands in her own.

'When I met your papa, we were young and full of ideals.' In spite of herself, Mrs Towers smiled. 'And he was so very handsome. However, what we did is not what I want for you, my dear. I must speak plainly. Your papa is not very worldly wise. Certainly, as a vicar, he is admired and respected for his good work ... but. ...' She walked over to the window and stared out at the dull February day. With her back to Kitty, she carried on, 'I do not want you to have to scrimp and save all through your life. There are seven of you children, Kitty, and all growing up fast. Our income can only stretch so far. It is your duty to make a good match. You cannot put it off any longer.'

'But, Mama, I am not at all ready for such a step ... there is so much work to do in the hospital; Papa needs me. ...'

Her mother sighed and took Kitty by the arm. She led her over to the mirror. 'Look.' She gestured at the reflection. 'You are young, with those glorious brown eyes, so like your father's; you have a beautiful complexion, a lovely slender neck and perfect white shoulders. You do deserve to be seen in the best circles.'

Kitty shook her head mutinously.

'Of course,' Mrs Towers went on, 'if you had shown a preference for any young man here – but our local society is very small.' She laid her cheek next to Kitty's and pointed to the mirror once again. 'Look at me, my dear, the years pass – more quickly than you think.'

'Oh, Mama!' Kitty threw her arms round her mother's neck. 'You will always be beautiful to us.'

Her mother shook her head. She looked Kitty straight in the eye and carried on with a little difficulty, 'A comfortable income is a necessity. Believe me, love will flourish better when you do not live in a constant worry about bills.' She picked up the dress she had folded and laid it in the trunk. 'That is why I wrote to your Great-aunt Picton. Now you have this one chance to spend some time in society. It is the only way for you to meet an eligible gentleman.'

Kitty swallowed a lump in her throat. Before she could speak, her mother added, 'It was certainly one care removed when she consented to my proposal. It wasn't easy to approach her after—' She stopped abruptly, coughed, then added hastily, 'After so many years without any contact. But she seemed quite pleased at the idea of having you to stay with her. And I am sure you understand that it depends very much on you whether your little sisters can have a decent opportunity in life.'

In the face of her mother's dreams, it was difficult to protest any more. She made one last attempt. 'Yes, Mama, but this is not a good time for me to go away. You really need my help now Charlie has broken his leg.'

A shadow passed over Mrs Towers' face. 'Thank heavens it was just a clean break. Whatever made him think he could ride Freddy's new brute of a hunter? I dread to think what he will try next.'

'Oh, Mama.' Kitty enfolded her in a hug. 'Do not fret, he will soon be well again. And at least he cannot get into mischief for a while. But it is an extra burden for you. Well, I won't say any more, although it is hardly going to be a glamorous come-out, is it?'

Mrs Towers smiled wryly. 'We certainly cannot compete with Amelia's preparations. If I know Mrs Warrington, she will have trunks full of the most splendid dresses for her daughter to go to London.'

'Oh, yes – and the sad truth is that Amelia is not even looking forward to it all. She is much too shy to relish going among strangers.'

'She depends far too much on you, Kitty. Amelia will never learn to manage while you are there to speak for her. A spell in Town should be the making of her. I am sure Mrs Warrington must hope so. No doubt she cherishes dreams of a splendid match for Amelia – and with those looks it is quite possible she will get many brilliant offers. . . .' She smoothed down the top garment in the trunk and smiled up at her daughter. 'Indeed, you are a very striking pair and should have a great success in town. Mrs Warrington will surely include you in some of their outings. Take every opportunity to enjoy what you can, my love.'

She looked around the room and gave a sigh of relief. 'Well, that seems to be everything. Now, bring me the tissue paper, if you please.' She held up the taffeta ball dress and smiled triumphantly. 'You will look lovely in this, Kitty. The sea-green colour is exactly right for you. I must say I am very pleased with the lace trimming. You have done it beautifully.'

They had just placed the dress carefully in the trunk when the door opened. In came a younger version of Kitty, her glossy brown ringlets cascading over her shoulders. Sophia stared enviously at the trunk. 'Mama, Charlie is reading. He told me I might leave him in peace,' she explained, before her mother could reproach her. 'He says his leg is not paining him and he will be glad of some food shortly.'

'Very good,' said Mrs Towers. 'You can help your sister to tidy up this room. It is high time I went to see what the children are doing.' She hurried out and Sophia pulled a little

11

package out of her sleeve. She unwrapped it, revealing some lengths of pink satin ribbon, which she held up against Kitty's chestnut curls.

'Yes, I thought these would look pretty on you,' she said. 'Why aren't you in raptures? How I wish *I* was going to London.'

'What, to stay with a crabby old great-aunt we have never even met? It is very sweet of you to give me these ribbons, Sophy, but I wonder if I will even need them.' Kitty pulled a face and sighed.

But fifteen-year-old Sophy refused to be daunted. 'You are bound to meet lots of new people,' she insisted. 'Even great-aunts have friends and neighbours. And Amelia will be there—'

'Oh, heavens! I promised to be at Amelia's house by three o'clock. I can just about manage to get there in time.' Kitty glanced down at her plain green gown and smoothed the skirts. 'This is fresh enough for a tea party at Millie's. Quick, Sophy, while I wash my face, be a dear and fetch me your boots – mine are soaking wet. I suppose it is still raining?' She wiped her hands and face, thrust her feet into the boots and rushed for the door.

Sophy gave a squeal of outrage. 'You cannot go out looking such a fright. Come here, do.' She applied a hairbrush vigorously and smoothed Kitty's tangles into ringlets. 'There,' she said, releasing her at last. 'Now you look elegant.'

Kitty stopped long enough to kiss her sister's cheek. 'You are the elegant one in this family. Thank you.' After checking that it was, indeed, still drizzling, she sped down the stairs and shrugged into her hooded cape. It was only a short walk from the vicarage to the large new mansion that was Amelia's home.

She made her way along the road, leaping over the puddles and taking in deep breaths of the rain-chilled air. The trees were still black and bare but the grass was green and the first catkins showed in the hedgerows. Kitty gave a sigh. Life in London was going to be difficult for someone used to the open spaces and the freedom of country life.

'I will only stay for two months,' she muttered rebelliously, 'and that is certainly not long enough to find a husband.'

CHAPTER TWO

'Going away?' echoed Lord Frederick Lynsford. He stared in disbelief at the two young ladies on the sofa in front of him. Chestnut curls and blonde ringlets bobbed as they both nodded.

'Surely, Freddy, you must know that Amelia is going to London for the season. Why, she has been preparing since the summer.' Kitty looked reproachfully at their childhood friend. He had not changed much in spite of his modish appearance, she thought.

Lord Frederick swallowed. 'Well, yes – s'pose so – but surely not before our rout party next week? Why, I've come especially to solicit the honour of a dance with each of you.' He gave an apologetic grin and ran a hand through his carefully disordered curls. One lock of sandy hair flopped on to his brow. His eyes were on Amelia, who gave him her usual sweet smile.

'Thank you, Freddy. It is most kind, but it will not be possible. We will be leaving very soon.' She looked towards her mama, seated near the fire in conversation with Freddy's mother. Lady Lynsford watched keenly as Amelia's mother put down her teacup and turned to the young people.

'We depart on Monday,' she informed them. 'Mr Warrington feels we should take advantage of the present mild weather.' She turned back to Lady Lynsford, adding, 'February weather is so unpredictable. Of course, he only plans to see us settled into the house we have taken in Green

Street before he hurries back home. It is unfortunate, but with this war against the French continuing, he says his presence is needed at the manufactories.'

Watching this exchange, Kitty discerned a flicker of relief on Lady Lynsford's face. She glanced quickly at Freddy. His disappointment was genuine. It was for sure, thought Kitty, that he was becoming strongly attracted to Amelia. She smiled to herself, remembering their childhood squabbles when Freddy and her brother, Charlie, had scorned to let the girls join in their adventures. It had always been Caroline, Freddy's sister, who had resolved the quarrels and dried the tears.

Now Caroline was married and living in London. In the past year, Freddy had taken over the running of his large estate and was so busy that they hardly saw him except at the monthly assemblies in Chester, or the occasional dancing parties in their small neighbourhood. He had always been an amiable person and a little shy. Not surprising, thought Kitty, living with two such determined ladies as his mother and his elder sister.

Lady Lynsford was the daughter of an earl and very conscious of her aristocratic background. She had found a wealthy and titled husband for Caroline. And now it seemed that she was determined to find a titled bride for Freddy. Although she accepted her children's lifelong friendship with Amelia Warrington, it was plain she considered the family to be socially inferior because their money came from trade. This made Kitty very angry for her friend.

Gentle Amelia was as talented as she was beautiful and quite without vanity. Although she was always the centre of attention at dancing parties, she treated all the young gentlemen with modest politeness and shrank from so much admiration. She never made any comment on any of her swains. She was most comfortable in the company of her close friends and family.

However, in spite of their youthful squabbles, since her early childhood, she had shared a love of horses and hunting

15

with Freddy. This meant that they often rode out together, but, while it was plain to Kitty that Freddy now eagerly sought Amelia's company, she could not tell whether Amelia felt any special degree of affection for him beyond a sort of brother and sister-like ease. This was the one area where Amelia stubbornly kept her own counsel.

Now Freddy was saying, 'It's a dashed shame you should have to miss next week's hunt as well – and just to go to London!' He shook his head and sighed. Amelia nodded but said nothing.

How discreet she is, thought Kitty – surely she understands his meaning?

At this point Kitty realized he was speaking to them both. 'You'll visit m'sister, I s'pose?' As they assured him they would, his mother rose to take her leave.

'It seems no time at all since we took dear Caroline to London. She was a great hit! So many suitors' – she swelled with pride – 'but once she met Lord William Bannister, her mind was made up. And now she leads a life of high fashion. Well, you girls must be so excited. I wish you both a very successful stay in London,' she pronounced, with a meaningful look.

And that was a hint to Amelia, thought Kitty, trying to smile politely as she curtsied. 'I must be going as well,' she added out loud, when the door had shut on the visitors.

'Are all your preparations made?' enquired Mrs Warrington, settling herself near the window and picking up her sewing.

Kitty assured her that her trunk was packed. 'It has been quite difficult, ma'am, especially with poor Charlie breaking his leg. And then my father is busy with so many war-wounded returning home and needing help. My mother has had such a lot to do, I feel I should stay here to help her, but she refuses to hear of it.'

'Oh, I could not face the thought of going to London without you, Kitty.' Amelia turned pale at the idea.

Her mother frowned a little. 'You will soon change your

ideas, my love, when you get caught up in the round of parties and entertainments.' She turned to Kitty. 'We have to remember that Kitty will be the guest of her great-aunt and may not have very much time to spare for us.'

Amelia looked dismayed and Mrs Warrington added, 'Take Kitty up to see the new dresses that were sent home this morning. Susan will have unpacked them by now.'

The two girls raced up to the large dressing-room on the first floor. Kitty stopped short in the doorway. 'Good gracious, Millie! It is like a modiste's shop in here!' She looked from one muslin gown to another, then at the silk dresses hanging in the open wardrobe. The table and even the floor was littered with bandboxes. Bonnets, gloves, scarves and bags covered all the available surfaces.

'Well, you should certainly cause a stir in all this finery.'

Amelia's shoulders drooped. 'I would rather stay here,' she whispered. 'I much prefer to be amongst people I know. It seems ungrateful when Mama has gone to so much trouble, but it is her wish that I go to London, not mine.'

'That makes two of us, then, for you know how strongly I object to the business of trying to catch a rich husband.' Kitty gestured towards all the garments waiting to be packed. 'We must be the only girls in all England who are so unwilling to live a life of parties and excursions and . . . and set ourselves out like merchandise for the young men to choose from.'

Amelia nodded, her china-blue eyes solemn. 'That is exactly the problem. I cannot bear the thought of being scrutinized like a horse in the market. All the grand ladies inspecting us and on the watch for the smallest fault. It is bad enough with Lady Lynsford – that hawk-like stare of hers. When she looks down her nose she makes me feel like a little girl caught out in something naughty.'

'She is a formidable matron,' agreed Kitty, 'but she was just the same with Caroline.'

Amelia's face brightened. 'Oh, that is one comfort. We will be able to visit her. I am sure she will find time for us. And now she has a dear little baby as well. It will be so pleasant to have someone from home down there.' She looked around the room and sighed. 'It seems I shall be spending most of my time changing my clothes. Morning dresses, walking dresses, evening gowns. . . .'

Kitty moved over to the wardrobe. 'This is really exquisite.' She indicated an evening dress of ivory silk, so soft it felt like a caress. The neckline and hem were embroidered with rows of tiny sparkling beads. She smiled at Amelia. 'You will certainly be the belle of the ball when you wear this. It is quite perfect for your delicate colouring. Make up your mind to it, Millie, if you have to be part of this courting game, you must be the best.'

'No, that role is for you,' protested Amelia with a gurgle of laughter. Kitty swept a deep curtsy, fluttered an imaginary fan and sailed out of the room.

CHAPTER THREE

'The whole courtyard is completely white now,' Kitty informed the Warringtons. She was standing at the window of the private parlour of the coaching house where they had taken refuge, looking out at the whirling snow.

'We were fortunate to arrive before the inn filled up,' Mr Warrington remarked. The landlord tells me that when snow comes in these parts it can last for several days. You girls will have to wait a bit longer for your first ball.' He looked from one to the other over the top of his reading glasses.

'At the moment, sir, we're very glad to be warm and dry.'

'And not struggling along, wondering if the horses could pull the coach up the next hill,' put in Amelia. 'How much further is it to London, Papa?'

He put down the letter he was reading. 'We are at Streatley, so from here we should reach London in the day – if the roads are clear.'

'I cannot believe that any travellers are still out in this weather. They must all have sought shelter from such a blizzard.' Kitty was just turning away from the window when a movement under the archway caught her eye. 'No, I do believe there is one more.' She peered at the darker shapes behind the thickly falling snow. 'Oh, dear. He is on foot – and limping badly. And his horse is lame, poor thing. The groom seems all right, though.'

The man went straight to the stables. Kitty imagined the fuss that would be made over the horse's injury. What about the man's lame leg? She smiled, thinking of how she would help if he were a patient in her father's hospital. But no doubt this man had just bruised himself on the icy road. She was still staring out absently when gradually she realized that the gentleman was battling across the yard towards the inn door. His left leg was dragging as he waded through the snow.

Kitty blinked and looked again. She saw a lean face with dark, straight brows. He was tall and even though he was muffled in a long, caped riding coat, she judged him to be well built. Suddenly she realized that he was looking directly at her from under those black brows. Kitty blushed and whisked herself away from the window. But the image of a remarkably handsome young man stayed in front of her eyes.

'What has made you leap away?' Amelia was watching her with an eager smile.

Kitty shook her head. 'Nothing.' She knew her friend was not deceived, but this time she was not prepared to describe the incident. Something was different here. Kitty had never felt so drawn to a man before. She was almost angry with herself being bewitched by a total stranger. For the first time, she began to understand why the young men flocked so helplessly round Amelia.

Mrs Warrington was seated close to the fire, shivering. 'I fear I have taken cold,' she said. 'Would you girls go up to our bedchambers and ask Susan to put a hot brick in my bed? I shall go and lie down shortly.'

The girls hurried to the door. As they mounted the stairs Amelia asked again, 'What was it, Kitty? What made you blush? That is not like you.'

Kitty put a hand to her lips. 'It was so strange. But wait until we can be private – oh!' She stopped short.

A gentleman had drawn back to let them reach the upper landing. Kitty recognized the young man from the courtyard. Close to, he was even taller than he had appeared from a distance. Kitty eagerly inspected his appearance. She noted the many capes on his riding coat and his shining topboots. Here was a real town beau, but behind the fashionable clothes she could detect the strength of a splendidly built man.

His lean, tanned face with its high cheekbones and firm jaw was extremely handsome. But his eyes were narrowed and his expression was grim. She was just dwelling on his straight, dark eyebrows and aquiline nose when she felt a pinch. Amelia was prodding her to make her move on.

'Thank you,' said both girls together, as they reached the top step. The gentleman inclined his head rather absently. Kitty wished he would not affect this exaggerated unconcern. She sensed an energy and power in him that fascinated her. In addition, his physical beauty was having the kind of effect on her that she had always scorned when her friends swooned over the young men at the assemblies.

They passed on towards their rooms, Kitty with a burning face and Amelia trying hard not to giggle. Susan was already unpacking her mistress's night things so they went into the next chamber. Amelia's blue eyes sparkled.

'If you could see yourself.'

'I have no wish to do so.' Kitty pressed her hands to her hot cheeks. 'What came over me?'

'I know what came over you; he was handsome – in spite of his gloomy air.'

'I expect anyone would feel gloomy after twisting their leg and injuring their horse.'

'Yes, dear Kitty,' added Amelia with a twinkle. 'You know all the young men at home consider that your heart is made of marble. How bizarre that one glimpse of a handsome stranger should make such a strong impression on you. Your mother was right to send you to London.' She dodged the cushion Kitty threw at her and laughed. 'Why, Kitty, I would have thought it impossible for your cheeks to get any redder than they were a minute ago!'

*

There could be no question of continuing their journey the following morning. When asked for his opinion, the landlord had informed Mr Warrington that it was likely the snow had drifted during the night.

'The last person to arrive were young Mr Weston – he comes by now and then and he knows the road well. But even he took a fall on the ice. Hurt his bad leg, he did, sir, an' his horse slipped as well. When it sets in like this, it be two to three days before the roads is safe to travel. Why, we've not seen even the mail coach come through – that just shows you, sir.'

'So, my dears, you will have to resign yourselves to a couple of days of inactivity. We are tolerably comfortable and warm in here.'

'Poor Papa,' Amelia put an arm affectionately round his shoulders. 'You have no newspaper.'

'No matter. I have plenty of letters to write.'

'In that case, as Mama is still resting, Kitty and I will take a short walk round the courtyard.'

Already concentrating on the first letter, Mr Warrington nodded abstractedly. As they put on their outdoor clothes, Amelia laughed. 'How easily we escaped. Mama would have been more difficult to persuade. Now come on, I am hoping for another chance meeting with your handsome gentleman.'

'This is very different from your usual attitude, Millie.' Kitty looked up from pulling on her boots. 'You are always so sweet and polite to all the young men who flock around you at assemblies, but you never show the least sign of interest in any of them. I had quite decided that you felt it to be a subject you would never discuss. And you tell me that I am hard-hearted,' she added, brushing her skirt down and pulling on her cloak.

Amelia finished buttoning up her pelisse before she answered. 'Well, there are always so many of them,' she said slowly. 'It is difficult to know if they want to dance with me out of admiration for my fair hair, or because they know my father is wealthy. If I were cross-eyed and spotty and they still offered to dance with me, we would know the answer.'

They both giggled at this idea.

'Yes, but have you never been really attracted to any man in particular?' persisted Kitty.

'Not among those we meet at the assemblies. Maybe I shall lose my heart to some dashing London rake. Pray hurry, Kitty, let us go outside before Mama sends for us. I really do feel the need for some exercise.'

They crept out of the bedroom and downstairs. As they emerged into the yard, Kitty felt a strange reluctance. She did so want to see the gentleman again, but not under Millie's observant gaze.

What is wrong with me? she thought crossly, I have only seen him twice and I find his face so attractive that here I am behaving like a silly schoolgirl. This has never happened to me before.

A path had been cleared in the yard and the girls walked briskly around it a few times.

'Shall we take a look at the state of the road?' suggested Kitty. 'Although indeed, I do not think we will stir from here today.'

They ventured under the archway and looked around at a hushed, white world. On the skyline, dark clouds threatened. The countryside sloped down to the river, a dark and winding line in the general whiteness. The coach road was hard to make out, just a dip between the trees and hedgerows. Close by, the snow was trodden down on the track leading to the centre of the village. Smoke was rising from the chimneys of a cluster of cottages nearby but nobody was about.

'How silent it is. Everyone is sitting close to their fire.' Amelia looked up at the heavy clouds. 'And I can see why. I fear there is more snow to come any minute. Oh, Kitty, we might be here for a week.'

'How could we bear being cooped up for so long,' groaned Kitty, as they turned back into the inn yard. 'No walks, no rides.'

A few flakes of snow sprinkled their faces as they set off again around their path. Kitty pulled the hood of her cape closer around her face. 'The wind is biting at my cheeks,' she said. As she tucked her hands deeper into her muff, the snow spilled down again. Laughing, they began to run. Then, as they reached the coach house an idea struck Kitty.

'I shall go and get my book out of the chaise. It seems there will be plenty of time for reading.'

Amelia giggled. 'Depend upon it, Mama will have lots of sewing to keep us occupied.'

A shrill voice called from an upstairs window. Susan was waving to them to come inside.

'You go,' urged Kitty. 'I will just get my book before I come in.' She darted off on the words and pushed open the heavy door into the high, gloomy coach house. She soon found the Warringtons' chaise. Without bothering to let the step down she climbed in and pulled the door shut to search in the pocket. Why had she stuffed so many things in here? With a sigh, Kitty pulled out the various items, set her novel on the seat and started putting the other things back more neatly. That done, she was about to climb down when someone spoke right behind the coach. Kitty froze, not wanting to be discovered there all alone.

'Nay, Mr Theo, I can't let you do that work, not with that leg an' all,' said a hoarse voice. This was accompanied by a long bout of coughing.

'Be damned to you, Jack. Of course I can manage. Get yourself inside the inn and keep to your bed until that cold eases.'

The voice was deep, smooth and it sent shivers down Kitty's spine. She could guess at once whose it was. He was speaking again.

'Do not go out this way, man. Just look at that blizzard. Go through the stables, you can get to the inn door in a few steps that way. Come on now. . . .'

The voices faded. Kitty sat on in the coach for a few minutes more. She wriggled her cold toes inside her boots. Well, she had learnt something useful. When she judged that the men had had time to reach the inn, she jumped lightly down from the chaise and hurried out of the draughty coach house into the stables. At once it felt warmer. She breathed in the reassuring smell of hay and horses. There was nobody in sight. A number of horses stood in their stalls, munching away. She was walking along the central path when her gaze fell on a magnificent black horse. Kitty stopped. This was his horse. She inspected the splendid beast. His coat was like silk and he held his head proudly.

Kitty remembered the animal limping on the previous day. She moved closer and leaned over the door to see what the injury was. The horse pricked his ears and took a step back. Kitty held out a hand towards his soft muzzle.

'Come on, be friends,' she coaxed. She heard a door open and looked round in alarm. It would not do to be found here all alone.

A tall figure emerged from a side room. She sensed immediately who it was even before she saw him limp. Why had she not guessed he would be tending to his horse when she had heard him send his groom away? He was in shirt sleeves and carrying a bucket. Kitty's gaze took in a pair of broad shoulders. He was coming closer. Hastily, she shifted her eyes to his face. Those black brows formed a straight line over a commanding nose and his lean features were grim. He obviously did not care to see a stranger petting his horse.

Scarcely breathing, Kitty watched as he continued to advance. His leg was dragging and from the set of his mouth he seemed to be in a lot of pain. Kitty knew she must move away, but she seemed to be rooted to the spot. Her heart was beating wildly. He appeared to grow more threatening as he came closer. His chest, under that fine, white shirt, was broad and well muscled. The column of his throat and the skin showing at the open neck of his shirt, was tanned, as if from an outdoor life. He had long, powerful legs.

Kitty gulped and brought her gaze back up to his face. Now

25

she could see that his dark hair was thick and curly, brushed back from a wide forehead. His face was long, lean and vivid. There was a devil-may-care look about the set of his mouth but his expression at this moment was forbidding – almost menacing, in fact.

It suddenly dawned on Kitty that she was quite alone here with a very big and hostile-looking man. With an effort she made to move back – but the book dropped from her nerveless hand and tumbled over the gate into the stall. At once the horse tossed his head and stepped backwards. His left hind leg was obviously weak. A furious exclamation broke from the young man. He had at last reached her. He set down his pail and straightened up again.

Kitty looked at the bucket from which came the warm, steamy smell of bran. He was going to apply a poultice to the horse's wound. It was a very ordinary, routine job. Yet this gentleman brought an atmosphere of tension and danger. Still, Kitty decided she would not be intimidated. She raised her face to look at him directly.

'What the deuce do you think you are doing?' he bit out. 'Can you not see that my horse is lame? He does not need to be startled?' Then, in a very different voice he said, 'Easy there, Nimrod. Be easy now.' He stretched out a hand to stroke the animal's glossy neck. Nimrod turned his head towards his master.

Kitty eyed those long, shapely fingers. A shiver ran through her. Cross with herself and with him for his lack of manners, she said, 'I certainly did not mean to frighten the poor horse. But I have dropped my book into his stall.'

He continued to soothe Nimrod. Without turning his head he said disdainfully, 'Have you indeed? I never heard that excuse before.'

'Accidentally,' insisted Kitty. 'I – you startled me. I did not think there was anybody here.'

He turned back towards her reluctantly. 'And what, if I might be permitted to ask, are you doing in here – especially in weather like this? It is no place for a girl.'

Kitty's eyes flashed. She was about to retort that she was entitled to keep out of the blizzard, but then she checked herself. She had startled his horse and she must retrieve her book. She drew a steadying breath. 'If you would excuse me a moment, sir, I will just pick up my novel and then I shall leave you to care for your poor horse.'

'A novel! Perhaps we should leave it where it is.' His tone implied that a girl who read novels was beneath contempt. Again, Kitty felt a surge of rage. He was deliberately insulting her and she did not deserve such hostility. She struggled with herself for a moment then decided to show him that she at least, had good manners.

'I trust you have not damaged your leg badly, sir,' she said politely. 'I could not but see how you limped into the inn yard yesterday.'

The gentleman's frown deepened. Now his lips were a thin line. 'It will mend, I thank you, ma'am.'

Well, what had she said there to make him snap her nose off? wondered Kitty. She bit back a sharp retort and glared up at him. Now he really was looking at her, actually seeing her. His dark brows lifted slightly. Kitty found herself gazing into the most intensely blue eyes she had ever seen. Fascinated, she just looked, feeling her heart jump as if it would force its way out of her chest. Her lips parted in silent surprise. She forgot what she had planned to say.

It seemed that time stood still, but at length she saw the corner of his mouth twitch and realized she was staring like an idiot. He was laughing at her! Hastily, she turned her head away. 'My book,' she said in a husky voice.

Without another word, the gentleman opened the door of the stall and retrieved the thick volume. Kitty held out her hand but he turned the book over to inspect the title.

'Dear me,' he drawled. '*The Trials of Arabella*. Gothic romance!' He shook his head and glanced at Kitty's indignant face. 'Well, perhaps reading this is better than wandering around stables in strange inns. You never know who you might meet in such places.'

27

'Indeed!' said Kitty in a freezing tone. 'Pray have the goodness to give me my book, sir.'

He took a step forward and stood right in front of her. 'Very well, ma'am. But there is a forfeit for frightening my poor Nimrod.'

Before Kitty could move he had put a hand under her chin and brought his own head down swiftly to kiss her, full on the lips. Surprise kept her motionless for a few seconds. Then she struggled wildly and he let her go, laughing as he handed her the novel. She gave him a burning look, put a hand to her mouth and raced for the door.

In the stable, Theo Weston set about applying the bran poultice to the grazed hock. 'No matter where we go,' he told Nimrod, through clenched teeth, 'the girls seem to find us. Even you cannot escape them.' He shook his head. Nimrod shifted as he felt the warm bandage on his raw wound. His master came round to stroke his nose and soothe him. 'Easy, old friend, easy,' he murmured. He gave a reluctant grin. 'But this time, at least, she was very pretty. . . .'

'If all the fine gentlemen of London permit themselves such liberties I shall be going home very soon, I can tell you,' Kitty announced, brushing her hair vigorously. She had confided her adventure to Amelia when they were finally on their own and preparing for bed.

'He sounds very disagreeable,' agreed Amelia. 'Maybe he feels angry because he took a tumble and dislikes females knowing about it. But his horse loves him, so he must have a kind side. And I know you found him handsome,' she added with a teasing glance.

Kitty shook her head in denial. However, she could not hide her feelings from Millie, who had known her all her life. She was attracted to this stranger, even while she was furious at his lack of manners. One look at his devil-may-care face and she had lost all her common sense. She had only herself to blame for that kiss. She wondered what was wrong with her that she still wanted to see him again more than anything else. But then, she thought, as she blew out the candle, it would be just her luck if they never met again.

The next day, much to the landlord's disappointment, the mail coach drove into the yard. The driver confirmed that the roads were now passable to the east. The Warringtons set off again and found that the weather improved as they drew nearer to London. They were all eager to finish the journey. However, Kitty soon laid her novel aside. She stared out unseeing at the view from the carriage window. She felt a growing anxiety at the ordeal ahead. She did not know what had caused the breach in the family, but it must have been serious to have lasted for so many years. What if her great-aunt was still angry and made life difficult for her?

In addition, she was struggling to cope with unaccustomed emotions. Was she just apprehensive of going amongst the fashionable people of London society, Kitty wondered, or had she been thunderstruck by a pair of bright blue eyes? He had treated her like the heroine in a silly romance and that was partly her own fault for dropping the book. He seemed to think she had done it deliberately. He was arrogant and had taken advantage of her, but it was a good lesson. She would not get into such a situation another time. She rubbed her lips. One kiss was not going to harm her in any way. Of course, it would be better if she never met him again.

Oh, why had she let Mama persuade her to come to Town? She thought wistfully of Papa, doing his best in the hospital. He needed her help and it would be so much more worthwhile than trying to make conversation with haughty town beaux. . . .

When at last the coach stopped in Grosvenor Square and the door opened, Kitty felt quite sick with nerves. She clutched at Amelia's hands. 'You will come and see me – soon?' she begged.

Amelia nodded, too overcome to speak. Kitty straightened her back and trod slowly up the steps to the open front door. Taking a deep breath, she looked up at the gloomy face of the butler waiting for her and stepped over the threshold.

CHAPTER FOUR

That same evening a tall gentleman was making his way upstairs to tap on the door of his friend's sitting-room.

'You are looking more like yourself this time,' said Gregory Thatcham, gripping his friend's hand warmly.

The Honourable Theodore Weston's face registered surprise, then delight.

'Where have you sprung from? Oh, but it is good to see you, Greg. You look very fit,' – he heaved a sigh – 'unlike me. Welcome to London. Take that coat off and tell me all the news.' His gloom lifted as he fetched another glass and poured brandy into it. For a little while he would be able to feel he was back in the army.

'So where is Wellesley based at present?' he asked, as Greg stretched out his booted feet to the fire and raised his glass to sniff its contents appreciatively.

'Portugal.'

Theo waited for more, but Greg said nothing.

'Come on, man, why Portugal and not Spain? What is our regiment up to? Any more battles after Talavera? You know I have been out of touch all these months.' He looked eagerly at his friend. Greg was frowning down at the glass in his hand.

'If you are trying to tell me my brandy is not the best. . . .'

Greg raised his head at that and smiled. 'What? Nothing like that. Prime quality stuff, this – especially after army fare! No, just wondering – tell me how things are with you, old

31

fellow. Is that leg better?'

Theo rubbed his left thigh. 'I still know where that damned Frenchman stuck his blade through it. And just a couple of days ago I managed to fall on it. I came off Nimrod on the ice. On my way back from Weston Parcombe. I have been visiting my father.' He pulled his mouth down and Greg nodded. 'But' – Theo swallowed some brandy, then went on – 'no more fever, my head is clear – and I am damnably bored.'

Greg nodded. 'Thought so. Good, because I have some work for you.'

Theo's gaze sharpened. He felt the old eagerness for action. Perhaps the future was not so grim after all.

'It is touch and go for the army in Portugal,' Greg began, 'but we mean to win.'

'Of course!'

'After Talavera, Wellesley was the hero of the hour. They made him Viscount Wellington but they still left him short of men and supplies. Then Boney sent another army under Marshal Soult. Our only option was to withdraw into Portugal, to a position we can defend.'

'Oh, God, don't I wish I could be there!' groaned Theo, raking a hand through his dark curly hair.

'You gave of your best, old fellow. With such wounds, you had to come back to England.'

'It was the damned fever – the last six months are mostly a blur. And when I was obliged to sell out, I felt so reckless I did some foolish things – got myself into debt and had no choice but to go home.' He looked at Greg bleakly. 'You know what my father is like – no welcome for me there.'

'Still favours your brother, does he?' Greg frowned and looked closely at his friend. His open face reflected his deep concern. He knew that Viscount Hethermere had never been close to his stormy older son.

'It was not important while I was a serving officer,' said Theo gloomily, 'but now I am just a crippled ex-soldier. . . .' He glanced at Greg and added quickly, 'That does not mean I am not grateful to you for saving my life—'

'Just stop there.' Greg wriggled with embarrassment and rubbed at his short brown hair. 'Can't see a friend filleted by those damned cuirassiers and not help him.'

There was a silence as they both remembered the battle of Talavera – the final desperate cavalry charge and the heavy French counter attack. Theo absentmindedly felt his leg where the French horseman had inflicted such a deep wound. Unhorsed and bleeding heavily, he had only been saved by Greg's swift help.

'Well,' he said eventually, coming back to the present, 'my fighting days are over, but are you saying I can help Wellesley – Wellington, I mean – with something at this end? It makes me feel I am still useful.'

Greg rubbed his chin, a sure sign, Theo knew, that he was anxious. 'It's dangerous work,' he warned.

Theo's blue eyes lit with genuine amusement. 'As dangerous as galloping into battle? The risks are what makes it worthwhile.'

Greg frowned. 'No galloping, Theo. This is diplomatic work and the devil of it is, it could quite likely end with a dagger in your back. Wellington has very few friends at Horseguards – and then Boney's agents are all over the place, desperate to find out our plans.'

Theo grinned at him. 'My cautious friend, I see why Wellington chose you for this mission. But why exactly are you here, Greg? You have not come all the way from Lisbon just to ask for more soldiers, have you?'

Greg shook his head. 'We have enough men. What we need is money – you would not believe how much.' He chewed his lip as he pondered the problem. 'But it will be worth it, we are building a complete network of defences around Lisbon. It is certain we will drive the French back – if only these fellows at Horseguards don't take fright and call off the campaign. That is where you come in. You can be very persuasive.'

Theo's eyes shone. 'Oh, I can do that for you; it will be a pleasure. I am frequently down at Horseguards anyway – my cousin Tom is under secretary to Lord Sheldon and so he is always there, with the pro-Wellington people, that is. We have to see that Wellington gets his money. What do those other fools think will happen if they recall him? Lord! We would have the French Army on our doorstep within the year.'

He got up abruptly and limped over to the window. He turned to see Greg watching him critically. 'Oh yes,' he said in a bitter tone, 'heart-rending, isn't it? No dancing for me these days.'

'What about riding? You said you came off your horse. . . .'

'Oh, that was only because of the bad weather – it gets very icy on the hills near home. But poor Nimrod suffered more than I did.' He shook his head. 'It was just the finishing touch to a charming visit.'

Greg looked enquiringly at him.

Theo's eyes narrowed. 'I told you I got into debt. I had a scheme and needed a large sum of money to set it up.' He shrugged and held up both hands. 'Never was any good with the cards.'

Greg grinned and nodded. 'Don't I know it!'

'So that made matters worse.' He wandered over to the table and poured himself more brandy. Scowling, he added, 'Ironic, really! Since the fever, I am a reformed character. But my father was furious. He misliked my scheme even more than my debts. All I wanted was to have some purpose in life, so I set up a hospice to help a few poor souls. Injured soldiers, mostly. He told me I should have had all this army nonsense knocked out of me by now.'

Greg preserved a discreet silence, but kept watching him intently.

'Oh damnation,' said Theo, 'then I tried to please him by offering to learn how to run the estate, but he didn't want that. Doesn't want me near Alexander.'

'As bad as that?' Greg looked appalled.

'He is afraid the boy will get army mad,' explained Theo. 'But he did suggest it was time I settled down. He even had a girl lined up.'

When Greg raised an eyebrow Theo nodded grimly.

'Exactly! If I ever do get shackled, I want a girl it is not a punishment to look at. When I refused his choice, he fell into the devil's own rage. He had even invited the girl and her mother to visit. So' – he shrugged – 'I beat a hasty retreat – and here I am, back in Stratton Street.' He tossed off his brandy and reached for the bottle to refill his glass. His hand was not quite steady.

It was not necessary to explain to Greg how much it hurt to always see Alexander preferred to himself. For years, Theo's home and family had been the army. Now, due to his wound he had lost it. Life was lonely and boring and he was back in the reckless mood of his youth. But maybe this new mission would put some meaning back into his life. His eyes gleamed at the idea of persuading the few men of influence likely to support Wellington in his latest efforts to defeat Napoleon.

He came back to his chair and held out his glass. 'Well,' he said with a smile, 'let us drink to my new career.'

'And to success in the Peninsula.'

They savoured their drinks. Then Greg stirred. 'I have a few letters to deliver. From the great man himself,' he added, as Theo looked a question. 'I can deal with all of them person-ally except the one to the Prince of Wales. Can you help me there?'

'You want to see him privately?'

Greg nodded. Theo pursed his lips. 'Think I can organize it, but it may take a while. How long are you staying?'

'I must go back as soon as I can get a favourable response to these letters. I tell you, old fellow, the situation is mighty serious out there. But most important of all is to keep every-thing secret from fellows like Lord Dalbeagh and Sir Thomas Knight. They have influence at court and they are set against allowing Wellington to continue fighting this Peninsular campaign.'

He got up and looked round for his coat.

Theo considered him frowningly. 'Are you sure nobody will try to disrupt your mission?'

Greg gave a bark of laughter. 'Oh, they will try. But they

cannot know I am here yet. Only reached Town this evening,' He pulled on his coat and adjusted the capes. 'and I am off again at first light for a few days, so with luck, I shall have all my replies before they can organize any opposition. But before I set off for Portugal again I plan to enjoy myself a little.'

'Well, then, let us meet at Lady Caroline Bannister's ball next week. I should have made arrangements for an audience with the Prince by then. It is always better to talk in a crowd.'

Greg nodded agreement. The door closed behind him. Theo stared into the fire. He took a deep breath. Was it possible that things were going to improve at last?

CHAPTER FIVE

Kitty followed Amelia into the barouche. She settled into her seat and let out her breath in a long sigh. 'Escape – at last!'

'Why, Kitty, it has only been two days,' laughed Amelia, 'and there is so much to do and see—'

'Maybe for you, Millie,' interrupted Kitty, 'but I am staying in a household of elderly people.' She pulled a face.

'Is it so bad?'

'Well, you must have noticed when you came to call just now. Broome – the butler, is old and slow. It takes him ages to lead the way upstairs. My aunt is a little old lady and her maid is nearly as old as she is. The house is so quiet, it is as if it is asleep. I dare not make a sound in there.'

Amelia leaned forward and squeezed Kitty's hand. 'Not at all like the vicarage, with all the children running around. But you will cope with the situation better than I could. And at least you are here in London.'

Kitty gave her a speaking look and heaved a sigh.

'I agree, everything is new and strange,' went on Amelia, 'and I feel intimidated by the number of fashionable events that Mama says we must go to. I really need your support, Kitty.'

'Nonsense! You will soon be at ease. They are only people, after all.'

'But Mama says they are on the watch for any sign of bad breeding, or lack of correct manners. It makes me feel so clumsy and ignorant.'

'You silly goose.' Kitty smiled. 'If they are staring at you, Millie, it is because they are struck by your sweet face and golden hair – not to mention this charming outfit.' She indicated the sky-blue velvet coat, trimmed with swansdown. 'Have you been shopping already?'

'Oh – yes. We spent ages trailing from one modiste to another yesterday. That is how I got my first taste of these intimidating grand ladies and their haughty stares.'

'Of course they are staring. I am sure none of them has a daughter who can compete with your looks. Now then, what monuments are we going to visit? My aunt only gave permission because this visit is educational.'

Amelia rolled her eyes. 'That does sound a bit frightening. Mama is waiting for us in Green Street. We want to show you the house and then pay a visit to the British Museum and see some of the sights in that area.'

'Well, that sounds like an interesting day – I shall be able to put it all in my letter home. Will your father take the letter for me?'

'Of course he will, but you will have to write it quickly. He sets off on the return journey tomorrow.'

Kitty found her spirits rising again. She could not admit, even to Millie, how she had cried herself to sleep on her first night in the large, sombre house in Grosvenor Square. Her aunt had seemed cold and unwelcoming. Kitty felt herself to be under inspection by every member of the household. She sensed the disapproval, the mistrust of something that was going to change their routine.

The two days she had spent there so far confirmed that everything was done according to a rigid code of etiquette. Used to the lively atmosphere of her own home, Kitty felt stifled in the solemn formality of Lady Picton's residence. Her aunt had still given no clue regarding the long quarrel with Kitty's mother. However, she had become a little less chilly and, when Mrs Warrington sent a note asking if Kitty might accompany Amelia on a tour of the principal monuments, she had given permission.

So today Kitty was determined to enjoy her few hours of freedom. And she was genuinely excited to be visiting the sights of the great city. Together with Mrs Warrington, they drove first to Westminster Abbey, where they explored the nave and chapels thoroughly, greatly awed to see the tomb of Shakespeare.

This was followed by visits to St Paul's Cathedral and the Guildhall, after which all three ladies agreed they would save the British Museum for another time. As they returned along the more modish streets, Amelia described the wonderful creations to be found in the elegant shops she had visited with her mother the previous day. Kitty knew she would never be able to afford such gowns with their bead or floss trimming and lace but still, if she could see them, maybe she could get ideas to embellish some of her own plain dresses.

She thanked Mrs Warrington for the pleasant outing, and ran up the steps to the waiting Broome. 'Lady Picton is in the drawing-room, miss,' announced the butler. 'She wishes to see you at once.'

Was it good or bad? wondered Kitty as she made her way upstairs. She wanted to set about writing her letter, while the impressions were still fresh in her mind. Everyone at home would enjoy the account of her day's excursion. But first, she must see what her aunt wanted.

She pushed open the door and went into the vast room. Her aunt was sitting in her usual armchair near the fire. To Kitty's great surprise, there was a gentleman seated opposite her. He turned his head; then, as Kitty came forward, rose to his feet. She was amazed to see that he was a young man, perhaps in his late twenties. A second glance confirmed that he was extremely handsome and well made.

'*Mademoiselle.*' His bow was faultless.

Mechanically, Kitty responded with a slight curtsy. She registered his fashionable appearance. As he looked at her with his lively brown eyes, she suddenly felt shabby in her simple gown. She felt her cheeks reddening and was annoyed with herself for caring. Clothes were not the measure of a person's worth.

'Pray sit down, both of you,' commanded Lady Picton. 'I see I have taken you by surprise, my dear.' She turned to Kitty, 'You must know that this young gentleman is Etienne de Saint-Aubin. He is the grandson of my dear schoolfriend, Hortense de Rochefort. And he is kind enough to visit me whenever he comes to town.' She turned towards Etienne. 'And this is Miss Katherine Towers, my great-niece, who has come to stay with me.'

Etienne stood up again and came to grasp Kitty's hand warmly. 'It is a great pleasure to make your acquaintance, Miss Towers.' He looked appreciatively at her face and smiled again. Kitty could not help feeling flattered. She smiled back, hoping that her cheeks were not too red. Then she turned her attention to her aunt. Lady Picton looked far more animated than Kitty had yet seen her.

Sitting down once more, the young Frenchman resumed his conversation with Lady Picton. Kitty took the chance to examine his classically beautiful face and smoothly brushed dark hair. His voice was pleasant, with just a trace of a foreign accent. She was delighted to find that such a personable young man was a frequent visitor in her aunt's house. That certainly promised to liven the place up.

Etienne had plenty of stories and items of gossip to tell and kept Lady Picton highly amused. Kitty was surprised to find how quickly the half-hour went past. Etienne rose to his feet and bowed himself out, expressing the hope that they would soon meet again.

Lady Picton surveyed her niece with a satisfied smile. 'I'll wager you found him a good-looking young man.'

'Indeed, ma'am. He has a very striking appearance and in addition, he is so smartly dressed.'

'Always. . . .' Her sharp gaze ran over Kitty. 'I was much impressed by your little friend's beauty and her style. Her mother obviously has excellent taste. That blue coat was superb – and the swansdown muff. . . .' She nodded and clasped her hands over the ivory head of her walking cane.

There was a long pause. Kitty waited, her eyes wary.

'The pair of you look very attractive together ... but you must accept what I am saying, my dear Kitty, as I know the world far better than you do – there is a big difference in the presentation.'

'Amelia is far too good a friend to mind my clothes.'

'That is to her credit, but society will judge you on your appearance.'

Kitty flushed. 'That is v-very shallow and I have no patience with such things.' Her voice shook. With an effort she bit back the hot words. 'I beg your pardon, ma'am, but that is what I think.' She cast a burning look at the old lady, who remained calm, watching her carefully.

'You yourself have just commented on Etienne's fashionable dress. There is no doubt that fine feathers make fine birds.'

The angry reply died on Kitty's lips. Indeed, she had felt shabby just now when she saw his elegant appearance. She realized that smart clothes did indeed convey a message. But now her feeling of humiliation grew. She could not afford to buy new dresses.

Her aunt nodded. 'I think you are sensible enough to understand what I am saying. Now then, child, I would not bring this subject up if I did not plan to do something about it. It vexed me very much to see you set off on your trip today at such a disadvantage.'

She rose painfully, leaning heavily on her cane. 'I declare, the idea of a shopping expedition is most entertaining. We shall take Miss Dilworth with us.'

CHAPTER SIX

That night, Kitty dreamed of new dresses and bonnets. She smiled in her sleep and woke with an unusual feeling of pleasure, knowing she was going to have some really fashionable clothes. But before she even opened her eyes, she felt that something was wrong. There was the sound of shovelling and brushing as the housemaid cleaned away the ashes and made up a new fire in the grate.

Kitty listened and frowned. Surely she could hear crying in among the other slight noises. Quietly, she raised her head. She saw a small figure, hunched over the grate, a hand pressed to her lips as she tried to stifle her sobs. Kitty sprang out of bed and knelt down beside the weeping girl.

The maid gasped in dismay. She shrank back from Kitty, rubbing a hand across her eyes.

'Whatever is wrong? Are you ill?' asked Kitty gently. 'Come now, do not be afraid.'

'Sorry, miss, fer disturbin' you,' whispered the girl, 'I won't be long gettin' this fire to light.' She fumbled with the coals. Another tear ran down her cheek.

'What is your name?'

The maid looked terrified. 'Oh please, miss, you ain't gonna tell the 'ousekeeper on me. I'll get the fire goin' in a moment.'

Kitty put a hand on the thin shoulder. 'Of course I will not say anything to anyone. Just tell me your name. I want to help you.'

The grey eyes widened. 'Why?'

Kitty smiled. 'I cannot see you in such distress. Are you unwell? Do you have the toothache?'

The girl shook her head. 'No, miss. It's me little brother, Sam. 'E's terrible poorly with a fever.' She choked back another sob.

'And can your parents not take him to the hospital? But you still have not told me your name?'

'It's Martha, if you please, miss – an' no, me dad's gone fer a soldier an' me mam 'as no money.'

'Very well, Martha, I will help you.'

Martha stared at her in disbelief. She shook her head. 'You can't,' she said with conviction. 'I 'as to work 'ere an' you can't get to my 'ome.'

'Oh, I think I can see how to organize that,' replied Kitty cheerfully. 'When I go out, I need a maid to accompany me. I shall ask my aunt if you may go with me. Everyone else is so old, they find it difficult to walk very far.' She gave a little laugh. After a moment Martha smiled back at her. 'So that is agreed,' said Kitty. 'Do not cry any more. It will take a day or two to arrange but I promise you we will go to your home and help your brother.'

Martha could not say a word but her face shone with new hope.

At the start of the shopping expedition Kitty felt very uncomfortable. She was torn between the embarrassment of accepting this generosity from her aunt and the dread that any clothes chosen for her would be hopelessly old-fashioned and make her plight even worse.

On first entering Madame Louise's boutique, Kitty's heart sank because this lady also looked rather stricken in years. However, she quickly noticed that the balldresses on display in the showroom were extremely elegant. Kitty stared in awe at them while her aunt and Miss Dilworth held a long conversation with Madame Louise.

Kitty was then ordered to parade up and down in an endless selection of coats before all three ladies exclaimed at the bottle-green pelisse.

'*Ravissante!*' exclaimed Madame, 'but it needs a dress also in green.' She beckoned an assistant forward, and selected a pale-green cambric gown, which, they all agreed, completed the outfit to perfection. Lady Picton appeared to be enjoying herself even more than Kitty, who, to her own dismay, had soon suppressed her usual opinion concerning the vanity of expensive clothes.

Her embarrassment returned, however, when, instead of going home, her aunt ordered the coachman to take them to a milliner's shop. Kitty felt she had tried on every bonnet in the shop before her aunt and Miss Dilworth were satisfied they had chosen the most becoming hat and muff to match her new coat.

During the journey back to Grosvenor Square, Miss Dilworth offered to run up a couple of gowns from lengths of material stored in the house. 'It will be a pleasure to put them to good use, my lady,' she assured her mistress. 'I know we have a bale of primrose-yellow silk, which will suit Miss Kitty very well – and there is also some checked muslin for morning dresses.'

'Such excitement!' exclaimed Lady Picton, when Kitty had helped her back into the house and she was settled in her favourite armchair. 'This is a welcome change from our usual routine, and I sense that the staff want to play their part in turning you into one of this year's most fashionable young ladies.' She took a sip of sherry and added, 'If young Etienne can be modish – and on his tiny income, my dear – so can you.'

'How does a Frenchman come to be in London at this time of war between our two countries, ma'am?'

'His family were *émigrés*, my dear. They lost everything during that awful revolution. His parents had to leave all their estates and possessions behind. I fancy they have led a wandering existence between here and Holland over the last twenty years.'

That evening she sent for Kitty to come to her dressing-room. Kitty had just tried out a new hairstyle, combing her hair back, with a few curls allowed to fall over her ears, then sweeping the rest into a knot on the top of her head. Lady Picton considered the effect and nodded.

'Excellent! You have achieved the current fashion and it suits you well. Now then, what jewels do you have?'

'I have a coral necklace, ma'am. Or else I use a knot or two of ribbon.'

'Very becoming, but I think you need a little more than that.' She opened a massive jewellery box on the table beside her and fumbled in it with her rheumaticky fingers. 'Now, let me see... Sir Geoffrey was always most lavish in his gifts. But heaven knows, it is long enough since I've worn any of 'em. The only parties I attend are card parties.' She looked up at Kitty's horrified face. 'It's all right, girl, they are only for you to wear while you are here,' She picked up and discarded a number of heavy, old-fashioned brooches and collars.

'Ah, here it is.' She pulled out a small bag and put it in Kitty's hand. 'Put 'em on.'

Kitty clasped the pearl necklet round her throat and peeped in the mirror. 'Oh, Aunt, how pretty they are.' She turned her head, admiring the lustre. 'Oh, *thank* you – I promise you I shall take great care of them.' Impulsively, she bent and kissed the old lady's cheek.

'There, there,' said Lady Picton, blinking rapidly. 'Just the thing for a girl to wear. And now you have arranged your hair into this new-fangled style, you are beginning to look smart.'

Kitty tied the strings of her new bonnet under her chin. She looked at her reflection in the long mirror. Her eyes sparkled back at her and she could not resist a smile of pleasure. Surely M de Saint-Aubin would find her sufficiently modish in this outfit. The bottle-green cloth pelisse with its black braid trimming fitted her tall figure perfectly.

'Well,' she told her reflection, 'I hope I am smart enough to impress Monsieur de Saint-Aubin. I saw him sizing up my dress when he was introduced to me. For all my ideas on valuing the inner worth of a person, I am being influenced by this fashionable world.'

She wrinkled her nose over the dilemma. But it was time to join her aunt for a drive to Hyde Park. They were soon seated in the landaulet, which was drawn by a matched pair of horses. Kitty wondered if they were also elderly. She noticed that the rather portly coachman had grey hair.

As the coach set off at a sedate pace, Kitty said impulsively, 'You are being very kind to me, Aunt. I do hope this is not too fatiguing for you.'

'Nonsense, child. I frequently go out to take the air or to visit friends. This is a luxury for me to have company. It has been a long lonely time since your great-uncle died – we never had any children. If only your mother—' She broke off and then added quicly, 'The house is far too quiet. Does us good to bestir ourselves.'

If only my mother – what? Kitty longed to ask but did not feel she knew her aunt well enough yet. But she took comfort from the knowledge that her aunt had definitely warmed to her over the past few days.

They now turned into the park and the coach slowed down to a crawl.

'It seems as if all of London is here.' Kitty's gaze wandered over the throng of people walking or on horseback, all mingling and exchanging greetings and gossip with each other and with the occupants of the many coaches.

'This is where you have to be seen, girl, if you want an entrée into society.'

They had made only one turn around the carriageway when Kitty spotted Amelia. She was riding in a phaeton driven by a very fashionable lady. Kitty waved and the two carriages drew to a halt abreast of each other.

'How very smart you are, Kitty,' said Amelia, but Kitty was

staring at her companion.

'Caroline!' Kitty saw at one glance that Freddy's older sister was dressed in the height of fashion. Her braided pelisse of light-brown velvet enhanced her guinea gold hair, elaborately curled under a dashing hat with ostrich plumes clustering round the brim.

Lady Caroline Bannister inclined her head to Lady Picton, then turned her gaze to Kitty. She smiled. 'So in the end, you gave in to the lure of London, Kitty. What was it you used to say about more worthwhile causes?' She took in the new green pelisse and bonnet as she smiled teasingly at her young friend.

Kitty decided to ignore this comment. 'Oh, it is good to see you, Caroline. You look well – and so smart.'

Caroline raised her delicate brows. 'Of course, I am always in the latest mode. And you see I have persuaded Millie to join me, so she can make some new acquaintances.' She looked back at Lady Picton. 'It would give me great pleasure, ma'am, if you and Kitty would join my dancing party on Thursday next.'

Lady Picton looked pleased. 'Why thank you. For myself, I do not go out to evening events any more, but if Miss Warrington's mother will chaperone Kitty, she may attend.'

Everyone was pleased with this arrangement. They were just bidding each other farewell when a smartly dressed young man approached Caroline's phaeton, raising his hat with a decided flourish.

'Why, Etienne!' Kitty noticed that Caroline looked very pleased to see him. 'I thought you were out of town.'

'I was, but am so glad to be back.' he said with an expressive look. He now registered the occupants of the other carriage and bowed with exquisite courtesy to Lady Picton. Kitty had the satisfaction of seeing his eyes widen, then gleam with appreciation as he took in her new finery. He liked it. She would not give up her principles, but at this moment it was important to be able to compete with Millie and Caroline. She felt a rush of gratitude to her aunt.

Etienne came over to take her hand and kiss it. Amazing, decided Kitty, what a smart new bonnet could do. Before he could speak, Caroline was inviting him to her soiree. When he accepted, Kitty's happiness was complete.

CHAPTER SEVEN

'Deuce take it, Weston! That is the fifth wafer you have hit in a row. Are you practising for a duel?'

Theo looked up from inspecting his silver-mounted pistol. There was a gleam in his blue eyes. 'If you are offering me one, Johnny. . . .'

'Oh not I, not I,' spluttered Mr John Denton, his pale-blue eyes bulging with horror. 'No match for you, assure you. Just fascinated, watching you demolish those wafers.'

By now, Theo had reloaded. He aimed again and hit the sixth wafer.

'It is no use to be a soldier if you are not able to hit your target,' he remarked, turning away from the shooting range. He sighed. His leg was still damnably sore and stiff after the fall from Nimrod on the ice. Impatiently, he dragged himself back towards the bench and sat down.

Another young man stepped forward to the stand, ready to shoot. Theo watched in silence for a few minutes as the newcomer fired several shots. Somewhat to his surprise, Johnny Denton sat down beside him.

'He is not in your league either,' remarked Johnny, nodding towards the red-faced young man, who had not yet hit a wafer. 'In fact, you are one of the best. Good job too,' he added darkly, 'if all they say about you is true.'

Theo glanced at him frowningly. 'What do they say?'

Under that stare, Johnny drew back a fraction. 'Oh,' he stammered, 'it is well known that you are quite a wild blade

49

– and the ladies all mad for you.' He coughed, 'Fact is, they are all in a twitter now word has gone round that you are back in town.'

Theo's lips thinned. 'Thank you for the warning.' By this time he had reloaded his pistol once more and he slipped it into his belt.

Johnny eyed him warily. 'Do you always go around with a loaded gun? Makes you look like a pirate.'

Theo shrugged into his greatcoat and took his hat from the attendant. 'I always keep my gun loaded,' he said, 'wherever it is.'

There was a moment's silence, while the other man digested this.

'I fear I have offended you,' persisted the sweating Johnny. 'Pray let me make amends. A glass or two at Brooks's will soothe your feelings.'

They walked along the street together. Theo did not tell his companion that he was on his way to Brooks's in any case. He was seeking a certain person and had not found him at Manton's Shooting Gallery. It was obvious that Johnny was going to stick close to him. He frowned thoughtfully; he had never heard Johnny spoken of as an agent for any political group. But an instinct for danger warned him that this sudden friendliness had a hidden reason.

Once in Brooks's they made their way through the crowd to a table in an alcove, a little apart from the clusters of gentlemen discussing the topics of the day. A bottle of port and glasses were set before them. Johnny poured the ruby wine into the glasses. 'A toast to your skill, Weston.'

Theo raised his glass and sipped. He watched as Johnny downed the contents of his own glass and picked up the bottle again.

'Oh.' In the act of pouring, Johnny checked himself. He stared at Theo's nearly full glass. 'I say, is there something wrong with this bottle?'

'Not at all. It is excellent. But I have to make a visit to a friend of my father's shortly. I must keep a cool head.' Theo stretched out his long legs, schooled his face into a bland expression and looked casually round the room. It was crowded and there was some matter causing a lot of laughter near the door.

'I think they are placing a bet on something.' Johnny followed the direction of Theo's gaze, 'Must be a new heiress in town or some such stuff.' He sipped his wine again, then turned his rather protuberant eyes back to Theo. 'Is it true you sold your matched bays recently?'

'And my curricle.' Theo's voice was hard.

Johnny hesitated for a moment. 'Heard you lost a large sum at play last month.' He stopped, quelled by Theo's forbidding scowl. He gulped some more of his wine then cleared his throat. 'Fact is, Weston, if you need more cash, perhaps you would consider selling me that black stallion of yours? Just name your price.'

Theo set his glass down sharply. 'Never.'

Taken aback by the fierce tone, Johnny blinked. 'Well, then, I would wager you for him. A hand of piquet, say?'

Theo gave a bark of laughter. 'You must know I have no luck with any games of chance. I have been physicked enough at the tables.' He looked at Johnny's red and anxious face. 'I do not play cards. And thank you, but I have settled my debts.'

Johnny's expression was dismayed enough to make Theo wonder just what the man's plan was. Perhaps he was one of those who drew wealthy newcomers in to be fleeced at the card tables. But that would not happen in a club like Brooks's. The only other possibility was that someone was already aware of Greg's presence in London.

Another gentleman came up to them at this point and chatted a little. This gave Theo an opportunity to look round the room again. At last! The man he was seeking was seated at a table in a corner nearby. He wore spectacles and was reading the newspaper. Theo considered how to shake off his companion. When the other person bowed and left them, he raised his glass.

'Come,' he said with a smile, 'you cannot have Nimrod, but let us drink to you finding a splendid horse anyway. Maybe at Tattersall's next sale.'

Johnny brightened, he raised his own glass eagerly and gulped down the contents. He called for another bottle. They discussed the good points of hunters and carriage horses. It was not long before Johnny was beaming happily and propping his head up on one hand.

Meanwhile, Theo discreetly observed the gentleman reading *The Times*. Eventually, he shook out the paper and folded it neatly, then took his spectacles off his nose, polished them carefully on his handkerchief and tucked them into a case.

So it was yes. Greg would be granted an audience with the Prince of Wales. Now to find out when and where. The gentleman rose, picked up his hat and coat and made for the door. Theo leaned forward. 'It is high time I went to pay that visit to my father's friend,' he said softly, 'You will have to excuse me now.' He pushed the bottle towards Johnny. It was doubtful if the latter even noticed that Theo had picked up his own coat and hat as he moved away.

Theo came down the entrance steps and proceeded as fast as he could along St James's Street. His limp was pronounced and he walked slowly. At the corner with Jermyn Street, he stopped for a moment. He leaned against the wall to rest his leg. The evening chill was penetrating. A slight fog that smelled of soot was dimming the outlines of the buildings. A number of well-dressed men went by, making for their clubs. Some coaches rumbled past. A few clerks and errand boys, all muffled up against the cold, hurried along without a second glance at him.

At last Theo felt satisfied that he could move on. He walked faster now, crossed Piccadilly and soon reached a covered arcade, where the lamplight welcomed him in. The bow-fronted shop windows displayed elegant wares. He halted outside the second shop, which sold tasteful ornaments and items such as brushes, tiepins and fobs.

Inside, a respectful salesman was showing a middle-aged

gentleman a selection of seals. Theo pushed open the door and stood at the counter, apparently absorbed in inspecting a tray of snuffboxes. When the customer had made his choice and the salesman was wrapping the parcel, the gentleman turned towards Theo.

'I trust I have not kept you waiting too long, sir?'

'Not at all,' responded Theo politely with a slight bow, 'it gave me time to make my choice.'

The salesman now returned with the package. The gentleman took it, raised his hat to Theo and left. A tiny slip of paper had changed hands meanwhile.

Theo breathed a sigh of relief as he made his way back to the main street. The audience would be granted in ten days' time, after the much publicized prizefight at Richmond. Not the best of times, he thought but that could not be helped. Greg was to wait in the Tower Inn at Weybridge until summoned by a member of the Prince's staff. With any luck, Greg would have received all his other replies by then so he could set off for Portugal immediately afterwards.

It was quite dark now and a drizzle held the fog down between the houses. The streets were emptying. Theo decided to return to his lodgings. He had no wish to run into Johnny Denton again. Who had sent the fellow to keep him under supervision? He was still pondering the question as he emerged into Bond Street. He was recalled to the present by a child's voice addressing him.

'Spare a penny, mister?'

Theo blinked at the ragged urchin. She did not look more than seven or eight years old. Her face was sharp and sallow but the eyes were still those of a small child. He dug a hand in his coat pocket and fetched out a sixpence.

'Why, Theo Weston, I declare it *is* you!' said a feminine voice behind him. 'It has been an age since I saw you.' The speaker was a bold-eyed young lady, fashionably dressed and holding out both hands to him.

Theo remembered her name with an effort. 'Miss Harling.' He bowed formally, avoiding taking her hands.

The lady darted him a sharp glance. She took in the tiny beggar and recoiled. 'Oh, do tell her to go away,' she exclaimed in a tone of disgust. 'It is quite shocking the way these creatures intrude even into Bond Street. It makes me nervous.'

Theo handed the coin to the child, with a wink. The grubby little claw closed fast around it. 'Thanks, mister,' and the urchin ran off.

'How can you encourage such vermin?'

Theo gave her a freezing look. 'We are fortunate not to be so poor.'

Miss Harling gave a tinkling little laugh. 'Your pet subject, is it not? But why so cold? You were eager enough for my smiles when you were last in London.'

'That was a long time ago. I trust you are well, ma'am? Excuse me, I cannot stay.' He raised his hat and walked on. Perhaps Johnny was right about these feather-headed females. Had he really been on good terms with this artificial creature in that time before the fever? Nowadays he would only associate with ladies who showed some genuine understanding for the problems of the real world.

CHAPTER EIGHT

Kitty felt quite breathless with excitement as she entered the ballroom on Thursday evening. After all, she reminded herself, it did not go against her principles to enjoy a party. Her eyes searched the crowd for Etienne de Saint-Aubin. Would he be impressed? She had taken great pains with her appearance.

'It will not just be Millie turning heads tonight,' Caroline had murmured, as she greeted them at the entrance to the ballroom. Kitty was dressed in the sea-green taffeta dress trimmed with lace. She had piled her hair high on her head and clasped the string of pearls around her neck. Excitement had added an extra glow to her cheeks and her large brown eyes were sparkling.

A number of heads turned to stare at two such pretty young ladies as Mrs Warrington led them towards an arrangement of potted palms halfway down the vast hall. A dark-haired gentleman rose from the bench by the plants. Kitty's heart beat faster – but it was not Etienne de Saint-Aubin.

This young gentleman was taller than Etienne and had a more athletic build. He was elegantly dressed but his handsome face was marred by a decidedly stormy expression. Her eyes widened. Her heart missed a beat. It was the disagreeable gentleman from the inn. And she had thought she would never see him again. She drank in every detail of his appearance. His evening clothes were moulded to his tall form and his hair was swept back. A splendidly tied cravat enhanced his smart appearance.

As Mrs Warrington reached the bench he executed a formal bow and moved aside. He was in such a hurry to get away he did not even cast a glance at the two girls. Kitty felt aggrieved. His leg was still lame but that was no excuse for ignoring them completely, she thought. This was a formal ball. He could have said something – a simple polite remark. Why was he so impatient with everybody – except his horse?

Well, she shrugged, there was another young man who was just as handsome and far more good-humoured. She turned her attention to checking the room. There was still no sign of Etienne, so she kept glancing towards the doorway, while nodding politely at Mrs Warrington's comments.

'Do not sit down,' she was instructing the two girls, 'you must not crease your dresses.'

Amelia fidgeted with her fan. 'We do not know a single person,' she said in a low voice, 'it makes me feel such an outsider.'

'Nonsense!' Mrs Warrington's tone was sharp. 'Lady Caroline will perform a few introductions and you will soon make friends. That is what these occasions are for. And hold your head up! Can you not see how many people are glancing at you?' She smiled with satisfaction, 'I should not say it, girls, but you do make a striking pair – and so very smart.' She surveyed her daughter's pale-blue silk robe with its over-dress of spangled gauze. 'Not even Lady Caroline looks so fine.'

Another gentleman strolled into the room – not Etienne, registered Kitty, looking away again. Then she realized that this man was walking in their direction. He was tall and had a pleasant, open face. Kitty watched him exchange greetings here and there but he kept moving towards them. Suddenly he noticed Amelia and stopped in his tracks. He blinked and looked more closely. Kitty hid a smile. She had seen this happen many times at the assemblies in Cheshire.

He recollected himself and walked past them. Kitty heard

him address someone close by. His voice was clear and she could not help overhearing.

'Hello, old fellow, as you see, I made it back in time.'

A deep voice replied, 'How did you get on? Everything satisfactory?'

The only answer to this was a grunt. Kitty glanced over her shoulder. The newcomer was talking to the man with the limp.

'As for the other matter,' he was saying in that attractive deep tone that sent shivers down her back, 'you will be glad to hear I have been able to arrange a meeting, but it will not be for another week or so yet—' His eyes met Kitty's at this point and he broke off. His brows snapped down over his aquiline nose. Hastily, Kitty whisked her head back. She knew her face was going red. Amelia eyed her in astonishment. Kitty plied her fan and went back to watching the door.

Lady Caroline came up at that moment. 'Let me introduce you to William.' Her husband, a tall, fair man, shook hands and gave them a friendly smile. 'Caroline has talked a lot about you,' he said, 'I feel I know you already.'

Caroline brought a couple of young ladies to speak to them and suddenly they were part of a group of friendly young people. Lord William's easy chatter soon had everyone laughing. All at once he called out, 'Greg, Theo. Where have you two been hiding yourselves? For shame – talking secrets—' He stopped abruptly as Greg put out a hand to silence him. 'Sorry, dash it!' he muttered, 'Keep forgetting.'

Kitty, still keeping an eye out for any sign of Etienne, saw the three laugh as the pleasant-faced Greg said, 'That is why we have to leave you out.'

Her heart gave a leap as she saw the lame man's face transformed by his sudden smile. That strange feeling of attraction stirred deep inside her again. Her lips tingled. Then Lord William was addressing Mrs Warrington. 'May I present two of my oldest friends to you, ma'am. This is the Honourable Theodore Weston. As you see, he is still recovering from injuries received—'

'That is of no interest,' interrupted his friend, with more haste than manners. Lord William grinned and gestured to the other young man. 'And Mr Gregory Thatcham.'

With an effort, Greg turned his gaze from Amelia and bowed to Mrs Warrington. 'Do I understand there is to be dancing?' he enquired of Caroline. She nodded. 'Then, may I beg you to save a dance for me?' he asked Amelia eagerly.

Mrs Warrington gave her daughter an approving smile. Kitty exchanged a glance with Caroline. 'The usual Millie effect,' she murmured.

'It is always fun to watch their faces when they see her for the first time,' replied Caroline, 'and she is so sweet to them all.'

'Yes, but she never shows any preference for one above another. . . .' Kitty shook her head.

Caroline glanced at her but said nothing. Kitty was surveying this group of fine London gentlemen. Secretly she was impressed by their stylish appearance, but she still felt sure they wasted a lot of time in frivolity and idleness. That was a pity, as they all looked fine, strong and intelligent.

During an interval in the dancing, Kitty was sipping a lemonade when Caroline appeared again. 'I see that Greg Thatcham is totally *épris* by Millie. That means poor Theo Weston is scowling more than usual. He cannot dance at present, as you can see. So sad for one of our greatest rakes, you have to agree. Would you be a dear and keep him amused for a while when the music starts again?'

'He most certainly looks like a rake,' said Kitty, not daring to say she already had experience of his rakish ways. She turned to look at where Theo sat at the side of the room, long legs stretched out, frowning into space. From time to time he rubbed his left thigh, seemingly without realizing he was doing so. She looked enquiringly at Caroline, who shrugged.

'He is a wounded soldier, darling. Just like the ones you nurse in the hospital in Deneford.'

'But do you think he will be pleased to talk to me?' asked Kitty doubtfully, 'He looks so grim! I would have expected a rake to be more . . . interested in people. This man seems so moody. And why is he all alone?'

'I suppose he is looking rather forbidding – but that will not worry you. Darling, he has been through a very hard time. You will . . . please?'

Kitty let herself be persuaded. In fact, she was torn between her anger at his rudeness and the unexplained fascination he exerted over her. So when the dancing started she made her way to where Theo was sitting. He stood up at her approach and bowed automatically. Kitty again registered his height and elegant appearance and told herself that it was no punishment to be obliged to spend a half-hour with such a handsome man.

She sat down and when he had settled himself beside her with his left leg stretched out in front of him, she put on the friendly smile she used when visiting injured soldiers at the hospital.

He glanced at her briefly then looked away again. 'Has Caroline sent you?'

Kitty's eyes smouldered but she kept the smile in place. 'Perhaps she did suggest it, yes. You seemed to be rather isolated.'

He took a deep breath. 'As you can see, I am not yet able to join in the dancing.' His left hand began rubbing at his thigh once more.

'After falling from your horse on the ice, I am not surprised.'

He gave her a puzzled frown. 'How could you know that? We have not met previously.'

'Oh, indeed we have, sir. But not formally – and not in Town.'

He looked at her more closely and shook his head. His frown deepened.

Kitty detected a strained look on his face. She tried not to take offence at his strange, abrupt manner. It seemed his wound was still troubling him. Then she was glad she had kept silent as he said rather hesitantly, 'If it was a long time ago, I may have forgotten. You know – I have had a spell of bad health and fever. . . .'

Kitty's heart melted. 'Our previous meeting took place because of the snow last week.' She watched his dawning look of recognition and hurried on, 'I trust you had no further problems in reaching town, sir – after the snow at Streatley, I mean.'

He turned to look at her fully. Kitty was transfixed by a piercing sapphire gaze. Her own eyes widened. She caught her breath. She did not know how long it was before she heard his deep voice saying, 'Nothing worse than having to leave my horse at the inn there.'

'Oh,' she stammered, the colour rushing into her cheeks at the recollections called up by the mention of Nimrod. 'Indeed, that was hard for you, but such a noble animal needs every care.'

His heavy frown did not lighten. He nodded but offered no other comment. He seemed to be concentrating on her mouth. She noticed his long thick lashes, hiding those sparkling eyes.

'I remember you now,' he said slowly, 'it was the day after the snowstorm. The day after—' He broke off, still frowning. He gave a deep sigh.

Kitty sought hastily for another topic of interest. 'Do you in general enjoy these evening entertainments?' It was lame but she must avoid any reference to that kiss. And now she was sitting by him, she knew she was succumbing to the fascination of his lean good looks, his voice and especially those blue eyes. He continued to stare moodily into the distance. Kitty cleared her throat and wafted her fan at her heated cheeks.

Slowly, he focused on her again and his eyes crinkled into a smile. 'Shall we say that they are a necessary part of society life. But surely every young lady considers them to be essential?'

Kitty shook her head. Her ringlets bobbed vigorously. 'As an occasional treat, I find them enjoyable.' She glanced at him a little shyly. 'However, there are many more worthwhile things to do—'

His gaze was very keen now. 'Such as?'

'I have seen such shocking poverty since I came to London. I wish I could find a way to organize some help.'

Theo nodded, his face thoughtful. 'A most unusual young lady,' he murmured. Suddenly he gave her a real smile. The way his eyes danced did strange things to Kitty's heart. With the scowl gone she found him wickedly attractive. She was shaken out of her usual composure. 'I-I should not really be talking about that,' she stammered, 'it is just that I do feel strongly—' She looked at him earnestly.

He bent his head forward, nodding encouragingly. 'Do go on.'

At that moment a voice close by, said, 'Hello, Kitty.'

Raising her head, she saw a beaming Freddy, looking very smart in his evening clothes. Beside him was Etienne, impossibly handsome in a perfectly cut evening coat and snowy cravat. Kitty laughed and jumped up, holding out her hand. 'This is unexpected. You did not tell us you planned to come to Town.'

Freddy blushed and pushed back the lock of hair from his forehead. 'Wasn't sure of it m'self, but managed to sort out all the business of the estate. . . .' He coughed. 'Came to see how you girls are getting on.'

Kitty saw his face light up as Amelia came towards them, closely followed by a dazzled-looking Greg.

'Freddy!' She held both hands out to clasp his. 'How lovely to see someone from home. Do tell us all the news.'

The other young men stepped back politely. It was several minutes before Kitty looked round. Greg and Theo had disappeared again. However, Etienne was still close by. His eyes met hers and he came up to her. 'I must compliment you on your elegant appearance,' he said, with that slight accent that fascinated her. 'This – you say sea-green, yes – is perfect for you.' He waved his hands expressively.

Kitty struggled not to feel too flattered. Admiration was a heady tonic and tonight at her first society dance she felt a little drunk. That very evening, she had learnt from Caroline that Etienne's judgement on all things to do with fashion was highly respected. And what added to her pleasure was the fact that she had sewn this dress herself from an old one that had belonged to her mother.

She danced two dances with Etienne and the sensation was exquisite. He moved lightly and made her feel as if she was floating across the dance floor. From the admiring glances cast at them by other couples, Kitty knew that she and Etienne were making a good impression. His admiration seemed genuine and when he bowed over her hand at the end of the second dance, she was conscious of disappointment that they now had to separate.

Her world had been turned upside down. With a twinge of remorse, Kitty remembered how she had scorned her mother's dreams of society events. It had not taken long for her to be converted. But was it just the pleasure of dancing and dressing-up – or had she already found that special person with whom she wanted to spend the rest of her life?

At this thought she checked herself. She was not going to allow herself to fall in love. This excitement was simply due to the novelty of society life. Once she became used to it, she would feel how empty it all was. She was determined to go back to Cheshire and help her father.

CHAPTER NINE

'Do you feel more comfortable now we have friends?' Kitty asked Amelia. It was the day after Caroline's dancing party and they had just been visiting their new acquaintances, the Walmseley sisters. The sky was blue and in spite of a sharp wind, neither of them was in any hurry to return home. They set off to walk at a brisk pace along one of the main paths in Hyde Park towards a display of early spring flowers.

Amelia considered the question. 'Well, yes,' she admitted at last, 'of course, it is more pleasant to know people. But I find I think more and more about home and our household. And I miss my horses and riding in the open countryside. London is so built up.'

'You really are a sad case, Millie. You are supposed to be enjoying your season here. And already you have set all the young men's hearts beating but do none of them make *your* heart beat any faster?'

Amelia did not answer although her cheeks showed more colour than usual. They walked on in silence for a few minutes.

'You certainly made one notable conquest last night,' persisted Kitty. 'Caroline commented on how struck he was – and he is a particular friend of hers.'

'I could hardly fail to notice,' replied Amelia. 'I found him very pleasant and gentlemanly.'

'But he has not made any impression on your heart?

Indeed, you showed far more pleasure at seeing Freddy again.'

Amelia adjusted her bonnet. 'Now that was an agreeable surprise. It just felt like being at home again.'

She will not betray any feeling she has for him, thought Kitty. Out loud, she said, 'There are not many people about this afternoon. I do not think we will meet anyone else we know.'

Amelia indicated a curricle approaching them. 'You spoke too soon. Here come two more of our new friends. Please note, I said friends,' she added with a mischievous glance at Kitty, 'but I do wonder if your heart is beating any faster at the sight of them?'

Kitty looked round towards the roadway. Flustered, she turned back to Amelia. 'Whatever I feel, I am determined to go back home at the end of two months and carry on with my usual life. You know my opinion on the subject of the marriage mart,' she hissed, as the curricle came alongside and pulled up.

Greg was beaming down at them. 'How pleasant to meet you again. Good afternoon, ladies. Miss Warrington, I see you are admiring my bays. I hope you like my outfit well enough to join me for a turn around the park?' He smiled down at her as she inspected the beautiful horses.

'Oh, indeed, I would be delighted,' Amelia's face showed her enthusiasm. 'They look to be wonderfully smooth steppers.'

Even as she was speaking, Theo climbed down, bowed and took Amelia's hand, more or less obliging her to take his place in the carriage.

'I can inform you that he has not overturned me yet,' he told her, 'but as for *smooth*. . . .' He glanced at his friend, who laughed.

'I shall pay you back for those slurs on my driving skills,' said Greg cheerfully. He tucked the rug around Amelia's knees. 'I assure you, Miss Warrington, you are in for a high treat. Just a couple of turns around the park. See you shortly,' he called down, setting the horses in motion. The other two stood watching the curricle move away.

'She cannot help it, you know,' said Kitty, seeing the frown settle on Theo's face.

His eyes turned to her sharply. 'I beg your pardon?'

'Being so beautiful – and sweet-natured.'

He shook his head. 'If you say so. She has certainly made a deep impression on my friend.'

Kitty gave him a reproachful look. 'Just consider it from her point of view. Constantly stared at, always the object of unwanted gallantry – and of spiteful comments.'

A reluctant smile replaced the frown. 'You are certainly a loyal friend, Miss Towers. Come, we shall take cold if we stand still any longer.'

Kitty found herself walking with her hand tucked in his arm. How neatly he managed that, she thought, I do believe he is every bit as big a rake as Caroline said. She was very aware of his splendid height and fine broad shoulders.

'I should be glad to continue our interrupted discussion of last night,' he was saying.

'Discussion?' she stammered, trying to collect her wits.

'Do tell me more about your interest in the poor, Miss Towers.'

This was very direct. Kitty hesitated. She hardly knew him. She looked at his aquiline profile, wondering how much to say. Then she received another dazzling sapphire glance and threw caution to the winds. 'It grieves me very much to see the poverty all around us,' she confided, 'especially when contrasted with the extravagant habits of the rich.'

He nodded. 'Oh, I agree. So many young lives are wasted when with a little training they could earn a living.' He sighed. 'If only a few rich landowners would give a little help to set up schools. . . .'

Kitty beamed at him. 'You care about them as well . . . but it is not just the children, what about the poor crippled soldiers, sent home from the war to beg and gradually starve to death?'

Theo's face registered astonishment. 'How could you know about the hospice? I did not think Lady Caroline would speak of this?' His voice was angry.

Kitty looked at him in bewilderment. 'I have not spoken of this with Caroline. Do you have a special charity for soldiers, sir? I was not aware, but I think it is splendid of you.' She smiled at him warmly. Someone who worked to help the poor must have a good side, even if he was a rake.

Theo drew in a deep breath and spoke more mildly. 'I see we are at cross purposes here, Miss Towers. But now I am puzzled, what do you know of these poor wretches?'

'Why, sir, they are there for those to see who will!' Her tone was too sharp. She bit her lip and darted a sideways glance at him. He did not look offended, however. He acknowledged a greeting from another gentleman on horseback, then turned back towards Kitty. 'This is an unusual interest for a young lady in London for the Season?'

'I am only staying with my great-aunt for a short visit,' retorted Kitty. 'It is very enjoyable but I do feel a lack of purpose in this way of life. At home there is always plenty to do. One gets involved in trying to find ways of helping people in need – wounded soldiers included.' She turned towards him eagerly. 'But you spoke as if you also help these poor souls, and I know you are a soldier—'

'Was!' snapped Theo. The scowl descended on his face again. There was an awkward silence. His limp was not too noticeable today. Kitty, undeterred by his sudden change of temper, decided to find out as much as she could. 'Did you break your leg?' she enquired.

There was a long pause then she felt him heave a sigh. He looked up at the sky as he answered in a neutral tone, 'No, that would have been easier to deal with.'

She sensed a big tragedy behind those few words and wished she had not spoken. 'Oh, I beg your pardon, I did not mean to pry. It is just that Charlie – my brother – broke his leg a few weeks ago. I-I was wondering how long it would take to mend.'

He bent his head to look directly at her. 'There is no reason to be worried. I take it your brother is a very young gentleman? He will be up and about soon, I am sure.'

Kitty gave him a grateful smile. 'I do worry,' she admitted. 'I wanted to stay at home to help nurse him but Mama . . . Mama said. . . .' Her voice trailed away. She swallowed hard.

Now he stopped and turned to face her. She was tall, but she had to raise her head to meet his eyes. Once again she was drowning in that sparkling blue gaze. 'You are a truly kind-hearted young lady,' he said in his deep voice. 'You have a lot of compassion. But your mama is right. At this moment, it is time for you to enjoy your visit to London.' He smiled warmly and Kitty nodded, but whether in agreement or just in helpless pleasure, she was not sure.

The sound of voices calling made them both look round. Two ladies, one young and fashionable, one older and dressed in plain clothes, were coming along the path towards them. Theo turned to face them and Kitty reluctantly realized that their discussion was over.

'So we meet again,' the young lady exclaimed, as soon as she was within earshot. 'My dear Theo, how I have missed you.'

Kitty sensed him stiffen but he replied calmly, 'Good afternoon.'

The bold-eyed young lady looked Kitty over from head to toe. She then put a hand on Theo's arm. 'Why, you have been making a new acquaintance.'

'Miss Towers, Miss Harling,' responded Theo.

Miss Harling gave Kitty the tiniest of nods. She fluttered her lashes at Theo. 'How splendid that you are now back in town. I look forward to resuming our former good understanding.' She glanced at Kitty as she spoke with a decided challenge in her eyes.

Kitty smiled politely and transferred her gaze to a clump of snowdrops. She did not think Theo was delighted to meet this pushy young woman – no doubt a former flirt. But she told herself it was a good lesson to see how quickly he could tire of the young ladies he had once admired. Those blue eyes that she found so attractive obviously had the same effect on many other females.

She darted a quick look at Miss Harling. Smart rather than pretty and with a very bold manner. Listening to her conversation, Kitty thought she was only interested in parties and entertainment. Did she really feel anything for Theo? She was probably more concerned with his future title than with him, the real him, that Kitty felt she had now glimpsed.

Miss Harling lingered. It was obvious she was determined to keep Theo's attention focused on herself. At last Kitty heard the welcome sound of horses' hoofs and coach wheels. Greg was approaching. He pulled up his curricle. Now another young man was walking towards them at a fast pace. Kitty saw it was Freddy, slightly out of breath. He reached them just in time to hand Amelia down. He stood and glared while she thanked Greg for the ride.

Theo gave Miss Harling a slight bow. He turned to Kitty and took her hand. He raised it to his lips, giving her a smile. 'Miss Towers, I have to go out of Town tomorrow but I look forward to continuing our discussion another time. We have not said everything yet.' He bowed, mounted into the curricle and touched his hat to Amelia as Greg set his team in motion again.

With a mere nod of the head to Kitty, Miss Harling and her companion immediately resumed their walk. There was a pause as Kitty stared after the curricle.

'Well, Kitty, are you coming home today?' Amelia and Freddy, arm in arm, were watching her interestedly. Slowly, Kitty roused from her pleasant dream. She had discovered another side to this society rake and she wanted to learn more about him. It seemed some of his ideas matched hers. She allowed Freddy to take her arm but bore no part in the conversation as they walked back to Grosvenor Square.

CHAPTER TEN

Lady Picton sat in her armchair while Kitty practised her music. As her fingers coaxed the melody out of the old pianoforte, she was thinking back over the busy whirl of the week since Caroline's soirée. That event had marked their real entry into society life. Both she and Amelia were now on friendly terms with several other young ladies. Invitations kept flooding in for walks, tea parties, concerts, dances and visits to places of interest. In fact, Kitty did not see how they could fit any more events into their days.

And how much she had learnt even in this short time. Society life was not the simple, pleasure-seeking round of activities she had supposed. Beneath a light and pleasant surface, many important matters were being dealt with. Caroline had warned her that diplomatic business was almost certainly being discussed at any large gathering. Kitty at once remembered Lord William's accusation of 'talking secrets' at the ball and Greg's immediate warning to him to be quiet.

Greg Thatcham made no secret of the fact that he was an officer in Viscount Wellington's Peninsular Army. He was home on leave, or so he told everyone. But in wartime, would any officer be home on leave unless he was wounded? Kitty suspected he had some hidden business to conduct as well. However, he certainly had time to attend every event that she and Amelia went to. Kitty sighed. He seemed to be completely bowled over by Millie. He always had a starstruck look on his face after any moment spent talking to her.

His friend has seen it as well, she thought, frowning at the sheet of music as she played a difficult passage with too much emphasis. She concentrated, got through it with a little effort then allowed her thoughts to drift again. There had been no further opportunity for any discussion with Theo. She had looked for him in vain since their conversation in the park. Kitty heaved a sigh. If he would allow her to help him in his hospice, she could forgive his arrogance at their first meeting.

But even if she was obliged to live this constant round of social entertainments, Kitty had realized that there were many things to enjoy. She was looking forward to her first visit to a London theatre this evening. It was a big event in her life. Her family would experience the occasion through her description of it in her next letter home. A smile crossed her face as she pictured them all sitting round the fire while Papa read out her letter.

She would simply name the members of their party and make no comments on Greg's adoration of Amelia. But, she thought, they might notice that whenever she wrote about Millie, she also mentioned his name.

At this point Kitty played a wrong note.

'Come and drink some of this excellent tea, my dear,' said her aunt, 'and let me look at Miss Dilworth's latest creation.' She nodded approvingly as Kitty pirouetted for her. 'You look very well in primrose – and I like the ruffled neckline and cuffs. And what will you wear to go out tonight? The amber crepe gown? And do you have a suitable fan?'

When they entered the theatre that evening, Kitty was in a sparkling mood. 'What a change a mere fourteen days has brought about in my life,' she said to Amelia and Caroline, as they got out of the coach and went up the steps of the imposing entrance.

'Whatever you do with your life in the future, I think this is an excellent way to show you how most young ladies have to start out in the world' Caroline remarked. 'Yes, I know you consider it to be a market but how else can they find a husband and set themselves up in life? And some people do

70

marry for love. Look how fortunate I was to meet my dear William.'

'You certainly did find a treasure,' agreed Kitty, 'but admit, Caroline, that it takes great wealth to maintain this lifestyle.'

'Now, don't start telling me about how many poor people I could feed on the money I spend to give a dinner party,' implored Caroline. 'I have told you how all these social events serve many important purposes as well.'

Kitty nodded. 'I have grasped that.' A smile lit her face. 'And I would be less than honest if I did not confess that I am enjoying it all far more than I expected to.'

'Well, that is an admission! What about you, Millie?' Caroline turned towards Amelia, who was following them in silence as they made their way up to where the gentlemen awaited them. When there was no reply, Kitty glanced round to see that Amelia was smiling up at Freddy.

'Oh,' she stammered, realizing that they were both looking at her for an answer, 'I-I still prefer to be among friends. That is why I am feeling happy tonight.'

Greg and Lord William were also in their party. There was no sign of Theo. Kitty gave a tiny sigh of disappointment. The discussion would have to wait a little longer. Still, she consoled herself, there was plenty to enjoy on her first visit to a London theatre. Everything was very grand, the large building, the décor and the elegant costumes of the crowd.

She felt a flutter of excitement as William ushered them all into their box. She stood quite still, gazing round at the other boxes with their gilding and red plush curtains rising up in tier after tier. They were all filling with elegant ladies and gentlemen. Silks and satins shone and jewels flashed, fans quivered and the sound of voices and laughter seemed to fill the air.

She looked at Caroline who smiled. 'Well, Kitty, I can see you are impressed. But do sit down.' It was then Kitty noticed that Freddy and Greg had taken seats one each side of Amelia.

She looked to see what Caroline thought of this, but

Caroline was inclining her head at someone on the opposite side of the theatre. Kitty realized, with surprise, that a great number of people were exchanging bows and smiles with them.

'I told you, I am always in the very latest fashion, darling.' Caroline raised a hand to acknowledge a greeting from a turbaned dowager nodding to her from another box. 'Oh look' – she gestured with her fan towards a box in the upper row – 'there is Etienne, in Lady Kent's box. If he sees you, Kitty, we shall certainly receive a visit from him in the interval.'

Kitty shot her a startled look, but Caroline serenely continued her survey of the company. 'Freddy, will you stop monopolizing Amelia, the Walmseley sisters are trying to catch her eye.'

Freddy reluctantly sat back and looked towards Kitty with an apologetic grin. While exchanging a few polite remarks with Freddy, Kitty managed to keep Greg under observation. His eyes were on Amelia, his face so softened that nobody could doubt his infatuation. How could Millie remain so calm and unmoved at such devotion? Then Greg seemed to recollect himself. He turned his head towards Kitty and forced a smile. Then he looked away.

She had an odd feeling that he had just recollected a problem. He was twisting a ring he wore round and round on his finger and sighing as he stared at the wall opposite. He glanced at Kitty again and seemed about to speak when the lights were dimmed. At once, Kitty's attention was drawn to the stage. She leaned forward, her eyes sparkling with delight and gave her full attention to the play, following every word and gesture eagerly.

At the interval, William laughed at Amelia and Kitty's spellbound expressions.

'It was tolerable,' he teased them and they protested hotly that it was wonderful and the actors magnificent.

'Come on, everybody,' he said, rising to his feet, 'refreshments.' He tried to get everyone out of the box quickly, but, as she reached the door, Kitty exclaimed that she had lost her fan and turned back to look for it.

'You carry on,' said Greg to William, 'I will wait for Miss Towers.' He stood by the open door. As she peered under the chairs, Kitty was surprised to hear him address her in a whisper.

'Miss Towers, do not look up, there are people still in their seats overlooking us. Can you help me? I am sorry to ask this, but it is a very urgent matter.'

'What do you want me to do?' whispered Kitty after a moment, still searching round her seat.

'If I drop this packet near you, can you keep it safe for me until tomorrow?' His voice was so low she only just made out the words.

'Yes,' she breathed, wondering what could be so desperate. She remembered his clenched fists and tense face earlier. At once a slim package slid to the floor. She picked it up and at the same moment saw her fan by it. He must have had it!

'Kitty darling, do hurry.' Caroline put her head round the door just as Kitty slipped both items into her reticule. Several times during the second act Kitty wondered why she had so unhesitatingly agreed to help Greg. Whatever could be in the packet? She stole a glance at him. As if he felt her gaze, his eyes met hers. He smiled faintly. But there was an air of anxiety about him.

Well, Kitty sighed, I have to go through with this now. She found it a little harder to concentrate on the play during this act. But she must follow the whole of the story, Aunt Picton as well as her family, would want to hear all about it.

At the end of the evening there was no opportunity to speak to Greg alone. How was she to return this secret packet to him? They reached the steps and Caroline's carriage was waiting for the ladies. As they said their farewells to the gentlemen, Kitty asked loudly, 'Do you think we shall be able to meet at Hookham's Library at eleven tomorrow?'

Across the general chatter, she saw Greg look relieved.

CHAPTER ELEVEN

The clock in the entrance hall struck two. Theo roused from his thoughts and reached for the brandy glass on the drum table by his armchair. It was empty. He stood up and stretched. There was nothing he could do at the moment but the feeling of unease was hard to overcome. He had spent the evening in discussion with his cousin Tom, who worked at Horseguards. Tom had confided in him that Lord Dalbeagh was determined to end Wellington's campaign in the Peninsula. Lord Dalbeagh, said Tom, had plans for a new military campaign in Holland. Besides, he disliked Wellington and wanted to prevent him distinguishing himself any further.

Theo shook his head. The slack way they ran things at Horseguards, it was amazing any army got money and supplies. But Wellington was the only hope the country had of defeating Bonaparte. It was vital to see he got the funds he was requesting. Theo knew he must warn Greg urgently not to go about without protection. He grimaced. Since Greg had met that blonde girl, he had lost his common sense. He spent his time running after her at every social event.

Theo picked up his glass and wandered over to the sideboard by the window where the decanter stood. He pulled out the stopper and then changed his mind. As he set it down again he heard a tap at the window. He frowned and turned his head, listening intently. There was a second tap on the glass.

Who would come at this time of the night? Theo pulled the blind aside and peered down. There was a figure slumped against the railings by the basement steps. He was bent almost double. Then as Theo watched, he straightened up again and raised his arm to tap at the window again with his cane.

'What the deuce. . . ?' Theo exclaimed in horror. The blood-stained face gazing up at him was Greg's. On seeing Theo, he gestured towards the door. As fast as his lame leg would allow, Theo strode through the hall, slid the bolts back and made his way down the entrance steps to where Greg was clinging on to the railings.

'How bad is it?' he asked.

'I – knocked on the head . . . just a little dizzy . . .' mumbled poor Greg.

Theo braced his weak leg and pulled Greg's arm round his shoulder. 'Come on, old man. One step at a time. Lean on your cane. That's it. One more,' he encouraged, heaving his friend along, 'we will soon have you inside.' Slowly, awkwardly, they struggled up the steps, Greg breathing hard and Theo pulling him up as best he could.

At last Theo got him into the sitting-room and Greg dropped thankfully into the nearest armchair. He leaned his head against the back of the chair and Theo grimaced at the spectacle revealed. There was blood down the side of Greg's face as well as on his neckcloth and shirtfront.

'Here.' Theo thrust a glass of brandy into Greg's hand and guided it up to his mouth. 'This will make you feel more the thing.'

Greg swallowed, choked and swallowed again. He nodded. 'Better already,' he gasped, his eyes closed.

Theo left him to go and lock the front door. He went to the kitchen and returned with a basin of water and a cloth.

'Thought you went to the theatre with William and Caroline,' he remarked, as he began to wipe the blood off Greg's face, 'so when did this happen?'

Greg winced. 'Easy, old fellow. Must have caught me there.'

He put up a shaking hand to feel the side of his head tenderly.

Theo continued to sponge his face and neck. 'I cannot find any wound here,' he said at last. 'It must be on your scalp. But you have bled very freely.'

'Someone hit me here,' Greg felt the back of his head. 'Went back to my rooms after the theatre. Saw at once that the place had been ransacked. He must have been waiting for me. As soon as I got into my sitting-room I felt a mighty blow. Next thing I knew, I was lying there with blood dripping all round my face.' He drank a little more brandy. 'Whoever it was, he searched my pockets as well – they were all pulled inside out.'

Theo eyed him grimly. 'So you have lost those precious letters. My God, Greg, this could be a catastrophe.' He swung away and brought his fist crashing down on the table. He glared at his friend from under his dark brows. 'Only this evening I learned that Lord Dalbeagh plans to do his utmost to end Wellington's campaign. You have just handed it to him on a plate!'

'No, no, not as bad as that,' protested Greg.

Theo wheeled round and pointed accusingly at him. 'If you were not so taken up with following the golden-haired Miss Warrington everywhere, you would have been more careful. When that information reaches Lord Dalbeagh. . . .' He groaned and raked a hand through his hair. 'Oh, I cannot bear to think of all our soldiers betrayed by that fat and scheming politician. Just think of the sacrifices already made by our men out there. All those poor wounded wretches sent home to beg until they starve to death. It makes me choke with rage.' He darted a furious glance at Greg, clenched his fists and made a visible effort to check himself.

Greg tried again. 'Nothing was taken, I assure you. I had delivered all my letters except the one to the Prince of Wales.'

Theo's eyes sparked. 'That is enough to give that cur all the information he needs.'

Greg shook his head. 'No, I tell you! I did feel uneasy – just that instinct you develop to know when the enemy is close but hidden. Came over me at the theatre. But, thank heavens,

I found a solution. It helps me to feel better now.'

'You have not hidden the letter somewhere?'

'Not quite that. I asked Miss Towers to keep it overnight.'

'*What*? You asked an outsider – a *female*? How could you?'

'Miss Towers is a splendid girl, very level-headed. Feel sure I can trust her.'

'Just suppose you were seen giving her the letter. Maybe she is now nursing a broken head as well? And even if she is not,' he went on savagely, ignoring a mumbled protest from Greg, 'she is a female and she may be overcome with curiosity.'

Greg gave him a sharp glance. 'I do not believe you mean that,' he said, 'Miss Towers is a very dependable young lady.'

'It ought to have been kept strictly between ourselves,' raged Theo. He did not know why he felt so angry that his friend had involved Kitty. 'Now we have more complications.'

There was a silence. Eventually, Greg tried to rouse himself. 'I shall have to get myself decent again to go and collect my letter. She said she would be at Hookham's Library at eleven in the morning.'

Theo looked down at him and sighed. 'You are not fit to go out. Your face is swollen and you are going to have a fine black eye by morning. Anyway, you are still half dazed. Come, have another brandy then let's get you to sleep. I will see Miss Towers in your place.'

'But perhaps she will not give you the letter.'

'I shall persuade her, never fear.'

Greg allowed Theo to pull him to his feet and strip off his coat and bloodstained shirt. He tottered over to the sofa and gladly lay down again. 'See in the morning,' he muttered.

Theo watched while Greg wriggled about to make his sore head comfortable. As he extinguished the candles, his face brightened. He was going to see Kitty in the morning. He grinned suddenly – Hookham's Library, indeed. She was still reading novels.

CHAPTER TWELVE

From ten o'clock onwards Theo Weston was seated in Hookham's Lending Library, apparently absorbed in his newspaper. He was looking decidedly smart in a coat of dark-blue cloth and a snowy cravat. His buckskins were impeccable and his boots shone like mirrors. His black curls were neatly brushed. His face, however, warned everyone that he was in one of his grimmer moods.

It was a little before eleven when Kitty entered Hookham's. He recognized her tall figure and graceful movements and watched carefully from behind the camouflaging *Times*. She deposited several volumes on the table and walked through into the inner room. He sensed rather than saw her return then realized she was peeping over his newspaper at him. Theo lowered the paper and looked at her quizzically. Her face fell. He felt his temper rise another notch but he got to his feet and bowed.

'Good morning, Miss Towers. Are you all alone today?'

'I was expecting to meet some friends here, but I have arrived a little early.'

'Well, perhaps I may bear you company until they get here. Tell me, Miss Towers, have you come here quite alone?'

She looked slightly puzzled. 'No, sir, my aunt does not like me to go out unattended. I have my maid with me.' She sighed. 'I must say I find these London conventions very restricting.'

Theo's lips twitched. 'You prefer to be quite independent?'

She raised her face to his and nodded. 'In our part of Cheshire we frequently need to walk quite long distances; we could not be forever requiring a maid to go with us – besides, there is not the slightest need.'

'How pleasant to be so free. But, I fear, as you are realizing, in London, young ladies need constant chaperonage.' He said this with a wicked gleam in his eye. Her colour rose. It was obvious that she was remembering the one occasion when he had taken advantage of her lack of a chaperon. She was saved from having to answer by the sound of the door opening.

She looked round at once. Theo watched the way her head turned on her slender neck, enjoying the movement of her chestnut curls as they stroked against her white skin. How pretty she was and how well she looked in her green bonnet and coat.

After examining the newcomers she turned her large brown eyes back to him. He considered those eyes with a feeling of pleasure. So clear and honest, such speaking eyes, fringed by thick dark lashes. His mood lightened. This task was going to be more pleasant than he had expected. He gave her a courteous look and indicated the well-filled shelves.

'What type of book are you seeking today?'

Kitty eyed him suspiciously but he kept his expression polite. At last she decided he was in earnest. 'For myself, I hope to find some information on travel in Southern Europe, but I daresay my friends will be selecting all kinds of material' – her eyes challenged him – 'even novels.'

He inclined his head, trying to hide his amusement. So Miss Towers was on the attack!

'Do you often frequent this library, Mr Weston?'

'Only when I have business here.'

She puzzled over that. Her face became a little wary. She glanced towards the door and made as if to leave him.

'Miss Towers. . . .' Theo kept his voice low. 'I know you have a packet for Greg – er – Mr Thatcham. I am here in his place and you can safely entrust it to me.'

Kitty opened her eyes very wide. 'I am not sure what you

are talking about, sir.'

He breathed hard. 'Miss Towers, I assure you I am here on behalf of my friend.'

Her face was pale. 'I believe I will wait for Mr Thatcham. Excuse me, sir, my friend has just arrived.' She turned towards Amelia who was putting books down on the table.

Theo bit back an oath. He stood rigid, feeling foolish and burning with anger at her refusal to trust him. She had trusted Greg! Damn Greg for involving her in this business. Of course, she had no idea just what she was carrying. When he returned to Stratton Street he would have something to say to his friend about putting an innocent girl in such danger.

Still trying to subdue his rage, he pretended to study the books on the shelf nearest to him. He had to get that letter and fast. Who knew whether someone was even now following her. Theo repressed a shudder at the idea of seeing Kitty in anything like the state Greg was in.

There was a burst of chatter as a group of ladies entered the room. He saw two of them go over and greet Kitty and Amelia. For a few minutes he watched them opening books and showing each other different passages, with much talk and laughter. It gave him an idea.

Shortly afterwards, having found what he wanted, Theo limped over to the young ladies and nodded courteously to them all before addressing Kitty.

'Miss Towers, I believe I recently heard you express a desire to travel on the Continent. I feel sure this book about Italy will be of interest to you.'

Politeness forced Kitty to give him her attention. 'Come,' Theo went on in a light tone, 'let me place it on this table so I can show you the picture I particularly want you to see. It is of Venice.' He managed to draw her a little apart from her friends by laying the book on an empty table near a window. He turned the pages and bent his head close to hers as he indicated a large colour plate.

'How interesting.' Kitty exclaimed, leaning over the page. He almost forgot his mission when her curls tumbled forward and nearly touched his face. At the same time he breathed in the scent of roses. He cleared his throat. 'Please trust me,' he murmured, indicating the picture as he spoke almost in her ear.

Kitty glanced sideways at him. He could not resist a quick look at her mouth, so perfectly shaped with its full underlip and such an inviting shade of pink. He drew a steadying breath and cleared his throat yet again.

'Mr Thatcham is not well enough to come himself this morning. He was attacked on his way home last night. Do you really think,' he added hastily, as she gasped in horror, 'that I plan to do anything to harm my friend? I am trying to help him.'

'Was he robbed?'

Theo looked into her large, anxious eyes. 'You prevented that.'

'Is he badly hurt?' Kitty was looking appalled.

He shrugged. 'A sore head and a black eye. He will feel better when he has this letter back in his possession.'

'D-Do you think the villain is watching us now?'

Theo smiled grimly. 'It is quite possible. Can you give me the letter very unobtrusively? You do understand that you are at risk while it is in your possession?'

Kitty stared at him. He watched the colour fade from her cheeks as she grasped how serious the matter was. Then a fighting gleam came into her eyes and she nodded. 'Thank you, Mr Weston. I shall certainly consider this book,' she said quite loudly. She picked it up and rejoined Amelia.

Now it was Theo's turn to examine the people choosing their books. He had to admit none of them looked tough enough to overpower a big fellow like Greg, but someone was obviously determined to get the secret information about Wellington's war plans.

Theo grimaced as he thought of how Greg had looked that morning. One side of his face was horribly bruised and his eye completely shut. He had been only too happy to give up his place to Theo.

81

In a very short time Kitty was approaching him again. She had three books tucked under her arm and was holding out a fourth one to him.

'Thank you for showing me this travel book, Mr Weston. However, I shall not take it on this occasion. Would you be kind enough to return it to the correct shelf?'

'Of course.' Now he could smile. He was amazed at her reaction to this. Her cheeks went a most becoming shade of pink and she turned away hastily. Raising his black brows, he retreated to a corner seat, where he unfolded his newspaper again. The packet was tucked in the page showing the picture of Venice. Hastily he slipped it into his jacket pocket. He breathed a sigh of relief, as much for Kitty as for Wellington's letter. And Greg would be vastly relieved to have this back safely.

Over the newspaper, his eyes met Kitty's as she followed her friends out of the door. He nodded at her and this time was rewarded with a sweet smile. Theo felt a tug of attraction and, with it, an instinct to protect this unusual girl. If anyone threatened Kitty, they would have him to deal with.

He smiled as he recalled that she had not shown any fear when she realized she was involved in a dangerous business. But then, she had no idea how ruthless these people could be. He surveyed the growing crowd in the library. Appearances did not indicate any possible spies but, thought Theo, they were bound to be the most unlikely of people.

CHAPTER THIRTEEN

'No, miss, not that road!' Martha flapped her hands frantically. 'You don't want to go down there, miss, it's terrible rough. We goes through there.' She pointed to a small alley on the left.

'Oh, yes, I see now. I thought I had learnt the way.' Kitty frowned as she looked at the tangle of alleys leading from this open space in amongst the endless narrow streets. What had once been grand town houses had decayed into this higgledy-piggledy mass. Lean-to rooms had been added on to old walls. Doors and windows had been knocked into the crumbling walls. Often the only covering was a scrap of wood or rag.

Her gaze lifted to the upper floors, where faces stared out, idly watching her. Some of them were dulled by drink, some were grey with hunger. Everywhere there were tiny passageways, mysterious entrances and steps leading to yet more sinister little yards. It was an absolute warren, overflowing with ragged people. A few of them appeared to be selling objects from a shelf in front of a dwelling or doing jobs like repairing chairs but most just sat huddled together with their animals on doorsteps.

Partly clothed children swarmed around whining for pennies. All this added to her confusion. In addition she had to concentrate on avoiding the endless piles of unsavoury rubbish. The stench of rotten food and unwashed humanity was almost overwhelming. No wonder so many of these poor souls looked so grey.

She suddenly realized how alien this world was and felt a shiver run down her spine. Thank goodness for Martha, to guide her safely back home. Heads turned to watch as she went past. She could see the calculation in the eyes as they inspected her hat and pelisse. Still, she did not regret coming for this second visit to help Martha's little brother.

Lady Picton had readily agreed to let Martha accompany Kitty when she went out to the lending library or shopping. It was a pleasure to see how Martha's pale face brightened each time Kitty summoned her for an outing. And on two occasions their walks took them past the fashionable streets and eastwards into the stinking alleyways of the old city. Here, Martha's family had been forced to live since her father had been conscripted into the army.

Some roads were so narrow that a broad-shouldered man would have to turn sideways to get through. It was poverty on a scale that Kitty had never imagined. She felt stunned on her first visit. Then she began to wonder what could be done to improve the lives of these unfortunate souls. This was something she wanted to discuss with Theo, when they could have time for a serious conversation. But he had been absent from town since their meeting in the library.

Meanwhile, Kitty and Martha had taken fruit and bread to the single room that was home for all Martha's family. Kitty advised cooling the little boy's head by sponging him with wet rags, but in view of the family's poverty, there was nothing else they could do. On this second visit, it was plain that little Sam was still very unwell but he managed a smile on seeing his visitors. The girls felt more hopeful that he could recover.

Now they were hurrying to get back to Grosvenor Square by lunchtime. Kitty raised her skirts to step across another mass of stinking refuse where a pig was rooting. They crossed the street and took the alley to the left. This soon opened into a wider road, still dingy but less crowded with ragged children. The air smelt fresher. There were several shops and housewives with baskets were gossiping and bargaining. It already seemed a safer environment.

'Quick, miss,' Martha whispered, 'turn your face towards the wall for 'eaven's sake.'

'Why?' Kitty frowned at her. 'We must hurry.'

We must 'ide,' whispered Martha nervously. 'That *moosoo* is over the road.'

'Surely not! You must be mistaken.' But to her astonishment, it really was Etienne de Saint-Aubin, just ahead of her in the narrow street. He was in the act of coming out of a doorway, with a man each side of him. She swallowed hard. Etienne had sharp eyes and he noticed everything. He would certainly tell her aunt.

She did as Martha suggested and pretended to be looking at a shop window. Perhaps he would hurry away. Behind her she could hear the sounds of a struggle. Then there was a thud, a groan and some coarse laughter. Kitty turned sharply. Etienne was sprawling face down in the alley. He was close enough for her to touch him. The two men were standing over him. She shielded her face and edged away, pulling Martha with her.

People were rushing to watch the scene. As the crowd gathered, one of the bullies raised a fist like a ham and yelled, 'An' jes' see yer do as we tell yer, bejabers, or there's more to come.' Kitty noticed the man's shock of red hair. He spat, folded his arms and leaned back against the doorframe. The other man disappeared inside.

Etienne slowly got to his feet. He was clutching his ribs. He bent to pick up his hat. He cast a burning look at his tormentors in the doorway, which made them jeer at him again. He turned away at last and set off down the street. When Kitty looked round again, he had gone.

It was a subdued Kitty who made her way back into the more wealthy part of town. It seemed there were dark undercurrents to the lives of more people than just servants. She knew Etienne had very little money and wondered if he had been attacked because of debt. But she could not offer to help.

Her aunt would be outraged if she knew where Kitty had been and Martha would certainly be turned off without a reference.

'Why, Miss Towers. Good morning to you.'

The deep voice startled Kitty out of her thoughts. She raised her head to see Theo right in front of her. His eyes were keen and a smile tugged at the corners of his lips. She pulled herself together and nodded a greeting.

'Miss Towers, you have hurried along Bond Street without one glance at any of the smart displays in the shop windows. How is this possible?'

Kitty looked around. Indeed, they were in Bond Street, close to the entrance to Jackson's Boxing Saloon. She tried to push the image of Etienne and the bullies to the back of her mind. Theo was still watching her, one eyebrow raised. His teasing smile faded and his gaze became concerned.

Kitty cast him a wary glance. 'I fear I am late, sir. My aunt will be displeased if I linger any further.'

'Well, I, too, am on my way home. My route takes me past Grosvenor Square. I will accompany you, if I may.'

For once, Kitty would have preferred to avoid his company, but she did not see how to say so without giving offence. She gave him a tiny smile and began to walk on. He fell into step beside her. Martha followed behind. They reached the corner and turned into the quieter street leading to the square, still in silence. Kitty knew that Theo was looking at her closely.

'You seem rather preoccupied, Miss Towers. I would almost say you look as if you have had a shock. Forgive me, has anyone been pestering you?'

Why did he have to be so astute? She forced a little laugh. 'Not at all, sir. I am just anxious not to upset my aunt's plans.'

'But there is something wrong.' He bent his head to examine her face. 'Even the most frugal young lady enjoys looking at fashions. To be so preoccupied makes me wonder if you have perhaps seen a different kind of society. Have you ventured past the Haymarket and into the poorer parts of Town? Or perhaps you have been harassed by beggars?'

Kitty gave a little gasp, which she hastily turned into a cough.

'Well?' he insisted. 'Am I right?'

'I – er. . . .' She gave him a reluctant smile. 'Yes, sir. Oh, nobody pestered me. I went to the St Giles area. And there is a great deal of work to be done there.'

Theo stopped abruptly. He was frowning, but in a look of concern, not ill-humour. 'You have been into the slums of the old city? Into *St Giles?*'

She nodded. 'I have, but I would be obliged if you would keep that confidential. My aunt must not know anything of this.'

He nodded impatiently. 'Your aunt will know soon enough if you develop a fever. Those slums are full of disease.'

'I have only been into one home,' said Kitty defensively.

'One could be enough.' His tone was serious. 'I respect your interest in the welfare of the poor, but that is not a place where you can do any good. And you are putting yourself in danger.'

'I have my maid with me,' retorted Kitty. 'She knows the area; in fact, we have been to her home.' She was about to mention little Sam's fever but checked herself. He would say that it proved his point. She moved on. He still accompanied her. Now she felt angry. He was interfering. Of course she needed to see for herself what life was like in the slums.

He still had that heavy frown on his face. At last she could stand the silence no more. She stopped again and lifted her chin defiantly. Before his eyes could have their usual effect on her, she asserted, 'I know you mean well and I thank you for your concern. However, I am a vicar's daughter and I am accustomed to seeing poverty and slum conditions.'

'But I warrant you have not seen anything like the area of St Giles before. Come, Miss Towers, aside from the health risks, that particular area is teeming with rogues. Why, a group of gentlemen would fear to venture in. I shudder to think what might happen. You have been lucky so far.' He took her hand and held it firmly. There was a rueful smile on his face now. 'I mean it, you must not do that again. It is no place for a young lady – especially a pretty young lady, if I may say so.'

They looked at each other for a long moment. Theo's gaze sharpened. His dark brows drew together. 'You do not mean to follow my advice, do you?'

'I cannot.' Kitty held his gaze. She saw the spark of anger in his eyes, watched his lips tighten, then a polite mask hid his emotions.

He inclined his head. 'If you must go back, take a sturdy serving man with you. Good day to you.'

Theo strode away as fast as his aching leg would let him. How could this girl make him feel so angry and so anxious at one and the same time? Why should he care what became of her if she was headstrong and foolish? But he did care and – if he let himself admit it, he admired her determination to do what she could to help those less fortunate than herself.

The devil of it was that in those back alleys she would soon attract the attention of some ruthless crook. Then she would simply disappear. He had to make her understand that there were other ways to give help to the poor. He shook his head. He needed more time with her. She was stubborn; she was spirited, but she was intelligent and, in the end, he would convince her. The task was not going to be altogether unpleasant.

He dwelt on her wonderful brown eyes, honest and direct, warning him to mind his own business. Here was a young woman of principle, and at the same time she was a pleasure to look at. He drew in his breath, remembering how she smelled of roses. And that mouth... His frown disappeared. By the time he reached his rooms in Stratton Street he was smiling in a way that caused his valet to look at him twice.

CHAPTER FOURTEEN

Theo shook back the lace ruffles from his wrist and picked up a glass of wine from the tray the footman was holding out to him. He moved through the crowd to a position in the large alcove opposite the entrance to the ballroom. He scanned the brightly dressed dancers and the chaperons, who, for the most part, were not wearing masks.

It was Lady Stratford's masquerade ball. Theo had dressed in a deep crimson jacket and breeches of eighteenth-century style, with enormous cuffs, tight waisted and laced with gold. He had lace at his throat and at his wrists. It was the nearest he could get to his old military uniform.

Was it going to be another insipid night? He could not trust his leg enough to risk taking part in the dances. His lips compressed as he remembered those merry evenings in whatever Spanish village Wellington's army was encamped. There had always been music and dancing and Theo had revelled in the light-hearted atmosphere, the movement, the pretty girls.

Well, his leg was getting stronger and, one day soon, he would be able to dance again. But, for tonight, he needed some agreeable company to while away the time. Greg was out of town again. He had taken his groom, so Theo hoped he would be safe from any further attacks. And at least he was carrying out his official business. Better than moping around after that blonde doll. She would never make a soldier's wife, but there was no talking any sense to Greg on that subject!

As for himself, now, that was a different matter. Yes, he was hoping to see Kitty this evening, but only to talk her out of her determination to wander the streets of the slum areas. He would force her to realize just what dangers lurked in those narrow alleys. He took another sip of his wine and glanced around the room once more.

His eyes brightened behind his mask as he recognized Lord William in a costume from the time of Queen Elizabeth. Close to William, he could see a group of females. There was Caroline, dressed to match William, in a wide skirted robe and a huge gauze ruff. Her bright hair was curled and dressed with pearls. They were all masked but he had no difficulty in spotting the blonde-haired girl who was causing Greg to be such a dead bore.

But more importantly, next to her was a taller young lady. Theo's spirits rose as he spotted the shining chestnut ringlets. He considered her slender form in the charming gown. All sense of boredom vanished.

'Can you spare me the time of a dance?'

Kitty turned her head towards the tall gentleman who had appeared at her elbow. She inspected his magnificent red-velvet costume very thoroughly before looking up to his black mask. She saw the blue eyes sparkling at her and exclaimed, 'I thought it must be you.'

'Do you approve of my disguise?'

He sounded amused. She gestured at his ruffles. 'Indeed, sir, you have captured all the style of the last century's costume. It is splendid.' She glanced at the other guests. 'I had no idea that people dressed in historical costumes. And there must be plenty of suitable garments in my aunt's attics,' she added regretfully. She indicated her mask of feathers and silk leaves. 'My friend made this; she has such clever fingers.'

He was looking at her attire, his head on one side. She was wearing a simple yellow gown that toned with the leaves of her mask.

'I see nothing amiss. You look very elegant.'

Kitty eyed him warily. They had not parted on the best of

90

terms that morning, but now he was charm itself. He wanted to talk to her. Perhaps he was going to tell her that he had decided she could be trusted to manage her own affairs. Somehow, she did not feel that he would see things in that way.

Meanwhile, she found it very agreeable to be in his company once more. Their conversations were always interesting and always too short. She fanned herself, aware that her heart was bumping against her ribs with anticipation. Theo acknowledged greetings from several new arrivals but still remained by her side. He gave her another long look.

'Will you consent to sacrifice a dance for me – you know I cannot take my part on the floor?'

'It is no sacrifice,' said Kitty warmly, 'but I know what you are planning to say to me.'

She could tell he was smiling behind his mask. He tilted his head to one side and quizzed her. 'Someone has to say it.'

They were interrupted by their hostess, who sailed up to greet the whole of Caroline's group.

'What splendid costumes,' she said, 'you are all very fine. I just wanted to remind you to take a walk through the conservatory. You know my husband is a most enthusiastic collector of foreign plants and there are some exquisite blooms open at present.'

'How interesting, ma'am,' exclaimed Amelia. 'It is a favourite hobby of my father's, also. I shall be able to tell him about your collection.'

Lady Stratford beamed at her. 'In that case, come at once, before the crowd gets there.'

She swept them through the ballroom and along a wide passage, discussing rare blooms with Amelia.

'So your little friend does have other interests than horses and fashion,' Theo murmured as he walked beside Kitty.

She shook her head crossly. 'Why are you so determined to dislike her? She is a very talented young lady – and kind.'

He shrugged, but made no reply. They had reached the conservatory and were all loud in their praises of the splendid display. There were many exotic flowers and strange, spiky leaved bushes. They wandered round in genuine admiration for the patience and care that had gone into producing such a beautiful environment.

The lush greenery created a calming atmosphere. Kitty lingered in a quiet corner. What a contrast with the scenes she had seen that morning in the slums. She sighed. It had been a tiring day. Now she needed to gather her strength to counter all the arguments that Theo would shortly put forward to prevent her going to Martha's home again.

The others spread out and drifted away. Gradually silence fell. Still Kitty stayed where she was. She untied the strings of her mask and pulled it off. She was looking at a shrub, bearing a dozen brilliant red tubular flowers with vivid yellow stamens. Which part of the world had that come from? Somewhere she would never have the chance to visit. With a faint smile she reached out to touch the delicate petals.

'Here you are,' Theo's voice was soft. Kitty glanced over her shoulder. He also had taken off his mask. A warm smile lit his features and Kitty's heart turned over in her chest. He was irresistibly handsome. His costume suited his tall figure perfectly, setting off the hard planes of his face and his dark hair. She determined not to quarrel with him tonight, whatever he said about her visits to the Rookery.

She smiled back and indicated the flowering shrub. 'How strange, is it not, that this fragile plant can survive the journey from its home country and be brought right across the world to grow here in such beauty?'

Theo nodded. He took a step closer. His eyes were on her lips. He breathed hard and seemed to recollect himself.

'Miss Towers, – Kitty – never mind the flowers for the moment. I must make you understand how dangerous it is for you to venture into the slums unprotected, but I am determined not to quarrel with you tonight.'

Somehow he was holding her hand and Kitty was conscious of the latent strength in his grasp. His clasp was so comforting that she did not attempt to withdraw her own hand. She waited for him to continue. He waved his free hand impatiently. 'I am impressed by your courage and determination to do what you feel is right for the poor . . . but—'

Kitty pouted. 'I knew there would be a but.' She looked up at him, her face serious. 'It is something I have grown up doing. I help my father. Once you understand how it is possible to assist helpless people, it would be wicked not to try. Do you not feel the same?'

Theo sighed. His eyes searched her face. 'Do you have any idea of the risks to a young and pretty woman in those slums?'

She drew back slightly. 'Well, there are certainly some villains there, but I came back safely.'

'You have been lucky so far!' he said in a harsh tone. 'Next time it may not be so easy to avoid them – and there is always the risk of disease.'

It seemed as if they were going to quarrel after all. Kitty transferred her gaze to the red flowers, trying to recapture the sense of peace. She attempted to pull her hand free but he held on to it. She turned her head and looked up into his face. He stared back very intently. With a groan, he let go of her hand and pulled her into his arms. Kitty knew she should resist, but she was already melting against his broad chest. It felt so good to be held like this, to smell the tang of his citrus cologne, his clean linen, the scent of himself.

She raised her face without any urging and a moment later Theo's lips were on hers, warm and firm. His kiss was gentle at first, quickly becoming more passionate. Kitty felt the thrill of it right through her body. She leaned against him, her knees too weak to hold her upright. She felt his hand at the back of her neck, urging her closer still.

Her eyes closed, her mind spun away from everything but the sweet sensation of his kiss. Then abruptly, he broke off and even as she reached for him again he had turned his back on her. She was standing behind him and he was facing the entrance.

A light step could be heard coming nearer and Freddy's

voice, saying, 'I believe I can see someone here. Oh, hello, Weston. Are you alone?'

'No,' replied Theo, 'I have been trying to rouse Miss Towers from her contemplation of these flowers.'

Kitty had whipped her mask back into place. Her whole body was aching for another kiss. Her breathing was uneven. Her lips felt swollen and hot. She clasped her hands behind her back to hide her trembling fingers.

'Is Caroline looking for me?' she asked, 'I had not realized how long I had stayed here.'

'No matter,' said Freddy cheerfully, 'but you should rejoin our group now. You are supposed to be dancing with me at this moment, y'know.' He offered his arm. As she took it, Kitty glanced at Theo. His face was studiously blank but his eyes were burning into hers.

CHAPTER FIFTEEN

'You seem to be a trifle weary this afternoon.' Lady Picton surveyed Kitty critically. 'Did you find the masquerade ball tiring, my dear?'

'Oh, not at all, ma'am.' Kitty set another stitch in her work and examined the effect. She looked up. 'It was a fairly small gathering, but most amusing. Many of the guests had dressed in historical costume.' Kitty thought of one particular costume and smiled to herself. She rubbed a finger across her lips. How vexatious of Freddy to arrive just at that moment.

'It is very fortunate that you are acquainted with Lady Caroline. It has meant that you are included in so many invitations. Really, things have worked out far better than I had hoped.'

'Indeed, ma'am, most fortunate,' answered Kitty, almost at random. She was trying to recapture the sensation of Theo's strong arms around her.

'Did you get many invitations to dance?'

Kitty laid aside her embroidery and concentrated on answering. Her aunt was always anxious to know which young men were showing an interest in her great-niece. It amused Kitty that she seemed to know all the families and could assess at once whether the young man was a good prospect as a husband.

Not that it mattered, thought Kitty again. She was not intending to get married. What she had seen in the Rookery had shown her that there was far too much work to do in such

95

places; it would be quite impossible to be trying to run a household in addition to that.

Great-Aunt Picton finished her commentary on the young men named by Kitty. She shook her head. 'No new faces at that ball then.'

'Well, none that I could see, dear ma'am. They kept their masks on—'

'Hah! I am sure you know who is who by now. Well, let us have some music, child, if you please. It will not do to be neglecting your pianoforte practice.'

Obediently, Kitty went to the instrument and opened it. She played a selection of the old tunes that pleased Lady Picton. Eventually she sang a ballad and looked up at the end to see that her aunt was smiling – but not at her. The door of the sitting-room was open. In the doorway was Broome, beaming proudly in Kitty's direction. Just inside the room, his eyes fixed on her, was Etienne.

Kitty was embarrassed at so much attention. She rose abruptly, putting out a hand to close the music. To her annoyance the sheets fell to the ground. At once Etienne sprang forward to retrieve them. The door closed discreetly behind the butler.

'Please do not stop,' begged Etienne. 'it was so delightful. I would very much enjoy to hear a little more.'

Lady Picton smiled and nodded. Reluctantly, Kitty sat down at the pianoforte once more. She played several airs and sang one more song. Then she rose again. Etienne also rose to his feet.

'Thank you,' he said simply, 'I cannot say how much I enjoyed your performance.' His face showed his pleasure.

Kitty could not doubt his sincerity. 'Why, thank you, sir, but my skill is not so great. Just enough to entertain my family.'

'It was charming,' he replied, his brown eyes glowing. 'Believe me, I do appreciate good music. Do you know that Signor Alberti is in London? He will give a recital at the beginning of next week.'

She inclined her head. 'Indeed, I will be there with Lady Caroline.'

Kitty was amazed to see him looking as smart and unruffled as if his beating of the previous day had never happened. Surely he must be sore and bruised? But there was no visible sign of it. She watched as he turned his attention to Lady Picton, enquiring after her rheumatism. He exerted himself to entertain her with his usual mixture of gossip and funny stories.

Kitty picked up her embroidery again. She took little part in the conversation, content to see her aunt so well entertained. Then she realized that Etienne was on his feet once more and coming towards her.

'May I see?' He levelled his quizzing glass at the delicate flowers she had worked on the gauzy material. 'Ah,' he exclaimed, 'this is for an evening gown. How exquisitely you sew.'

'You are very complimentary today. But do not tell me you are an expert?'

He raised his shoulders with a mocking smile. 'I cannot make the stitches, but I can appreciate the result. Your sewing is so even.' He looked at Lady Picton. 'It reminds me of my mother. She was a fine needlewoman. My sister also—' He broke off and went back to his seat. There was a silence.

Eventually, Lady Picton said, 'Have you had any news of your sister recently?'

There was a distinct slump to Etienne's shoulders. 'Not for a long time, *madame*. In fact, she has only sent one letter since she went to Moscow.'

'We have to hope that all is well,' said the old lady bracingly. She looked at him with sympathy. 'At least, by marrying Prince Yevgeny, she is far away from that monster Bonaparte and his armies.'

He inclined his head. 'As you say. And she is no doubt used to that dreadful climate by now.' He made a determined effort to brighten up and announced, 'Maybe, one day, I shall go and visit her.'

Kitty raised her head at this. 'It must be a long journey to Moscow and quite adventurous. I am always fascinated by distant lands.' She smiled at their visitor. 'Have you travelled much?'

He gave a dry little laugh. 'You see before you a person who has spent his life wandering from one country to another. It becomes a little monotonous.'

'Oh. I suppose so.' Kitty thought about it. 'But I should find the variety in the scenery and customs so interesting.'

He shook his head. 'You can always find that information in books and pictures. Travelling is not really suitable for a woman, in my opinion.'

'Why ever not?' she asked indignantly.

He shrugged. 'Women are better off in their own homes. They are too delicate for the hurly-burly of long journeys and there are many dangers involved in travel.'

'But what about your sister? She has made a long journey, surely?'

Etienne nodded. 'In our circumstances, I had to agree to her marriage to a Russian prince. We have no estates any more, you understand. In short, it was the lesser of two evils.'

'But it means you have to live far apart.'

He opened his hands in one of his expressive gestures. 'She is well established with her husband. And there are plenty of servants to ensure her life is comfortable.'

Kitty considered the matter. 'She will have a great deal of responsibility then for the welfare of her household.'

Etienne gave a short laugh. 'You speak as if the welfare of the lower classes was of importance. They are there to save my sister any exertion. That is all I care about.'

Lady Picton intervened before Kitty could make a sharp retort. 'Kitty, my love, would you ring for Broome to bring the sherry. I declare, he was so entranced by your performance on the pianoforte that he has quite forgotten us.'

Kitty rose to pull the bell rope. By the time she sat down again, she had overcome the desire to argue with Etienne. She wondered if his experience of the day before had some bearing on his contemptuous attitude to the working classes. She examined him again and this time, noticed dark shadows under his eyes. He was suffering. She could only admire his efforts to appear as smart and as bright as usual. His visits to her aunt were an act of kindness, whatever his opinions.

CHAPTER SIXTEEN

'Oh, I am so *cross* this evening!' declared Caroline to Amelia. 'You have no idea how provoking the gentlemen have been since they went to their horrid prizefight yesterday.'

'But they were looking forward to the event for days – they talked of nothing else,' Amelia protested. She took the glass of lemonade Caroline was holding out to her. 'You are looking as immaculate as always, Caro. I love this hooped trimming on your gown – and the little silk roses.'

'Darling, I know your sweet ways, Millie but your flattery does not stop me from feeling cross. You have not had to sit through a meal with two men who do nothing but frown and snap if you ask them a question. I am certain they have all had a big quarrel but we ladies are not to know.'

'Well, that makes me glad we ladies do not bother with such sporting events if that is how it ends,' declared Amelia, turning towards Kitty. 'Do you agree with me, Kitty?'

Kitty looked at her blankly. 'I am so sorry,' she said, 'I was not paying attention.'

'Oh, really! Whatever has come over you?' exclaimed Amelia, half laughing and half cross. 'Ever since the masked ball, you have been lost in thought. Goodness knows what set you off.'

'Those wonderful flowers have given me a craving to travel the world,' replied Kitty. It was the best excuse she could think of. Until she saw Theo again, she felt unable to make any decision about what that kiss had meant. Had he just been flirting with her? She knew Caroline would think so, but to Kitty it seemed that he had given in to his feelings spontaneously, as she had. But why had he not made any effort to see her in the five days since the ball?

The memory of that kiss still made her go hot whenever she thought of it, which was very frequently. She stifled a sigh and roused herself to answer Millie's question.

'I wonder if they had other things to discuss,' she said, sipping her drink thoughtfully.

'Whatever can you mean?' squeaked Amelia.

'Oh, gentlemen have all kinds of business,' said Kitty, thinking of the mysterious letter that had been so important to two of them, at least.

Caroline raised her glass to her lips. 'They could be quarrelling over you, Millie.'

Amelia looked startled.

Caroline shook her head. 'Poor Greg Thatcham is certainly smitten. And Freddy always was your champion, so he has been bristling like a guard dog.' She gave a wry smile. 'Of course, we are so used to you and your beauty we do not always appreciate just what the effect is on strangers. But no, it was not a duel between those two – nothing of that kind. Poor William, he never can keep secrets so I know the problem involved Greg and Theo. He said everyone saw them arguing in a very heated way.'

'And that spoiled the atmosphere for the whole group!' said Amelia.

Kitty would have liked to ask for more details. But at least she knew where Theo was. He is still arguing, she thought, hiding a smile. A movement close by drew her attention.

'Here comes one gentleman who seems still to be in a good humour.' Kitty kept her gaze on Etienne, who was approaching with his light step.

'Ladies.' His smiling gaze embraced them all. 'The second half of the recital is about to begin. I have come to escort you back into the hall.'

They stood up and began moving along the corridor. Kitty

found Etienne by her side. As always, he was faultlessly dressed. She stole a glance at his classic profile and thick, sleek hair. It was now several days since she had seen him manhandled by the Irish bully. It was hard to believe it had really happened.

Suddenly he stopped and lightly took her arm, obliging her to stop also. Standing so close to him, Kitty could smell the faint scent of vetyver. She looked into his eyes and slowly registered that his expression was serious. Had he seen her on that day, after all?

'Have you come across Mr Thatcham today?' he asked, in a low voice.

She had not expected such a question and blinked at him in surprise. She shook her head.

'In that case. . . .' He bit his lip, not seeming to know how to go on.

Kitty was puzzled. 'Surely, sir, you were all together at a – a sporting event yesterday?'

He flashed her a sombre glance. 'Indeed we were. But it was not a happy party, I fear. Mr Weston—' He checked himself.

'Yes?'

'Forgive me, *mademoiselle*, I should not be speaking of my concerns. You are a friend of Mr Weston, is it not so? Come, the other ladies have returned to the hall. We shall be late.'

'Never mind,' protested Kitty, thoroughly alarmed by his manner. 'Please do not leave me to imagine something dreadful. I can see you are worried.' She looked at him very earnestly. He cast a quick glance up and down the deserted corridor. Through the closed door, the faint sounds of a violin could be heard, shortly followed by a tenor voice singing.

'We are already too late. We cannot interrupt them for the moment,' she urged, 'you have time to tell me.'

Etienne sighed. 'Very well. Yesterday, a large group of us went to watch a prizefight. It was out of town – at Richmond. It was a large party but not very harmonious.' He raised an eyebrow and shrugged expressively. 'Lord Lynsford was not his usual cheerful self – but enough of that. Suffice it to say that we split into smaller groups to watch the event. That part of the day went well enough. We agreed to meet afterwards at a hostelry to refresh ourselves before returning to London.' He stopped for a moment and looked very earnestly at Kitty. 'However, Mr Thatcham did not appear.'

Kitty stared at him. 'Why was that?'

He shrugged. 'I cannot tell. At the start of the day he had a black eye. He was knocked down in his room a few nights ago.'

Kitty nodded. She clasped her hands together tightly. 'But surely he has recovered from that?' she faltered.

'He said he felt well enough to come along to the prize-fight.' Etienne stopped and took a few steps away. He turned back towards Kitty and pressed a hand to his brow. 'I am not sure I should mention this, but. . . .' He hesitated.

Kitty's heart was thumping uncomfortably. 'Please do not stop there. I am full of suspense now.'

He shrugged. 'Very well, then. I could not help overhearing Mr Thatcham and Mr Weston arguing. They became quite heated. There was some mention of a letter. When Mr Thatcham did not join us at the hostelry after the prizefight and Mr Weston had a face of – of thunder—'

'Like thunder,' corrected Kitty. 'But please go on.'

'Well, since the end of the fight, I cannot discover anyone who has seen Mr Thatcham. He is definitely not in London. And now Mr Weston' – he grimaced – 'has not shown his face in town today.'

'Oh!' Kitty pressed a hand to her mouth. A cold knife of fear twisted in her stomach. She remembered Greg's plea for help and his grateful look when she hid the letter for him. Was it so important that he had been attacked a second time because of it? I am involved in this, whatever it is, was her next thought. She walked jerkily over to a seat and sank on to it.

Etienne followed her. 'Are you unwell? Can I get you a glass of wine?'

Kitty shook her head. 'I just need time to think.' He had

mentioned Theo and in a way that suggested suspicion. Surely ... but Kitty could see no reason to doubt Theo's loyalty to his friend. 'I am sure it is all a mistake,' she said firmly. 'No doubt we shall meet Mr Thatcham around Town tomorrow.'

Etienne inclined his head. 'Let us hope so,' he replied ironically. 'However, sometimes debt can make a man desperate.'

'How could attacking a friend solve a problem of debt?'

'If that person was carrying a valuable secret, and the other needed money. . . .' Etienne raised his hands expressively and shook his head. He leaned forward, his face very close to hers. 'I am sorry to give you such bad news.' Suddenly he seized her hand and kissed it. 'Miss Towers, do you know how delightful you look with your beautiful eyes so thoughtful. You are a very brave young lady. And now I will get you a glass of wine.'

The next morning, Kitty managed to drink her breakfast cup of tea but the slice of bread and butter remained untouched on her plate. She had spent a restless night worrying over her part in this unpleasant situation. Etienne had implied that Theo was connected with Greg's disappearance. That meant she was in part responsible because she had handed the letter to Theo. She had felt at the time that he was very tense – could it mean he was plotting something against his friend?

Kitty shook her head instinctively at this idea. He had told her he owed his life to Greg – surely no one would forget such a debt? Yet Etienne had hinted at money problems. It seemed that lack of money forced men to do bad things. Kitty suspected that she had stumbled into one of these areas of complicated diplomatic business that took place in amongst social events.

She pushed away her plate and rose from the table. Someone very ruthless was following Greg. How could she help to find him? She shrugged away the idea that this might put herself in danger. Deep in thought, she mounted the stairs to her room.

'Of course!' she exclaimed out loud, making the maid jump. 'Caroline!' She dressed in another new gown made by Miss Dilworth, a fawn twill morning dress trimmed with braid and with a double flounce round the hem. She smoothed her curls into a fashionable topknot and set her new bonnet carefully on her head. Soon she was on her way to Caroline's vast mansion in Cavendish Square.

When Kitty was shown into the dressing-room, Caroline's maid was fastening the buttons down the back of her very smart silk gown. Caroline adjusted the sleeves, considered herself in the mirror and nodded.

'That will do. You may go.'

The maid curtsied and slipped out of the room.

Caroline turned to the pile of shawls laid out on top of a chest. She held them up, one after the other, her attention seemingly focused on them. Without looking at Kitty, she said, 'So what brings you here at this early hour? Has your aunt heard about your indiscreet behaviour last night?'

Kitty shook her head. Caroline had already scolded her about her long tête-à-tête with Etienne. 'You know he is a great favourite with my aunt,' she reminded her friend. But what would Caroline say if she knew about Theo and the kiss that Freddy had interrupted? It did not bear thinking about.

Caroline finally selected a long, fringed shawl and arranged it over her elbows. She glanced up and fixed Kitty with a warning look. 'Whatever your aunt thinks is beside the point: she does not go into society nowadays. After your lack of conduct at the concert last night, people are going to talk.'

'What was I to do? He said it was an urgent matter.'

'Darling, you just never – ever – allow yourself to be alone with Etienne. Everyone knows he is a rake and that he can only marry a fortune.'

'But he is so devastatingly handsome,' murmured Kitty, half to herself.

'You see!' Caroline cast up her eyes. 'I fear you will be his next victim.'

'Oh no!' To her annoyance, Kitty felt her cheeks go red. 'I

find him charming to talk to but—'

'To flirt with,' Caroline corrected, looking at her very sternly.

'I did not mean it so,' retorted Kitty. 'Tell me, Caro, do you know what has happened between Mr Thatcham and Mr Weston? Apparently they have not been seen for a couple of days.'

'Do not talk to me about Theo Weston!' was the pettish reply. 'If he was not such an old friend of William's, I would keep my distance.'

Kitty looked at her in amazement. 'But you all seem to be on such easy terms with each other.'

Caroline lifted one shoulder. 'Darling, he is William's oldest friend. But he has a devil-may-care reputation. He is very wild, or he was until he was so ill.'

'Is that what makes him moody?'

Caroline looked closely at her. 'You are taking a keen interest in him. I thought you were encouraging our dear Etienne in his attentions.'

Kitty sighed. 'Are they all such sad rakes?' she asked. 'And do they quarrel often?'

'How can I tell? Men have such odd notions – a gambling debt, a bet, they have to settle these matters by duelling. They call it the code of honour. Then they all go to some prizefight together and become friends again.'

'Only it seems to have worked the other way round this time,' muttered Kitty. She was no wiser and left feeling as troubled as when she had arrived. She considered Theo's moody personality. He had a dangerous side to him, that was certain. But he genuinely cared about helping the poor. In a bad mood he was unapproachable, but even if he quarrelled with his friend, she felt in her heart that he would never harm him. There had to be a different reason why they had both vanished.

CHAPTER SEVENTEEN

'Good evening, Miss Towers.'

At the sound of that deep voice, Kitty stiffened. At last she had a chance to discover whether he was innocent of harming his friend. And there was also the matter of the kiss. She drew in a deep breath and slowly turned her head. Theo was smiling down at her. His lean face was unusually cheerful. Kitty noticed a dimple in his cheek. His blue eyes gleamed as he looked at her. Then the smile faded.

'You do not look pleased to see me.'

She stared at him rather fixedly. No; how could she feel pleased? She was afraid he had harmed his friend because of that letter. Even as she thought it, her heart felt like a stone. It was impossible to believe. But Caroline had warned her that Theo was a rake and that he had recently been in trouble with his father over gaming debts. At every level in society money caused problems.

By now Theo's smile had quite gone. He was watching her through narrowed eyes, his head tilted in that way he had of concentrating on her. Kitty forced her lips into a polite smile. 'Why, Mr Weston, it seems an age since we saw you in Town.'

'And in that time you have changed your opinion of me.' His voice was rough with suppressed anger. 'The last time we met, we were on much more friendly terms,' he added. Kitty felt the colour scorch its way up her cheeks. He was watching with a satisfied look on his face.

So he was just a rake, she thought, mortified. He just

wanted to make her fall in love with him. This was going to be a horrible evening.

As if to confirm her fears, he said, 'Come, Miss Towers, you are my dinner partner tonight. Let us take our place.' He offered his arm. After a tiny hesitation, she placed her fingers on it. To her dismay, even that moment's delay had its effect. She felt his arm stiffen and saw his jaw clench. Somehow, he kept the polite smile in place as they followed their hostess downstairs to the dining-room.

His left leg seemed to be dragging rather more tonight than when they had last walked together, on their way to visit Lady Stratford's conservatory. Kitty glanced at him from under her eyelashes. He was so tall and broad-shouldered and his evening clothes set off his athletic physique. She felt him to be her ideal – at least in his physical appearance. Her heart contracted with misery at the idea he could be a spy, working against his country.

It was in a very sombre mood that she sat down at table. Theo was seated on her left, which meant that for the first part of the meal, she did not have to speak to him. As etiquette demanded, Kitty began by exchanging small talk with the gentleman on her right. When the soup bowls were removed, however, she turned to her left and found Theo looking at her. Her heart jolted. His eyes were steady, questioning and as usual, their penetrating gaze caused Kitty's heart to beat faster.

Her instinct was to trust him. But for the past few days she had heard so many warnings against him, all from people who knew him so much better than she did. She cleared her throat. 'You have been out of town for quite some time, Mr Weston?'

He nodded. His gaze fell to her mouth. He seemed to be breathing in deeply. Kitty felt a blush creep up again. Was this a reference to that kiss? She was horrified to realize that she wanted to kiss him again. Looking into his eyes, she was sure he had not done anything underhand, he looked so open and honest – it was just that other people were warning her against him. It would be no good to ask him. He certainly did not look guilty, but, of course, if he was a spy, he must be a good actor.

'Miss Towers, in spite of all your – er – visits, you appear to be in good health. However, I fear that will not continue if you do not eat at least something.'

Kitty looked down at her plate. The food lay untouched. She made a show of cutting up a morsel of chicken. To avoid actually eating it, she murmured, 'What a pity your friend, Mr Thatcham, cannot be present tonight.'

Theo's brows snapped down over his commanding nose. 'To waste his time gazing in helpless adoration at your friend?'

Kitty glared back. 'That was not my meaning. I believe I already said that it is unfair to blame Miss Warrington for the looks nature bestowed on her.'

'I do not blame her for that, but it irks me to see the effect she has on Greg. He is a moth to the flame and she is quite indifferent.'

Kitty opened her mouth, shut it again and looked at him. Before she could decide how to reply, Theo continued, 'I wish you could keep her out of Greg's way, poor fellow.'

'Poor fellow?' gasped Kitty, outraged. 'And, pray, how can I do anything?'

'Come now, Miss Towers. You are the stronger personality, you can easily persuade her.'

Kitty's eyes flashed. 'You are very busy on your friend's behalf—' She swallowed and added, 'even though he has not been seen around for several days now. I do not forget that he had one unfortunate accident. And now, he has disappeared completely. Did you have anything to do with that?' Did he understand her meaning. She watched his face darken and almost shrank from the anger she felt radiating from him.

'What are you implying?' he growled. There was a moment of painful silence. His head was bent down and he seemed to be struggling with himself. Then he took a deep breath and looked her firmly in the eye. 'This is a matter I do not speak

109

of but for now I will make an exception. Without Greg's help, I would have died on the battlefield,' he grated out, somehow keeping his voice low. 'He risked his life to snatch me to safety. That makes a debt I will spend my life trying to repay.' He grasped his wineglass and downed the contents.

Kitty glanced round the table anxiously. Everyone appeared absorbed in their own conversations. Her eyes burned with unshed tears at the sincerity in his voice. Looking down she gradually realized her food was still untouched. She cut up another piece of chicken, but it was impossible to eat it. Her hands trembled so much that it was an effort to lay her knife and fork down without clattering them on the plate. After a moment she risked another look at Theo. He gave her a cold glance then turned his head away.

The rest of the meal seemed like a nightmare to Kitty. She felt so many conflicting emotions that she hardly knew how to stay in her seat. The conversation rose and fell around her. At last the hostess stood up and the ladies withdrew. Kitty kept her head high as she followed, but it seemed a long journey from the table to the door.

In the drawing-room she slipped into a quiet corner, desperately needing time to compose herself. She had made a grave accusation based on gossip. Theo had reacted so angrily she could not doubt he understood what she was implying. The fact that he had told her about his rescue showed how deeply she had wounded him with her comments. Kitty closed her eyes in anguish.

She was miserably aware that Theo had withdrawn from her. Now she realized how much she valued his good opinion. In fact, she told herself, without his regard, the future seemed very bleak indeed. How did it come about that each time they met, it ended in an argument? When he had first come up to her, he had seemed so pleased to see her.

The sound of a lively tune broke in on her thoughts. The young ladies had already begun the musical entertainment. Just then there was a soft touch on her tightly clasped hands. Kitty opened her eyes to see Amelia's concerned face.

'You are terribly pale,' she murmured. 'Do you have a headache?'

Kitty nodded. 'But it is my own fault.' Her voice trembled. 'I m-made him so angry. Oh, Millie, I wish we had never come to London.'

Amelia patted her hand. 'Do not feel too distressed. It will not seem so bad in the morning, I assure you. You know they will soon be asking you to play and it will cause comment if you refuse.'

Kitty drew a deep breath. She rubbed her cheeks. 'Does that look better?' Amelia sat down and kept up a gentle flow of comments about the meal, the guests and their fashions. It was soothing and gradually Kitty was able to focus her mind on the ladies and the music. When their hostess called upon her to play and sing for them, she took her place at the pianoforte with a polite smile on her lips.

She played a popular tune. Her voice was sweet and well trained. There was an enthusiastic request for her to play and sing again. She was halfway through the second ballad when she glanced up to see the gentlemen entering the room. Theo was standing just inside the door, his eyes fixed on her. Hastily, Kitty lowered her head. She finished the piece and rose from the pianoforte.

She could not help glancing towards Theo again. Her heart leapt at the softened look on his face. But then he blinked and turned away. Kitty watched as he joined a group of men chatting in an alcove. She made her way back to her seat and glanced around. He had disappeared. Her head throbbed unmercifully.

CHAPTER EIGHTEEN

'Do you really mean what you said last night?' asked Amelia, tucking her hands into her muff.

'About what?' asked Kitty wearily. The two young ladies were in Bond Street, where they had just been choosing new ribbon trimming to refresh their evening dresses. Kitty had spent another sleepless night and was hoping that some exercise in the fresh air would help to reduce her headache.

'About not coming to London.'

'Yes,' said Kitty with feeling. She walked a little way, her brow furrowed, then added, 'I am to blame. I have been carried away by our new life. I was too quick to make judgements without proper knowledge of the facts – and I can see no happy solution to the problem I have created.' She sighed. 'What about you, Millie? Are you ready to go home?'

She waited but Amelia did not reply.

'Have you met anyone you would want to spend the rest of your life with?' persisted Kitty.

The silence continued as they approached the corner of the street. Finally Kitty looked full at Amelia and saw tears in her eyes. 'Why, Millie, what did I say?' she asked in dismay. 'Please do not cry or, the way I feel at present, I shall start as well.'

'Let us look into this shop window while we compose ourselves,' whispered Amelia. After a few moments, she added in a firmer voice, 'Yes, I am aware of Mr Thatcham's infatuation. He is most truly a gentleman but I cannot feel any special attachment to him. . . .' She shook her head and sighed. 'It makes my life so much more difficult.'

They looked at each other mournfully. 'We were happier at home,' said Kitty. She stared unseeing at a chipstraw bonnet with long pink ribbons. The next moment both girls jumped as a familiar voice spoke from just behind them.

'*Mesdemoiselles*, are you choosing new bonnets ready for the Spring?' They turned to see Etienne sweeping his hat off and bowing to them.

Mindful of Caroline's scold, Kitty felt her cheeks going pink. If she was the subject of gossip, the people passing by must be watching out for any sign of indiscretion. A quick glance at Amelia reassured her that Millie was showing a more cheerful face than the moment before.

Etienne was politeness itself. He insisted on carrying their parcels for them and on accompanying them home. He kept up a lively conversation, telling them about a wonderful new opera singer he had heard at a concert the previous night. He was in the middle of this story when Kitty's eyes were drawn to a tall figure coming out of a shop just ahead of them. She had come to know Theo's height and broad shoulders now.

He looked in their direction. His eyes bored into hers, then narrowed as he glanced at her companions. He bowed slightly and turned away. It felt like an icy hand on her heart. To add to the chill sweeping over her, Kitty saw Miss Harling and her lady companion approaching from the other side of Theo. Miss Harling's eyes darted from Kitty's face to Theo's. She took on a smug look. Without even bothering to acknowledge Kitty, she greeted him loudly and affectionately.

Etienne had led Kitty and Amelia past by this time, so Kitty could not see how Theo responded to this. Her feelings were in turmoil. She could not bear to think she had lost his good opinion. He was the person whose views she respected the most and there would be no pleasure in going to parties and events if she could not share her ideas with him.

In her misery, she found it hard to listen to Etienne's amusing chatter. He made no comment about their meeting with

Theo until they had left Amelia at her front door. But as they walked back from Green Street towards Grosvenor Square, he suddenly said, 'When we met Mr Weston in Bond Street, he did not behave as a friend. He was very cold.'

'He is known to be moody,' responded Kitty in a neutral tone. She had no wish to discuss Theo with Etienne.

'Or else he is conscious of something bad and wanted to avoid any questions.' Etienne gave her a searching look. 'Miss Towers, again you are very pale. Are you quite well?'

'It is just these city streets,' she assured him, 'You know I am used to life in a small town – and we frequently ride or drive in the countryside.'

He beamed at her. 'So. . . . Now I know what will please you. I will take you for a drive to Richmond Park.'

'If my aunt permits,' stammered Kitty, dismayed. What would Caroline say?

He laughed. 'But of course she will permit it.'

And so it turned out. Lady Picton was delighted to learn that the friendship between her great-niece and the grandson of her dear schoolfriend was progressing so well.

'You make a very handsome pair, my love,' she assured Kitty. 'If only that young man had sufficient wealth, I do declare I would consider him a perfect match for you. Of course, he is French but from a very old family.'

'Caroline says he is a dangerous flirt, ma'am.'

'Oh, pooh! What does she know? When I was young, we were not so namby-pamby in our notions, I can tell you. Next she will be saying that driving out in an open carriage is not the thing to do.' Seeing that Kitty was still doubtful, the old lady tapped her cane on the floor and added in a sharp tone, 'Before she passes judgement on Etienne, Lady Caroline would do well to consider some of her other friends. One or two of those young men have reputations that do not bear scrutiny. Take Julius Hethermere's son – what's his name, now—?'

'Theodore Weston, ma'am.'

Lady Picton gave her a shrewd glance. 'I see he has wasted

no time in making your acquaintance! Well, he's been raking around town for years. *He* was a dangerous flirt, if ever there was one. Then he went to be a cavalryman and became a hero.'

'It is plain he misses his military career,' agreed Kitty, laying out her new ribbons on the little work table and opening her sewing-box, 'he must have looked splendid in his uniform.'

'Maybe so, but keep a proper distance, if you please. He has broken enough hearts – a handsome boy of course, takes after his mother.'

'I notice he has a very changeable temperament,' Kitty said, looking down at the tangle of threads in her sewing-basket. She added thoughtfully, 'I wonder if it is because of his wounded leg that he is so moody.' She pulled gently at a length of green silk and began winding it round a paper. She glanced up to see her great-aunt watching her with her head on one side. Kitty continued to sort and wind the silks. She knew her cheeks were red.

'Since it interests you so much,' snapped Lady Picton at last, 'it is common knowledge that his father prefers the younger son – this young man's half-brother. His own mother died when he was small.'

Kitty looked up at this. 'How sad, ma'am. It is as if he lost both parents.'

Her aunt made a sound between a grunt and a snort. She seemed ready to give Kitty a lecture on avoiding rakes when there was a welcome interruption. Broome came in with the sherry. There was silence while he set out the decanter and glasses. Kitty laid aside her work to go and pour out a glass for Lady Picton. She met her aunt's eyes as she put the glass down. Lady Picton nodded. 'So when will you go for this drive with Etienne?'

'The day after tomorrow, ma'am.'

'Very well. Now, if you will be so kind as to write a note for me to my friend, Jane Clemence, you can take it round as you go for your walk this afternoon. I must thank her for this new

115

novel she has sent me, *The Necromancer's Revenge.* It is most entertaining and passes the time wonderfully. You should try it as well, my love.'

CHAPTER NINETEEN

Kitty handed the note from her aunt to Mrs Clemence's butler and made her way down the steps of the elegant town house. At the end of Half Moon Street she hesitated. Her thoughts were in turmoil and she dreaded returning to the quiet of the house in Grosvenor Square to be shut up there for the rest of the day. How she craved the chance to walk energetically in the open air.

She really needed time to sort out her feelings about Theo. In addition to reproaching herself for her stupid accusations of the previous night, she was conscious of another new emotion burning in her breast. Miss Harling had made her feel jealous. If she had time to be alone in the fresh air she could convince herself that she still wished to return to Cheshire and continue helping Papa with his good works.

That was the best attitude to adopt now that Theo had shown he was no longer interested in her. And she was no Miss Harling, to keep pushing herself at a man. Kitty sighed. She cast a longing look in the direction of Hyde Park then reluctantly turned her steps towards Grosvenor Square. She heard a man's tread coming up behind her. In a very few minutes a gentleman drew level with her, looked her way and raised his hat. In consternation, Kitty stared at Greg Thatcham.

'Oh,' she stammered, drawing a shaky breath, 'y-you *are* in Town.' She took his outstretched hand, noticing the faint shadow of the bruise around his eye.

'Indeed. Got back last night.' He gave her his usual friendly smile. 'You are on your way home? May I escort you?'

'You have been sadly missing from our circle, Mr Thatcham,' said Kitty, putting a hand on his proffered arm. 'Indeed, we feared you were indisposed.'

'Oh, you are looking at my eye. Well, Miss Towers, as to that, I have been wanting an opportunity to thank you for the great service you rendered me in accepting that letter. It was very bad of me to ask you – but as you see, I was right to fear it might be stolen from me.'

'I assume I have been dealing in secrets of State?' Kitty said jokingly. She cast a glance up at him. His frank expression changed to one of shame.

'Theo was ready to murder me for involving you in the business. He did not approve at all. I am sorry for it, but indeed, at the time I was desperate.'

'Did he think I would betray you?' Kitty tried to keep the indignation out of her voice. Her eyes flashed. How dare Theo suspect her? No wonder he had been so persistent about getting the letter back from her in Hookham's Library. Then she remembered her accusation to him the previous night and bit her lip. A huge sigh escaped her.

Greg looked down in concern. 'You are unwell? By Jove, Miss Towers, now I come to notice it, you are very pale.'

'I am just a little tired,' admitted Kitty, 'this lifestyle is so different from the way we live in Cheshire. We are used to spending time riding or driving in the fresh country air, not to living in city streets. So you see, both of us are longing to go h-home.' Her voice shook.

Greg stared at her in alarm. 'I say, please don't be in a hurry to leave Town. If you wish to drive, I would gladly take you out in my curricle. And I am so looking forward to dancing with you – and Miss Warrington – at Caroline's next ball.'

Kitty's head was by now pounding so badly that it was an effort to speak. However, she remembered Theo's words. All too obviously, Greg was cherishing fond dreams of Amelia. It was only kind to warn him away. She forced a smile. 'You are very kind, sir. We shall certainly be at Caroline's ball, but I must tell you that Amelia is also eager to return to Cheshire. You see, she has such a gentle nature and is very attached to her home and friends. I fear she will never settle very far from them.' She held out her hand. 'Good afternoon – thank you for your escort.'

Greg looked at her dumbly. His face had lost all its colour. Mechanically he raised his hat as Kitty fled up the steps of her aunt's house and through the open door. She was sorry for the pain she had inflicted on him but now she needed time to sort out her own thoughts.

Did Theo really consider her to be untrustworthy, or was she misinterpreting Greg's words? In any case, Theo had made it clear that he was no longer willing to speak to her. The cold look he had given her this morning showed how angry he was. And if she had understood Greg correctly, Theo was a little suspicious of her.

As reasonable as her being suspicious of him! thought Kitty ruefully, remembering her remarks to him about betraying his friendship to Greg, but it just showed that dealing in secret documents meant a loss of trust even in friends.

Mechanically she removed her bonnet and smoothed out the ribbons. She hung up her coat with shaking hands and sat down on the window seat to stare out unseeing at the bare trees in the square. How had she allowed herself to get into such a terrible mess? She had lost sight of her true aims in life. Living in this constant whirl of social events and the constant obsession with high fashion, she had fallen victim to the habit of gossip.

Etienne's suspicions seemed ridiculous now. Wherever Greg had been, he was plainly well and on good terms with Theo. She felt wretched at her own folly in assuming Theo was guilty of some sinister act. This secret letter had made her lose her common sense. And now she had lost more than that. She realized sadly that just when she seemed to be developing a deeper understanding with Theo, she had destroyed his trust in her. She rubbed a finger along her lips as she remembered his kiss. There would never be another one.

She stood up and paced restlessly round the room. The sooner she left London and returned to her former way of life, the better. Only now, she was not so sure she would be happy ever again.

Late that same afternoon, Theo emerged grim-faced from Jackson's Boxing Parlour to see Greg standing outside Angelo's Fencing Academy next door. They looked at each other.

'You too?' enquired Theo at last.

Greg nodded. 'Does it show?'

Theo took him firmly by the arm. 'If you haven't worked your feelings off after all that exercise, there's only one other remedy.'

They set off in the direction of Piccadilly, moodily contemplating the havoc caused in their lives by females. Neither spoke until they reached the narrow streets near Covent Garden. At the first congenial tavern, Theo guided Greg to an empty table. He called for gin and the two settled down to try and drown their sorrows.

Night had fallen when they emerged, in somewhat better spirits but not totally steady on their feet.

'W-what we need, ol' fellow, is a good dinner.' Greg slapped his friend hard on the back, causing Theo to stagger and fall as his weak leg gave way.

'Didn't mean to do that,' mumbled Greg. Carefully, he leaned over and pulled Theo up again.

Theo swore furiously, dusted his breeches and announced, 'Dinner be damned – this calls for brandy.' He waited for his friend to agree. 'Brandy!' he repeated, to be sure Greg had understood.

Greg nodded solemnly. They linked arms to keep upright and set off on an unsteady course down a very uneven street.

Theo heaved a deep sigh. 'Never been like this before. We are properly dished this time.'

They sought around for another inn. In the dark alleys their progress was slow. Finally, they spotted a lighted building at the end of the street. Before they reached it, however, a pair of ladies appeared from a doorway and barred their way.

'We got lucky ternight,' purred the first one, making for Theo, 'an' you'll be 'appy, I can promise yer that.' She reached up to slip her arms round his neck.

Theo peered at her painted face and muttered something under his breath. Her cheap scent assailed his nostrils. Suddenly he sobered up. 'No,' he growled, drawing himself up to his full height. His black brows snapped down in a deep frown.

'Jus' a quick drink wiv yer then,' coaxed the woman. 'Wot yer doin' 'ere if yer not come ter see us?'

Greg was holding the other woman off by the simple means of grasping her arms.

'Oi, lemme go!' she shrieked at him, 'I ain't gonna prig yer, no'ow.'

'Let's get out of here.' Theo found a coin in his pocket. He handed it to the first woman and pulled Greg away. With the women's coarse shouts ringing out behind them, they found their way to a larger street. After examining the place carefully, they decided on their direction and set off westwards. It took them a long time but at length they were in Pall Mall. Here, their pace slowed again.

'Dinner. . . .' said Greg thickly, 'we need dinner.'

'You are drunk, man,' replied Theo. 'I know you: always stick to one idea when you are drunk.'

'You not drunk, ol' fellow?'

'Not as bad as you.'

'She'd never make a soldier's wife' Greg exclaimed suddenly, in a tone of deep sorrow. He stopped and prodded Theo's chest with his forefinger. 'She's a-a – an angel . . . but she'll never b-be mine.' He shook his head slowly and pressed his lips together grimly.

Theo put a hand on his shoulder. 'She really bowled you over, but she is not the girl for you.'

They stood there, a little hazy. Greg raised his head and took a deep breath. 'What about you, ol' fellow?'

Theo's only answer was a harsh crack of laughter. He turned away, shaking his head. He put a hand against the wall to steady himself. The air was cold now and eventually they moved off again. Greg had relapsed into a gloomy silence and Theo was busy with his own thoughts. His face was bleak.

As they rounded a corner into the now deserted St James's Street, a door across the road opened. Light shone out. Theo blinked, shook his head to clear it and looked more closely. He pulled Greg to a halt behind a clump of bushes.

They both watched Etienne de Saint-Aubin descend the steps, glance around and slip away into the darkness. Theo frowned and looked again at the house where the young Frenchman had been visiting. Greg was blinking at him owlishly. Theo raised a finger to his lips. It was a long time before he signed to his friend to move on again. They walked the rest of the way to Stratton Street in silence.

'This ain't my bed,' complained Greg, as he lay down on the sofa. Theo pulled his boots off and found a blanket to cover him.

'No, but better than another black eye,' he muttered. Greg was already snoring.

CHAPTER TWENTY

Kitty stood in front of her aunt for that lady to inspect her clothes. Lady Picton examined her from head to toe and nodded. 'Very well,' she commented, 'you look very well indeed. That yellow dress sets off your pelisse better than I would have thought. Put your bonnet on, child. Etienne will be here any minute.'

In silence, Kitty tied the strings of her bonnet. Her aunt tapped her silver-headed stick on the floor impatiently. 'Well, have you nothing to say, child? Here's a handsome, elegant young man calling on you and you show not the least interest. You liked him well enough when you first saw him.'

'Indeed, ma'am, he is everything you say,' replied Kitty in a colourless tone. 'He is also much sought after at all social events and he has a great talent for witty conversation.' She pulled on her gloves. 'And I must admit,' she added thoughtfully, 'he dances beautifully and has the gift of always appearing charmed by his partner.'

'In short, he is universally pleasing...which leaves just one defect.' Kitty looked at her in mute question. 'His lack of fortune.' said Lady Picton, sipping her tea and watching Kitty over the rim of the cup.

'It is surely wrong to call that a defect,' objected Kitty, her eyes flashing, 'a lack of money is not a crime.'

'Fiddle-faddle, child. These are country notions. In society, a lack of fortune is a crime – or at the very least a major handicap. Etienne is thirty years old and should be married and setting up his family. But he cannot do so unless he finds a rich wife.' She took another sip of tea.

Kitty was a little uneasy. Why was her aunt insisting on this? If it was to try and make up a match for her with Etienne, it did not make sense. It could not work, as neither of them had any fortune. But her aunt had seen clearly. At first, she had found Etienne fascinating. More than that, she had found him exciting.

She remembered her first ball, and how she had dressed with such care, hoping to please Etienne. But that was where she had made friends with Theo. And little by little her opinion of the two men had altered. Both were extremely handsome but their characters were widely different. Etienne was all charm on the surface while Theo only revealed his good side when coaxed. The inner person was more important, thought Kitty.

She considered Theo. It was not his good looks nor his rakish charm that drew her, she was attracted by the hidden depths she sensed in him. He had great warmth of character under that cool exterior. She felt sure he could be a great social reformer – with proper encouragement, of course. There was a dreamy smile on her face when Broome came in to announce that *moosoor* was waiting in his carriage.

Etienne smiled at her as he helped her up into the curricle and set a rug over her knees.

'The horses are very fresh,' he warned her. 'I hope you do not mind a lively ride.'

'On the contrary, it will be such a pleasure. And I am so looking forward to seeing open green spaces.'

For the first few miles he was obliged to give all his attention to driving. When the streets grew quieter and the houses more spread out, he glanced at Kitty with a smile. 'You are not so pale today, Miss Towers. You are recovered, no, from your headache?'

'Oh, yes,' she assured him. 'and I am enjoying the treat. It is a pleasant change to see the grass and the trees. I had not realized how fast the spring is coming along.'

He returned a mechanical answer. Kitty glanced at his handsome profile. A few weeks ago she would have been delighted to be out in his company. Now she was more concerned that being seen out with him would harm her reputation, as Caroline insisted it would. But did the fashionable world know that he was such a favourite with Great-Aunt Picton? And how could she refuse to obey her aunt's express wish?

The horses slowed. 'This is where we enter the park,' explained Etienne, sweeping neatly through the gates. Now he exerted himself to point out interesting features and landmarks. But he lacked his usual sparkle. It dawned on Kitty that he was uneasy. Can it be to do with me? she asked herself. He looked a little pale and heavy-eyed and his manner was more forced, as if he had a weighty matter on his mind.

The fine day had encouraged other people to venture out. There were a number of vehicles and riders in the Park. Etienne drove on until he reached an open area where the land fell away in front of them towards the river. It was a very beautiful view and at the same time, Kitty noticed that he had selected a spot where they were sheltered on both sides by bushes and trees. Etienne pulled the bays up. He turned towards Kitty and now she could see the strain in his eyes.

'I trust this is sufficiently rural to please you,' he said, indicating the peaceful valley before them. 'We will allow ourselves a short space to contemplate nature.'

She nodded, forcing her lips into a smile. 'Indeed,' she replied, 'on a day like this it is delightful.' But her heart sank. If anyone had recognized her and reported that she had been in a secluded place with Etienne, Caroline would be furious with her. She hoped nobody else did come by to see them.

'I have become concerned about your safety,' announced Etienne.

Kitty jerked her head round. 'I beg your pardon?'

He fixed his large dark eyes on her earnestly. 'I fear your acquaintance with certain young men in your circle of friends could lead you into danger. I mean of course Mr Thatcham and his friend, Mr Weston. They are soldiers and I am certain they are dealing in political secrets.'

Kitty frowned and uttered a protest. Etienne possessed himself of her hand and held it firmly. 'No, please listen to me. You are too innocent to realize what is happening. You have seen how Mr Thatcham has a black eye, yes?'

She nodded. A shiver ran down her back as she remembered that morning in Hookham's Library when Theo had given her a dark warning of the dangers involved in diplomatic secrets. It seemed Etienne was also mixed up in these hidden political plots. Her throat tightened up. Now she really was in a very difficult position. She knew she would have to deny any knowledge of such matters and hoped she could do so convincingly.

Etienne watched her expression change and inclined his head. 'Someone attacked him to obtain whatever message he was carrying. That person could attack any of his friends, if he suspected they were helping him. Believe me' – his grip on her hand tightened – 'I have lived in dangerous places and have seen many political quarrels end in violence.'

'But how vital a secret could it be?' Kitty demanded. 'They are just two young officers. They would not be entrusted with important matters.'

A fleeting smile crossed Etienne's face. 'It is the young officers who do the hard work and risk their lives. But please, Miss Towers, just think. Have you not noticed how frequently Mr Weston disappears from town? Never for long, but long enough to be going to secret meetings, perhaps. . . .'

All Kitty's pleasure in the outing had gone. Something seemed to be clawing at her stomach. She pressed her free hand to her mouth as she considered the facts. Finally, she nodded. 'All that you say is true,' she admitted reluctantly. 'I thank you for your concern.'

For the first time, he seemed to relax. He gave her his usual beaming smile. 'You take a weight from my mind.' He released her hand and flung out his arms. 'In fact, I now feel quite light-headed with relief.'

She had to smile. He was so demonstrative, his immediate change of mood made her feel more relaxed. And yet a little doubt remained. Why did he want to bring her out here to say all this? The last time she had allowed herself to be influenced by him, she had made a grave mistake and alienated the man whose good opinion she valued most.

Etienne's excitement roused the horses and they started to move forward. He seized the reins and checked the bays. As he was doing so, Kitty stole a look at him. She sensed that he was still watchful, even though he continued to smile and make conversation. Then an idea occurred to her. She bowed her head a little, frowning in concentration. It did make sense. He was jealous on her account. That seemed the best explanation of his constant attacks on poor Theo.

Just as she reached this conclusion, Etienne leaned forward and studied her face. 'You are still very thoughtful,' he said in a gentle tone, 'can it be that I have frightened you? You are very close to Lady Caroline and her group of friends.'

Kitty shot him a sparkling look. 'I am not frightened, sir. I have done nothing to make me afraid. But these are new ideas – and not very pleasant.'

'Indeed.' He inclined his head. 'However, I felt it necessary to warn you because if you should be approached – for example, to hide a letter or a small packet, at once that puts you in danger.' He grasped her hand again. 'And I could not bear that. You are too beautiful, to precious to be a tool in the plots of spies.'

She withdrew her hand. 'You are very good,' she said, keeping her tone indifferent, 'and now let us leave this topic.' She hoped she was concealing her dismay. Could it be that he suspected her? The reference to the letter was very precise. Kitty gestured to the clouds thickening on the horizon. 'This is a beautiful view,' she said, 'and I am most grateful to you for the opportunity to enjoy it. However, I think perhaps it is time to return home.'

He showed his white teeth in a laugh. 'Oh yes, your reputation. Or rather, mine, is it not so?' He gave her a wicked grin. Suddenly, his mood had changed as if a weight had dropped from his shoulders. He gathered up his reins and turned the horses back towards the entrance to the park. They advanced at a trot, crossing several other curricles and groups of riders.

Kitty's heart sank as she heard a familiar and unwelcome voice hailing them. Etienne slowed his pair to a walk and another curricle came abreast. Miss Harling, smiling a very satisfied smile, was looking at Kitty.

'What a surprise,' she exclaimed, 'and to see you out with our dear Etienne.' She made no attempt to introduce the colourless gentleman driving her. Kitty and Etienne bowed and drove on.

'Ah, that one, she is always keen to gossip.' Etienne's accent was more pronounced in his anger. 'She is not a good person to have as a friend.'

'She is just a passing acquaintance.' Kitty wondered what sort of tale Miss Harling would tell. It was the last and worst blow since that wretched dinner party. Now she could not feel any comfort even in the open spaces and greenery of the park. Throughout the whole return journey Etienne kept up a flow of easy, amusing chatter. Kitty, who had more than enough to think about, merely responded with a few smiles and nods.

She was thankful when at last they reined in outside Lady Picton's house. Pulling herself together, Kitty politely thanked him for an agreeable drive. She was about to descend from the curricle when he put a hand on her arm. Surprised, she raised her eyes to his in a mute question.

'Please be careful.' His own eyes were dark and solemn, almost pleading. 'I would be desolated if harm came to you. I mean it, Kitty.' He said it so earnestly that she had to overlook his use of her name.

'Yes, er – th-thank you,' she stammered, climbing down hastily and turning towards the house. Etienne watched until she reached the top step before touching his hat and driving off. Kitty saw him disappear along the street. She felt sure he had just given her a warning. A cold shiver ran down her spine.

CHAPTER TWENTY-ONE

'I tell you, Greg, you are foolish to linger here.' Theo frowned at his heavy-eyed guest. They were seated at the table in Theo's room, a large breakfast set out in front of them. Greg's plate was laden but his appetite seemed to have deserted him. He lifted his tankard with a shaking hand and gulped down the contents.

'Don't usually feel like this after a few glasses,' he groaned.

Theo blinked to quell his own headache. 'Agreed, old friend. But when we were young officers in Spain, we had fewer problems to trouble us.' He gazed out of the window at the pale-blue sky behind the rooftops. 'Just the next campsite, the next skirmish, the dances, our horses – oh, it's no good to remember!' He brought himself firmly back to the present.

Greg cleared his throat. 'Your life is here now,' he ventured. 'And maybe between your diplomatic efforts and your charity work, your role will be more important for the outcome of the war.'

Theo's black brows snapped down. 'What do you know of my charity work?'

Greg propped his head on his hand to face the freezing blue glare. 'Who else would know your movements? Who else would have to be informed?'

'By Gad, who has been spying on me?' Theo leaned forward, eyes narrowed. 'Did William tell you?' All at once the anger faded. 'Sorry, Greg, I understand . . . all part of the dirty game we play. I told you myself, didn't I, that I wanted some purpose in life. It seemed that the best thing I could do was to help my fellow soldiers when they have been wounded so badly they cannot help themselves.' He pushed his chair back and strode over to the window. He drummed his fingers on the sill as he stood frowning across the street.

Suddenly he came back to the table and leaned both hands on it, looking Greg very firmly in the eye. 'And that brings me back to my argument. Wellington's campaign is on a knife edge. You have the letters that guarantee him the money for his new defences. His enemies here are wanting to know what has been agreed, so they can prevent him from gaining any further glory; the fools.' He tapped his finger on the table. 'It's time you set off. You are in danger now. What we saw last night tells me that.'

'Etienne de Saint-Aubin? He's an aristo. He's no supporter of Bonaparte.'

'Maybe, maybe not. But he came out of Lord Dalbeagh's house and he *is* violently opposed to Wellington, let me tell you!' Theo frowned fiercely. 'Lord, don't I wish I could go back to Wellington. I would not be hanging around here a minute longer than I had to.'

'I only received the letter from the Foreign Minister yesterday,' protested Greg. 'Agreed, now I can leave, but my boat does not sail for another two weeks. There is plenty of time to get to Portsmouth. Anyway, I won't go until after Caroline's grand ball.' His usually amiable face was stubborn.

Theo looked at him intently. 'Why prolong the agony?' When there was no reply he shrugged. 'Very well, five more days, then. But you do not go out alone. They are after you and they are desperate.'

With a sigh, Greg nodded and refilled his tankard.

The next day, both gentlemen were heartily glad to get out of the house. Very smart in their buckskins and caped driving cloaks, they climbed into Greg's curricle. The bay horses were restive after several days without exercise. Greg got rid of some of his own frustration in managing their high spirits.

131

'They are not really broke to town traffic,' he panted, as the horses sidled at every passing mail coach or barking dog. But Theo, wrapped in his own thoughts, only grunted. He stretched out his long legs to brace himself against the jolting of the carriage. Arms folded and face grim, he was dwelling on a pair of smiling brown eyes and a desirable mouth – and the scent of roses. His own mouth tightened.

They were driving into the City and the streets became narrower and more winding. At last Theo roused. 'That is the third time you have driven us past Hoare's Bank and on to the Mermaid Tavern,' he drawled. 'Are you checking if anyone is following you?'

'Not really, old fellow. I was looking out for a certain person. This last time he was there. All is clear and now we will meet up at The Mermaid.' He glanced at Theo. 'You were asking how I get my information. . . .'

'Oh, Lord! What else are you mixed up in?' Theo discreetly felt the pistol in his coat pocket. 'Why choose such an area of cutthroats and thieves to meet anyone? And who is going to look after your horses while we talk to this – person?'

Greg chuckled. 'Why, you are. My informant will disappear if I bring anyone with me.' He glanced at Theo's frowning face and added, 'Be easy. Jem won't let me down.'

Theo walked the horses slowly up and down the road, keeping an eye on the door of the tavern all the while. He was thinking about Kitty Towers again. Why had she accused him of betraying Greg? Who would put such ideas into her head? She was a clever girl and her determination to use her abilities to help the less fortunate aroused his admiration. For a second he closed his eyes and remembered how charming she looked and sounded at the pianoforte last Monday evening. He had been within an inch of approaching her again to try and sort out their quarrel.

The curricle dipped as Greg jumped up. 'You drive,' he said tersely. 'let's get back.'

'Bad news?' Theo turned the carriage and dropped the reins slightly. The horses set off willingly. There was a lengthy pause. Then Greg gave an embarrassed cough. 'Don't know,' he grimaced. 'Oh, dash it, have to say it. You will not like it though.'

'What will I not like?' But Theo already had an idea.

'Jem reports that – that Saint-Aubin took Miss Towers driving yesterday to Richmond Park.' He stopped and glanced warily at his friend. Theo's eyes were blue ice. 'It means,' went on Greg unhappily, 'that we have to consider whether – whether—'

'Whether she is a spy. Oh, for the Lord's sake, Greg, that is ridiculous. You trusted her with your most important letter.'

'I know,' muttered Greg, 'but people can be persuaded to change their views. And there is no denying she is on good terms with that Frenchman.'

Very upright, Theo frowned between the leader's ears as he drove back towards Piccadilly at a shockingly fast pace. Greg wisely kept silent, not even protesting when Theo kept on past Stratton Street, past Hyde Park and on into the main road to the south-west. By the time he reached the busy commercial area nearer to the river, the horses were sweating. Theo slowed them to a trot and shot a glance at his companion.

'I could fight you for your last remarks, you know.'

Greg gave a short laugh. 'Damn it, old fellow, that temper of yours is still as fiery as ever. Do you think I like to tell you such things?'

Theo shook his head. 'I understand – but you are wrong,' he ground out. Then, with an effort to control his temper, he added, 'Well, it was better to drive out here than to go back to my rooms. I would surely have throttled you there!'

'You could have tried,' retorted his friend cheerfully. 'You never managed it yet, old fellow. Er – where are you taking us?'

Theo gave him a rueful grin. 'You are going to see my hospice. It is not very big – I shall do more when I can raise the funds – but at least the poor devils here have a roof over their heads. There is enough land for them to grow vegetables and keep a few pigs and chickens. One or two are fit enough

133

to chop wood and maintain the building. Between them they are managing. I am learning as I go along how to organize the whole business.'

'It is a wonderful scheme,' said Greg, much moved. 'And I am honoured you are taking me there. This is also something to tell Wellington. You are doing as much for the war as when you were on active duty.'

CHAPTER TWENTY-TWO

'I can see by your smile that you have received good news.'
Lady Picton selected another slice of cold ham from the serving dish. Kitty raised her head from the letter and looked
across the breakfast table at her aunt.

'Yes indeed, ma'am.' Her eyes were sparkling with pleasure. 'My sister Sophy has written most of it but everyone has
added a few words. It brings them all close to me. Mama
sends you her very warmest wishes. Oh and my brother
Charlie – he is the one who broke his leg – is able to walk
about again – with the aid of a stick, of course.'

'Well, my love, it is very pleasant to have good news from
home. It has acted on you like a tonic.'

Kitty felt there was a reproach in this. 'It is very comforting
to know that they are all well. But they are all envious of me
for spending time in London and for being so spoiled by you,
dear ma'am.'

Lady Picton blinked rapidly. 'You have such sweet ways,
my dear. You have made an old woman very happy – all my
household has taken you to their hearts. Indeed they have,'
she asserted more firmly as Kitty shook her head, embarrassed. 'I can tell you about the matter now,' she continued,
'because I begin to understand why your mother said no to
my request all those years ago.'

Kitty froze. She had wondered for so long what this matter

135

could be. She fixed a painful stare on Lady Picton, unaware that her face had gone white. Unable to speak, she just nodded.

Her aunt tipped her head on one side, like a little bird. 'When I heard that Frederica – your mother – had given birth to a fifth daughter, I suggested to her that she could let me bring you up here. You were the eldest and I thought you would benefit from a little more attention while your parents were so busy. As I have already said, Sir Geoffrey and I had no children.' She sighed. 'We would have been so happy . . . but your parents declined. And I must say, my dear Kitty, that I do begin to understand now how much it means to you all to be part of a large family.'

'Yes,' croaked Kitty. She could feel herself trembling. It was a relief to have the secret laid bare at last. Her aunt was obviously waiting for some response to her disclosure. Kitty pulled herself together. 'That was a very kind offer, ma'am and I thank you for making it, but I will be honest and tell you that I would not like to be an only child – like Amelia.' She smiled. 'But she has always been like another sister to us all.'

'She is fortunate,' commented Lady Picton, laying down her knife and fork. 'Well, that is all in the past now. Pray pass me that dish of fruit, my love.'

Kitty obliged. She glanced at her letter again. 'My father mentions two books he wishes me to purchase for him from Hatchard's bookshop.'

'If you are going to Piccadilly, my dear, perhaps Miss Dilworth could go with you.'

Kitty cut up her bread and butter into small pieces before she answered. 'The little housemaid called Martha usually comes with me. She is neat and well mannered.'

'Martha? Oh, yes, I recall now. But you need Miss Dilworth for matters of your toilette. You still need a suitable fan and slippers to match your new gown.'

Kitty was already feeling embarrassed by her aunt's latest gift of an elegant pink silk ball dress. None of her protests –

and she had made many – had moved the old lady's determination. 'I think we have chosen exactly the right style and
colour for you.' she had insisted, 'I am determined you will
outshine all the other girls at this ball and have the fine beaux
falling over themselves to dance with you.'

Now Kitty rose from the table. 'Well, ma'am, perhaps I
could look at some possible fans this morning and go back to
make a choice in a day or two?'

'Very well, child,' approved Lady Picton. 'But do not be too
long. We have a visit to make this afternoon.'

As she passed her aunt's chair, Kitty bent to kiss her cheek.
'You are so generous, dear ma'am, that I am almost mortified.
Be sure I shall find some way of thanking you properly.'

Lady Picton shook her head. 'Well, well, who knows. That
may happen sooner than you think.' This mysterious remark
was accompanied by one of her sharp glances but Kitty
decided not to pursue the matter any further.

It was not long before Kitty, with Martha by her side, was
walking along Grosvenor Square. Martha was looking at her
hopefully.

Kitty smiled. 'I have some errands to do, Martha. But if we
hurry, we have just time to visit your mother. Maybe this time
we shall find Sam improving.'

The two girls quickened their pace, stopping only to
purchase some lemons and sugar for the invalid. They soon
reached the end of Piccadilly and the wide streets. They
plunged into the crowded narrow alleys, where the stench of
dirt and garbage caught in Kitty's throat. She was becoming
familiar with the route now and knew they did not have to go
too far into the Rookery.

The one room where Martha's family lived was clean if
sparsely furnished. The children knew Kitty now and clus-
tered round following every move as she looked at Sam and
talked to his mother. The little boy was still feeble and his
breathing was laboured but he was definitely improving.

'Lady Picton will be looking for you soon, Miss, we must
'urry back.' Martha was becoming anxious. 'If she ever learns

you was 'ere, miss, I'd lose me job an' then where would Mother be?'

Reluctantly, Kitty bade the family farewell. Soon they were back in Piccadilly and Martha could relax. There was a bench outside Hatchard's, where the little maid sat and waited while Kitty went inside. She took a glance at the day's newspapers, laid out on a table by the fireplace but quickly set herself to find the books for her father.

When she emerged with a neatly wrapped parcel under her arm, Martha greeted her with relief.

'Oh, miss, proper scared I be,' she gasped. 'I seen a man watching you through the shop doorway.'

Kitty laughed. 'Come, now, Martha, how can you be so sure he was looking at me? There were lots of customers in the bookshop. He was probably waiting for his master.'

Martha shook her head. ' 'E went off sharp-like, a few minutes before you come out.'

'Well, then, I expect he was looking for someone but they were not there.' Kitty set off towards home and Martha scuttled along at her side.

'Oh, no, miss. I seen 'im this mornin' already. 'E was in the street outside me mam's 'ouse. I looked out while you was talking to Mother about our Sam. Only thought about it when 'e showed up outside the shop. Then 'e went and spoke to a gentleman on the corner of the street. Maybe 'e's a pickpocket.' She glanced around nervously.

'It must just be a coincidence.' But Kitty quickened her step.

Martha kept glancing uneasily over her shoulder but saw no more of the mysterious stranger. It was a blustery day and Kitty was struggling a little with her bonnet, her coat and her books when, just as she rounded the corner into Berkeley Street, a well-known voice said, 'Good morning, Miss Towers. You appear to be in some difficulty. May I be of assistance?'

Kitty raised her head to see Theo standing in front of her. Wrapped in his caped driving coat, he presented a large and formidable bulk. When last she had seen him, he had given her a cold nod and turned away. That had been her fault, she reminded herself, but it was too late to apologize now. In any case, her heart was doing funny things and she felt too breathless to speak. Another gust of wind tugged at her hat and strands of hair blew across her face, making her blink.

Theo moved closer. 'I really think you need some help.' He gently removed the parcel from under her arm. Kitty murmured something inaudible and smoothed her hair back under her hat. Theo stood watching interestedly as she tied her bonnet strings more tightly and rearranged her pelisse. Kitty risked another glance at his face. His eyes met hers and crinkled into a smile. She was still gazing at him when she became aware of someone loudly clearing his throat. Reluctantly, Kitty looked round to see Greg, waiting to greet her.

'You are looking well today, Miss Towers,' he said blandly. 'I trust you have got rid of those headaches that were troubling you?'

Kitty felt the colour creep up her cheeks. 'Indeed, sir, I do feel better. As I said, I like exercise in the fresh air.'

Now they were all walking along the street, Theo shielding Kitty from the worst of the wind. He indicated the parcel he was carrying. 'A walk to Hatchard's hardly counts as exercise, but perhaps you have been further afield?' He raised an eyebrow. Kitty had the grace to blush and his expression turned more serious. He shook his head at her but merely said, 'This wind is tiresome and blows up a lot of dust.'

He was still trying to control her actions! She was perfectly capable of getting to Martha's home and back. She had made the journey into the slums so many times now and not been in any danger. Why did he persist in interfering? She was searching for a suitably cutting answer when he suddenly asked, 'Have you been buying some travel books?'

Was this a reference to that letter, or to the evening he had kissed her? Either way, it added to her annoyance. She felt there was something more behind his question. She remembered Greg's words – *Theo was ready to murder me for involving you* – and suddenly all the hurt came flooding back.

139

'There are no letters in those books – yet!' she flashed. She saw him stiffen and felt a perverse pleasure in making him cross. But when he turned towards her, his face showed not anger but dismay. Puzzled, she glanced at Greg and surprised a warning look from him to Theo.

Whatever is going on? she asked herself, feeling a flutter of alarm. They both seemed to think she was involved in something suspicious. How hurtful it was! For a moment she toyed with the idea of hinting at some mystery, just to worry them. They walked on in an awkward silence. Eventually Kitty gave a brittle little laugh. 'I have been buying philosophical treatises – for my father. Of course I will write a letter to my family to put in with them.' She glanced at Theo, her large brown eyes reproachful.

He gave her an embarrassed look. 'I was only funning,' he said, 'but perhaps you really do dream of travel?'

Kitty sighed. 'Yes, I should dearly like to see some of the places I have read about, but with this terrible war, it does not seem possible to visit the Continent.' She turned to Greg. 'Oh, I am sorry, Mr Thatcham, of course you have to brave the risks and make the journey back to Portugal.'

He nodded. 'Indeed, ma'am. But that is a soldier's life, you know.'

They had reached Lady Picton's house and Kitty was receiving her parcel from Theo. He raised his hat. 'Will we see you in Hyde Park this afternoon?'

Kitty shook her head. 'I shall be accompanying my aunt to a tea party at Lady Deane's house.'

The response to this was a puzzle. 'Lady Deane . . . oh – ah,' stammered Greg. Theo gave a smile but made no comment.

Once inside the house Kitty realized that Martha appeared even more agitated than she had been outside Hatchard's shop.

'Please, miss, the man what followed us, it was one of those two gentlemen 'e was talking to near the bookshop.'

Kitty stared at her, aghast. 'What? Who?'

Martha gulped. 'Not the one as is sweet on you, miss, the

other one, with the light brown 'air.'

'*Sweet* on me. Hah! Er . . . when did this happen, Martha?'

'Just before you came out of the bookshop, miss. Oh, miss, are you angry with me?'

Kitty realized she was glaring and her fists were clenched. She shook her head. 'No, not at all, Martha. But do not speak of this to anybody,' she warned.

In her bedroom, Kitty flung the books down and tore at her bonnet strings, wrenching the hat off. She twisted her fingers in her curls as she thought through the events of the morning. How dare he spy on her! Having her followed around town and then intercepting her.

It was bad enough that he could even suspect her of being in some way untrustworthy. But to behave in such a friendly way and make her feel that he was truly warming to her again. She had been so pleased to see him. And surely, she had not mistaken the softening in his expression when he spoke to her or the interest he showed in her.

This business of the secret letters, whatever they were, was becoming sinister. How could she be sure who was a friend and who was speaking the truth? Torn between anger and distress, Kitty pressed a hand against her mouth. She forced back the sob in her throat and set about making herself presentable for the visit to her aunt's friend.

CHAPTER TWENTY-THREE

Kitty and her aunt were the first guests to arrive in Lady Deane's elegant drawing-room that afternoon. Kitty rose from her curtsy to find that she was being examined with a keen eye. She knew her appearance was smart but again she felt indignant that clothes and ornaments were of such importance.

Her hostess was a neat, upright lady, who must have been a great beauty in her youth. She nodded and smiled as her eyes met Kitty's.

'I warrant you have made life more lively in your aunt's house, my dear.' She turned towards Lady Picton. 'It must be very agreeable to have such a delightful young lady to take about. I must confess, I long for the chance to do the same.' She looked back to Kitty. 'I had four sons, so I was never able to bring out a daughter. And my sons all had sons. In fact, I believe you know one of them.'

Kitty looked a question.

Lady Deane laughed. 'Do sit down, my dear. We older ladies survive on gossip, you know. My grandson is hopelessly infatuated with your little blonde friend. The most exquisite creature he has ever seen, he told me.'

Kitty darted a glance towards her aunt but received only a bland smile. She was not sure how to reply. Either Lady Deane was indeed a sad gossip, or she was trying to promote Greg's cause.

'Miss Warrington is a very modest person,' she said at last, 'and would not wish to be the object of undue admiration.'

'Well, Gregory is a level-headed young man. But on this occasion, he appears to be completely bowled over.' At this moment another guest arrived. Lady Deane moved away to greet her. Kitty sat down by her aunt, hiding her dismay behind a polite smile. Both she and Millie were in a tangle and Kitty could see no way out of it.

It was not pleasant to suffer a heartache when there was no chance of a happy outcome, she was thinking. The knot of pain in her chest seemed tighter than before. She could not forgive Theo for suspecting her. He must have been alerted by the man who had spied on her and he had come deliberately to check up on her. There was a bitter taste in her mouth.

Her aunt laid a hand on her arm. 'Lady Deane is speaking to you, my dear.'

Kitty looked up and tried to smile. She accepted the cup of tea and took a sip. The warm liquid slipped down and, as she drank, Kitty felt her determination harden. Her misery was a private affair. She would present a calm and dignified appearance to all these ladies. After all, she had only to sit quietly as they chatted. She focused her attention on the group listening to their hostess.

'So unlike his great friend Theodore,' Lady Deane was saying. 'Why, he told me how Theodore was always brave to the point of recklessness in battle. And of course, it was Theodore who led a desperate charge at the French cavalry and got cut down – and Gregory who rescued him. Lord Wellington mentioned his gallant behaviour in a despatch,' she finished, her pride in her grandson's bravery plain to see.

This was bittersweet news to Kitty, doing her best to appear unconcerned. She was aware that her great-aunt was watching her with a gimlet eye. She made a show of sipping her tea, keeping her eyes lowered to hide her admiration of Theo's gallant courage. No wonder he hated his lame leg so much. But then she quickly looked up as the conversation took another turn.

'Well, with that badly injured leg, his army days are over,' another lady remarked. 'He is back on the town, but not such a rake as he used to be. He is quite a catch, after all – heir to a very handsome viscountcy.' Her eyes gleamed as she added, 'I see that Augusta Payne has brought her daughter up to town – she is desperate to marry the girl to young Weston.'

There was a general scream of laughter at this point. Kitty looked at her aunt in bewilderment, which made the other ladies laugh even more.

'Poor Letitia,' Lady Deane said mildly, 'if only she had a little beauty.'

'Or taste!' said another dowager scornfully. 'Young Theo Weston's mother was such an exquisite creature. I cannot believe he would look twice at Letitia Payne.'

'Maybe not but the Paynes are often guests at Weston Parcombe. Lady Payne is a great friend of his stepmama.'

Kitty tried not to feel jealous of this unknown girl whose family were determined to turn her into Theo's bride. But I will never be anything to him, she thought miserably. Why did it all go so wrong between us?

'Are you going to call on your grandmother?' Theo teased Greg, as they drove past her house in Mount Street on their way to Hyde Park.

'When she is holding one of her tea parties?' Greg's voice trembled with horror. 'I would rather face a whole French division than those dragons.'

'Faintheart,' mocked Theo. 'There may be some rewards – pretty young ladies to talk to. And maybe you should be talking to them, just to reassure yourself about their loyalty to King and country,' he added, in a sarcastic tone.

Greg heaved a sigh. 'We have already discussed this. I accept she might be just an innocent party but there are two questions to answer. One, what was she doing in the backstreets? That is the sort of place any kind of agent would lurk. And two, why is she suddenly so friendly with Saint-Aubin?'

'Perhaps it is more the case that he is attracted to her.' Theo directed a withering look at his friend. 'We do not all go weak at the knees at the sight of golden ringlets. As for the back-streets' – he shrugged – 'I would guess she was helping the maid's family. It should be easy enough for your Jem to check that.'

They drove on in moody silence and turned into Hyde Park. As they proceeded slowly along the main avenue, Theo added, 'Now I come to think of it, every time I have seen Miss Towers at any social event, Saint-Aubin has always been hovering close by.'

'By Gad, I do believe you are right, old fellow. Perhaps he thinks she is to inherit her great-aunt's fortune and is trying to court her. It is certainly a reasonable explanation for his attentions.'

'And means that she has nothing to do with these absurd suspicions of yours.'

Greg looked at him thoughtfully. 'Point taken, old fellow. Consider the matter closed.'

Theo stared ahead grimly. 'Wish I could!'

Knowing his friend's state of mind, Greg simply gave a tactful cough and concentrated on guiding his pair of horses through the cluster of carriages ahead of them. The wind was still strong and the crowd was thinner than normal. One young lady in a phaeton was struggling to keep her horses from breaking into a canter. Greg pulled up to let her through. Suddenly, he heard Theo utter a curse.

'Get moving, man, quickly!' he urged. Just as Greg was gathering up the reins to urge his pair along, a strident female voice hailed them.

'Too late!' groaned Theo.

A barouche drew alongside. It contained a large middle-aged lady and a younger version of herself. Both were fussily dressed in strong colours that did not set off their high-coloured complexions to any advantage. Theo looked at them with a frustrated resignation.

'Lady Payne,' he inclined his head, 'and Miss Payne.' He indicated Greg. 'My friend, Mr Thatcham.'

The countess barely gave Greg a glance. 'Dearest Theodore. What an age since we saw you. We were so disappointed to miss you when we stayed with your parents last month. But never mind, I shall expect you to call tomorrow.' She indicated her daughter. 'Letitia is quite impatient for a chance to show you her progress on the harp: you must remember how delightfully she entertained us the last time we were all together with your dear father and stepmama at Weston Parcombe. I recall that your papa was most impressed.' She gave him a toothy smile and waved as the coaches drew apart.

Greg was helpless with laughter. 'What a dragon!' he gasped at last.

Theo's brows were one straight line over the bridge of his nose. 'I am going out of town,' he announced through his teeth, 'now!'

'Steady on, old fellow. What about protecting me?'

Theo gave a snort. 'This time, the boot is on the other foot.' He glared around moodily. 'Did my father send her?'

'Is that the – er – suitable match he was proposing to you?'

Theo nodded. 'And it seems he had discussed it with her mother.' He raked a hand through his hair and scowled at Greg. 'Why are you laughing at me?'

'It – it was your face when she mentioned the harp!' choked Greg, putting a hand to his ribs. He wiped his eyes and gave a wicked grin. 'Lay you odds the countess will nobble you at Caroline's ball.'

'Oh, Lord! As if I did not already have enough to do there. . . .' He heaved a sigh. 'Do me a favour, Greg, dance every dance with Miss Payne.'

'Sorry, old fellow,' his unsympathetic friend seemed about to give way to another fit of laughter, 'I could not face that prospect. She may have every quality, but beside Miss Warrington, the contrast is too awful.'

'As I said before, you are a faintheart,' growled Theo. 'Well, at least whip your cattle up and let us enjoy a decent drive.' He looked around and uttered a curse. 'As fast as you can, man. Just go!'

'Now what is wrong?' Greg obediently urged the bays to a canter.

Beside him Theo let out a long sigh of relief. 'That was Miss Harling trying to accost us.'

Greg burst out laughing again. 'You used to like the ladies, dash it! Couldn't get enough of them, in fact. What has come over you?'

Theo grimaced. 'These days I need something more than empty comments about the weather and the next party.' Which was true, as far as it went, he thought, bracing his feet as Greg took a corner a mite too fast. The image of Kitty with her honest brown eyes and sweet expression came into his mind. He compressed his lips. He did not like the role he had played that morning in intercepting her. He remembered her angry look. It was going to be a hard task to win back her confidence.

CHAPTER TWENTY-FOUR

When Kitty and her aunt returned from their tea party Broome tendered a silver salver with two letters on it.

'The messenger said as they was urgent, m'lady.'

Kitty took one look at the flowing script on the elegant, hot pressed paper. 'From Caroline,' she said, breaking open the seal.

The note begged her to not to fail in joining a group of ladies at Caroline's home that evening:

It is a meeting to discuss ways of helping orphans from the current war, so I know it will appeal to you, dear Kitty. I have informed your aunt and requested her permission for you to attend. Bring that funny little maid of yours if you wish.

'Oh, ma'am, it does sound interesting. May I go?' Kitty looked up from her letter, eyes and cheeks glowing with excitement.

'Why, certainly you may, if you still have the energy, my dear, after so many outings today. I shall be glad to retire early, I must confess. But you will take Martha with you and John coachman shall fetch you home.'

'Oh, thank you, but there is no need for him to wait up for me. Caroline writes that she will organize our return. Amelia is also invited.'

The group of ladies in Caroline's sitting-room seemed

genuinely concerned to do something constructive for the young orphans. They were mainly older ladies and it soon became clear that some of them had a good knowledge of how the current war was causing much hardship and suffering in society generally. After a lengthy discussion they agreed that the best way was to establish a school, in a healthful area on the edge of town. Then they debated on how many children could be admitted and how to select them.

Kitty was totally absorbed in all these ideas. She rejoiced that at last these wealthy members of a privileged society were showing a more human and practical side. Here was a prospect of organizing help on a scale she could never achieve alone. The time seemed to fly past as she listened and offered her own ideas. She could not believe it when Caroline rose to her feet and announced that supper was served.

'But we have not finished arranging everything yet,' she protested to Amelia, 'what about the financing of this scheme?'

'I believe the gentlemen have been discussing that,' replied her friend. 'And surely you can see that some of the ladies are getting a little tired now.'

Reluctantly, Kitty followed as they went through to the dining-hall. A buffet had been set out and tables arranged so that everyone could gather in small groups. There was a loud buzz of conversation as the ladies chose from the elegantly arranged dishes. Liveried servants filled their plates and once they sat down, wine was poured.

The door opened again and the room suddenly filled with a cheerful burst of laughter and the sound of deeper voices. The gentlemen appeared. They all seemed in good spirits as they headed for the buffet. Kitty immediately picked out Theo's tall form. Once again she noticed how elegant he was, his broad shoulders setting off his dark-blue jacket to perfection, his long, well muscled legs showing to advantage in the narrow pantaloons.

She watched him cross the room towards the food, talking to Lord William as he went. How different he looked, relaxed and smiling. She turned her eyes to William. Whatever tale he was telling, it was making them both laugh. It was rare to see Theo so animated.

But even as she acknowledged to herself that he was exactly the person she wanted to see at this gathering, Kitty felt all the hurt and anger at his conduct that morning in spying on her activities. This was going to spoil an evening when they really could be working together for charity. It certainly meant another quarrel. She gave a tiny sigh and picked up her fork. While she was considering whether or not she could fancy the lobster patty on her plate a figure appeared beside her.

'May I?'

Startled, Kitty looked up. It was Theo, smiling at her as if he had never had the least idea of suspecting her of being a spy. He did not wait for permission but took the seat next to her and settled a laden plate on the table. He cast an amused glance at her supper.

'Miss Towers, it seems you live on fresh air.'

'Are you trying to provoke me?' Kitty said with a snap. 'If we are to talk of portion sizes, it would appear you have not yet eaten today.'

He laughed out loud, throwing his head back. She kept her face calm, secretly pleased at his enjoyment of that quip. Even while his suspicion stung her, she could not deny the warm sense of pleasure at having him close to her once more. It was a dilemma!

'What is it?' He set down his wineglass and tilted his head, studying her face. 'I have the feeling that you are not quite pleased with me?'

Kitty looked him in the eye. 'Well, I always prefer to be honest. This morning before I met you, my maid tells me that a man was following me – a man who reported back to—' She was stopped by Theo laying a hand on hers. He shook his head slightly, warning her to be silent. His face was serious.

'This is not something we can discuss here.'

Her mouth formed a little 'o' of shock. She stared into his

eyes, her own kindling. 'Then it – it was true that you thought I—' She felt horrified. He had been suspicious enough to have her *followed*! She swallowed a sudden lump in her throat. How could he suspect her of doing anything against her country?

She felt a sudden pressure on her hand, which was still lying under his. Kitty looked up and saw a rueful smile on his face as he looked at her steadily.

'Will you please believe me when I say that it was all a big mistake? I know I owe you an apology.' There was no doubting the sincerity in his voice. He squeezed her hand encouragingly. Recollecting where they were, Kitty hastily withdrew hers. After a moment, she nodded.

'Perhaps we can find somewhere private where I can explain the matter to your satisfaction.' His eyes twinkled. 'If you would like to see Caroline's conservatory. . . ?'

A blush crept up, but she kept her eyes on his. 'How can you recall such an episode?' Even as she spoke, she felt a thrill run through her at the memory of his kiss. How much she wanted him to kiss her again. She caught her lower lip in her teeth, shocked at how quickly her body could respond to him.

'Oh, very easily.' He drank his wine and gestured to the servant who hastened to refill the glass. 'In fact,' he remarked thoughtfully, leaning back in his chair and considering her, 'I think of it often and with great pleasure.'

This was teasing. Was he trying to divert her mind from the spying episode? She was not sure and it made her feel cross.

'Or else I could escort you home at the end of the evening,' he added, breaking in on her already seething thoughts.

'Thank you, but I have Martha with me.'

'Ah, yes, Martha – the girl from the St Giles area. That is another topic we need to discuss.'

'Oh, not now, please. We shall soon be returning to the drawing-room to make out a plan of action for helping the orphans.'

People were already drifting out of the dining-room. Across the table, Amelia was politely conversing with Greg.

Kitty looked up a little guiltily. She had been totally absorbed in her own affairs and had neglected her table companions. Amelia wore her usual sweet expression but Kitty, who knew the signs, sensed that she was uneasy.

Greg was leaning one elbow on the table as he described something, tracing a pattern on the cloth as he spoke. When he glanced up at Amelia, he had a look on his face that Kitty could only describe as besotted. He radiated tenderness. She heard Theo give an exasperated sigh and knew he was looking at his friend. She pushed back her chair and rose.

'Shall we get back to work?'

The rest of the evening was animated. Now the gentlemen had joined them, a plan of action was quickly agreed and people appointed to oversee the job of finding a building and equipping it, while others undertook to select the most suitable children to benefit from the scheme.

Kitty was glowing with enthusiasm at this positive action to help people in need. Theo made a number of suggestions, which were well received. Kitty caught his eye and gave him an approving smile. After that, she found him looking at her each time she glanced his way. Decidedly he was in a better mood this evening than Kitty had yet seen. Her pleasure in the whole enterprise was increased by sharing the undertaking with him.

When the meeting was declared closed and people began to drift out of the saloon, Kitty jumped up and walked over to Theo. He was talking to Greg but turned readily towards Kitty.

'Do these plans meet with your approval?' he asked her.

Her eager nod was enough to bring a warm smile to his face.

'It quite reconciles me to living in society, when I see how much can be achieved,' Kitty told him. She noticed that his eyes were focused on her mouth. It made her feel a little shy and she looked away. She saw Greg ready to assist Amelia into her pelisse. She felt a pang for him. But Theo was claiming her attention again. 'It is a way of giving positive help,' he was saying, 'and I do hope you will agree it is better – and safer – than anything you could achieve in the St Giles Rookery.'

Kitty tossed her head at that.

He took her hand. 'I cannot let the matter rest, even if your eyes are warning me to keep silent.' He gazed at her, his face serious. 'It is intolerable only ever to see you in company,' he murmured at last. 'I absolutely must make you promise not to go into that hellhole again. Now you are going to slip away and leave me worrying.'

Still sparkling from the excitements of the evening, Kitty laughed at him. 'Indeed I am, sir. But at least we have got through an entire evening without a quarrel.'

He sighed. 'Yes, but without a kiss, either.'

CHAPTER TWENTY-FIVE

'Miss Towers?'

The deep voice penetrated Kitty's thoughts. She stopped and looked round, blinking a little. Theo was on the other side of the road, on horseback. He was frowning at her. Kitty gave a gasp of disbelief. It was as if she had conjured him up. She had been dwelling on his face as she walked and turning over his remarks from the previous evening.

She had just decided that he was only flirting with her. Probably he was so used to having all the young ladies fall in love with him that he simply wanted to add her to the list. Even her friend Miss Walmseley confessed to being a little in love with Theo, he was so handsome and elegant.

So Kitty had made up her mind to admire his work for his hospice but to keep him at arm's length as far as she was concerned personally. But now he was in front of her once again and, as usual, she felt her willpower melt away. She was completely absorbed in the pleasure of looking at him and the temptation of spending some time in his company.

She retained enough common sense to try and hide her feelings. She smiled at him brightly. 'Good morning, Mr Weston. I see you have at last got your beautiful horse back.'

His frown did not lift. He walked Nimrod across the road and came alongside Kitty. His face was serious.

'Miss Towers, this is a very strange part of town for you to be in – and quite alone as well?'

Kitty looked round a little vaguely. 'I have been paying a

154

morning call on Caroline. It seemed to be a very exclusive area, so I thought I would make a detour to the north – it looked to be more open land and I enjoy walking when there is a lot to think about.'

Theo gave her a keen look. He dismounted without any sign of weakness in his left leg, noted Kitty. As he pulled the bridle over his horse's head and stroked Nimrod's glossy neck, she secretly admired his smart appearance. Man and horse were splendid. She could perfectly agree with Miss Walmseley on both points. Her eyes lingered on his profile. She jumped a little when he turned towards her, tilting his head down to look at her very closely.

'You seemed to be in a world of your own when I saw you.'

Kitty blinked. 'I – er – I was deep in thought—'

'And now you are lost, are you not?'

She looked around. 'Well, I do not recognize this street, but no doubt I would get back to Grosvenor Square eventually.'

He was frowning again. 'Where is your maid?'

'Martha? She has a blister and could not manage the walk. I sent her home before I reached Cavendish Square.' He was even more strict than Great-Aunt Picton, thought Kitty. She indicated Nimrod. 'Your horse appears to be in excellent condition.'

'Indeed. He is fully recovered and craving exercise.' As if to confirm this, Nimrod tossed his head and stamped a hind hoof.

'Surely you would prefer to ride him in one of the parks to exercise him.'

'Oh, we have been out for some time already. I was just planning to pay a call on William before returning home.'

'May I?' Kitty looked at Theo for permission before putting out a hand to stroke Nimrod's velvety muzzle. Theo watched carefully.

'In general he is not too friendly towards strangers, but I feel sure you are the exception.'

'He is so handsome,' murmured Kitty, as the horse inclined his head towards her. 'No, I am afraid I do not have any sugar,' she told him, giving him a final pat and stepping back.

'We will accompany you,' announced Theo.

'But you were on your way to visit William.'

He shook his head. 'You should not be in these streets alone. And perhaps at last we have time to discuss your visits to the Rookery.' He indicated that they should move on and added, 'It does concern me closely, you know. If Lady Picton had the least idea. . . .'

Kitty checked the impulse to retort that it was nothing to do with him. She found it rather pleasant that he cared so much about her safety. She glanced up and found him watching her rather anxiously.

'Well, I do assure you it is just to help a sick child, and now he is getting better I will probably only go once more.' She could not help laughing at his dismayed expression. 'Surely, sir, you should be satisfied with that.'

'Every visit is a risk. I truly fear that someone in there will be bold enough to rob you.'

'The poor wretches seem too weak from hunger to do much. That is something we could discuss.'

He shook his head. 'You cannot solve all the problems of humanity. It is best to help where it can make a positive change. I admire your spirit, ma'am but sometimes you are too innocent to understand the danger to a young female of venturing out alone.'

Kitty sighed. 'Life is so restrictive in London. Sometimes I feel suffocated.'

'I do not imagine it is very different in any large town.' Theo looked at her keenly. 'And you seem to go where you want to in any case.' He paused for a moment, then added, 'Which brings me back to the thing I seem to keep repeating: it is dangerous for you to venture into the Rookery.'

Kitty bent her head to hide a smile. 'Would you venture in there?'

He gave a bark of laughter. 'Not I! Only in dire need, to help rescue someone.' He indicated a road running south-wards. 'We should take this direction now.'

They turned into a busy street. At once, Theo had to give all his attention to his horse. Nimrod was not very willing to walk through such a press of people and noise. Theo coaxed him along and by degrees they reached the other end of the street. Kitty was impressed by the unfailingly firm yet patient handling of the nervous animal.

As they reached the corner at last, she pointed to a couple of ragged children sitting in the gutter. 'They look like suitable candidates for the orphanage.' She smiled up at him and again was fascinated by his sparkling blue eyes. They were unaware that they had stopped. Theo caught her hand in his free one.

'That is not the only topic on my mind,' he murmured. He slanted her a look full of meaning. Kitty's lips parted. Her heartbeat quickened. She wanted nothing more than for him to kiss her, so she could drift away, surrendering to her senses in his strong arms. But with a great effort of will, she reminded herself of her decision earlier. She *must* stick to that.

She still did not feel certain that he meant anything other than flirtation. He never showed any deep emotion towards anyone. She remembered how cold he was towards Miss Harling, who kept trying to attract him. And then there was this Miss Payne, whose mother wanted her to marry him, but he was avoiding her. It seemed he was determined to stay free.

The pressure of Theo's hand on hers was getting stronger, he was pulling her towards him. His eyes were intent on hers; his face was pale. Then Nimrod tossed his head and sidled, still uneasy. Theo gave a start and dropped her hand. He looked a little dazed.

'We should carry on,' he said, indicating the road ahead. 'It is not much further now.'

Kitty felt her knees trembling. She gave a little sigh of disappointment. They walked along the next street in silence. She reminded herself once more that he had never said one word to show he felt any real attachment to her. She must act normally.

'Will you not tell me a bit more about your hospice?' she asked. He was so deep in his own thoughts that she had to repeat the question.

He shrugged. 'There is not a lot to tell. At present the hospice is a small house with enough outbuildings and land for ten poor souls to look after themselves, while they recover from their wounds.'

'It does seem to be an excellent idea,' said Kitty enthusiastically. 'I am sure my father would wish to do something like that.' She sighed. 'If he could find the necessary money.'

Theo nodded. 'It was difficult to set up at first but now all seems to be running smoothly.' After a short pause, he looked at her a little hesitantly. 'If you would like to see it, I will drive you there.'

'That would be splendid, but I doubt my aunt will give me permission.'

He looked down his nose, suddenly haughty. 'Lady Picton dislikes my reputation, does she? But she allowed you to drive to Richmond Park with Saint-Aubin.'

'Oh!' Kitty stopped dead and wheeled round to face him, her eyes flashing. 'And just how do you know about that?' She watched his look of surprise change to dismay and nodded grimly. 'Have you been gossiping with Miss Harling?'

Theo's eyebrows snapped down. His face became thunderous. 'Never!'

'Well then,' bit out Kitty, 'you were spying on me – in spite of what you said last night.' Her bosom heaved. Her eyes stung with sudden tears. He still did not trust her, so how could she trust him? Stupid her, she thought, to care so much for a man who considered her to be a spy.

Theo was looking bewildered. 'Miss Towers,' he protested, 'I swear to you that I have not—'

'Pray do not attempt to justify yourself, sir.' Kitty's voice trembled. 'We have both made mistakes in our judgements about each other in the past. It is of no importance what you think of me. I shall soon be returning to my home.' She swallowed hard and managed to keep the tears back by blinking hard.

Strange how she no longer wanted to go home. This man staring at her from under his dark brows was making her feel more miserable than ever before in her life. With a supreme effort she said, 'Thank you for your escort. I know where I am and can safely walk the rest of the way by myself. Good day, sir.' She turned away and set off.

Theo was left standing there, his expression a mixture of fury and dismay. Nimrod tossed his head impatiently as his master seemed rooted to the spot.

CHAPTER TWENTY-SIX

Caroline's ball was one of the big events of the season. The enormous room was already full of guests when Kitty, Amelia and her mother arrived. Mrs Warrington found a place for herself close to a tall urn.

'With such a crush of people, both of you need to remember where to find me when your partners bring you back after each dance.' She beamed around the crowded room. 'What a splendid gathering.' She nodded politely to another matron, approaching with several daughters in tow.

Mrs Warrington, herself very elegantly dressed in pale-green crêpe with bead trimming, could not hide her pride as she gazed at her charges. They looked a striking pair as they stood, exchanging smiling remarks while they took in the scene. Amelia was in the whisper soft gown of ivory silk. The tiny beads sparkled as she moved. With her golden ringlets and flawless complexion, she was already attracting admiring glances.

Kitty also looked charming. Her chestnut curls were dressed high on her head with several shining ringlets allowed to fall from a gilded clasp at the back of the knot. She held herself very erect, her slender figure enhanced by a deceptively simple rose-pink silk gown, which showed off her graceful neck and white shoulders, as well as rather more bosom than usual.

'What a difference with your first visit here, girls. You did not know a soul. But this evening I shall be surprised if you do not both dance every dance.'

Kitty was more concerned to try and make her peace with Theo. Why did she always seem to quarrel with him? Now she regretted her outburst on the day he escorted her home. She could not enjoy the ball without seeing him and apologizing. However, it seemed that Mrs Warrington was right and both she and Millie would dance throughout the evening. The young gentlemen were all anxious to partner her, but as she went through each dance she could not help looking round often, hoping for a glimpse of that tall, dark-haired figure with his broad shoulders.

A conversation with Theo would give her more pleasure than a dance with anyone else – if she could coax him out of his moodiness. Her eyes sparkled at the challenge. But where was he? The next time she searched the throng for him she saw Miss Harling right behind her. Before she could look away, Miss Harling gave her a slight nod.

'No Etienne de Saint-Aubin?' she enquired loudly. 'I thought you two were inseparable.'

Kitty turned back to her partner. Her eyes were sparkling with rage, especially when she heard the wretched woman telling her own partner how she had seen Kitty and Etienne in Richmond Park. 'Just a little fast, do you not agree?' she heard the spiteful voice commenting. Then the steps of the dance took her down the room and out of earshot. Well, at least she knew Theo was not with Miss Harling.

As dance followed dance, Kitty smiled and made polite conversation with the never-ending succession of partners. She hoped every minute to see a dark, handsome face smiling at her but there was no sign of him. It was becoming more of an effort to maintain her bright appearance.

The evening drew on and the crowd continued to grow. It seemed as if the whole of fashionable society had come to Caroline's ball. At the supper interval, Kitty's spirits revived. Surely Theo would have arrived by now. But there was no sign of him in the dining-hall. She began to worry that he would not appear at all. Her heart sank. Then she realized that she had not seen Greg either. There was still time, so she forced herself to smile and chat politely with her friends around the table.

After supper, Etienne led Kitty out for the cotillion. She sensed the jealous eyes on her and knew she had the best partner in the room. Etienne made it clear he was delighted to be dancing with her. Fortunately Kitty had learnt the steps well and gradually she forgot the onlookers as she gave herself up to the pleasure of the rhythm and the company of the handsome man smiling at her as they floated dizzily around the floor.

Etienne bowed low over her hand at the close of the dance. 'Exquisite,' he murmured, giving her a lingering look from speaking dark eyes. 'You are made for such dances, Mademoiselle Kitty. And I must compliment you on your charming appearance.'

She was still breathless when Freddy claimed her hand for the boulanger.

'Have you remained in town especially for this ball, Freddy?' asked Kitty, when she could speak again. 'How are they managing without you at home?'

He was gazing at something over her shoulder and did not answer.

'Freddy!' said Kitty crossly, 'I am talking to you.'

'Eh? What? Just look at that, Kitty. How *dare* he upset her.' Freddy was bristling with anger. He nodded towards a couple standing by the edge of the dance floor. Kitty saw Amelia in earnest conversation with Greg. Her heart beat a little faster. If Greg was here, surely Theo was with him. But when she glanced again at Amelia she could see the telltale signs of distress. Whatever was Greg saying? Finally he raised her hand to his lips for a long moment and then turned away abruptly. Both looked very white.

'Deuce take it, he has made her cry!' growled Freddy through his teeth. He seemed inclined to go after Greg there and then.

Kitty held on to his hand firmly. 'Do not draw attention to

them,' she whispered. 'It is not surprising she feels upset. You know how tender-hearted she is.'

By the time Freddy led her back to Mrs Warrington's urn, he had changed the focus of his anger. He looked at Amelia's wan face and frowned. He bowed stiffly and turned on his heel without a word. The girls watched him stride over to his sister and start talking to her. He was not coming back. Kitty saw Amelia go even paler and blink rapidly. Up to this moment, she had always been able to rely on Freddy's support. Perhaps it would help her to examine her own feelings properly at last.

She stood still, waiting to see what Millie would do. But then, the voice she had been waiting to hear all evening spoke from behind her. She lifted her head, her heart seemed about to leap out of her chest. Millie was forgotten as she turned to face Theo.

He was looking particularly fine this evening, his tall figure moulded into a severely cut evening suit in midnight blue. His cravat was tied in an intricate style. His thick curly hair was smoothed back. Kitty eagerly took in every detail of that lean, vivid face.

He was smiling down at her. She noticed the dimple in his cheek and smiled happily back at him. She felt a rush of delight. He had forgiven her accusations. She determined to start afresh. For a few moments they stood there, oblivious of the swirling crowd around them. Theo's gaze slowly drifted down to her slender neck and white shoulders. He swallowed then gazed appreciatively at the smooth white swell of her bosom revealed by the fashionable gown.

'May I compliment you on your charming appearance, Miss Towers.' His voice was a little husky. His blue eyes sparkled at her. 'I am very glad to have found you at last. You see, I want to ask something bold. . . .' He raised one black brow and smiled in a way that made her understand why he was considered to be a dangerous flirt. Whatever he asked, she knew she would agree.

Theo's smile grew broader. He took her hand and pressed

it slightly. 'I know you have a kind heart so I will dare to continue.'

Kitty nodded, biting her bottom lip in anticipation. He stilled, his eyes on her mouth. At last he blinked and added, 'It seems to me that I can now manage to perform a simple dance again – oh, just a country dance, but I fear I may be somewhat clumsy. . . .'

'And you are hoping I will dance with you? But of course I will.' Kitty beamed at him, her whole body thrilling at the idea of being so close to him. Theo offered his arm. Kitty placed her fingers just above his wrist, very correctly. They smiled at each other and moved forward to join the line of dancers.

At first she was a little hesitant in case his weak leg should give way. To her relief and delight, however, he did not limp at all. They were well matched for height and in a couple of minutes it was clear that they moved in harmony.

Kitty gave him an elated smile. 'You dance very well. It is so easy to follow your lead.'

He grinned triumphantly down at her. 'You cannot imagine how pleased I feel – and flattered at your judgement. It has been a very long time. . . .'

They said no more but followed the rhythm of the music, instinctively moving as if they had danced together many times before. Kitty slipped into a state of dreamlike pleasure. Her enjoyment was all the more intense because they had put their quarrels behind them. She roused reluctantly, realizing that the music had stopped.

With a broad grin, Theo took a firm grip of her arm and led her back towards Mrs Warrington. 'Do you really think I passed muster?' he murmured, eyes mischievous.

Kitty nodded, still regretting that the dance was over. He raised her hand to his lips and pressed a kiss on it, his eyes never leaving her face. He smiled as he saw her eyes widen and heard her give a little gasp of pleasure. 'My deepest thanks for your trust,' he said. His face became serious. 'In fact, I—' He broke off, cast her a rather embarrassed look and was about to add something when they became aware of someone very close by.

They looked round unwillingly to see Etienne, looking very grave.

'Pray excuse me,' he said, addressing himself to Kitty, 'your friend is not well and wishes to speak to you. It is urgent,' he added, when Kitty showed no inclination to move.

'Oh, very well. . . .' said Kitty reluctantly. The spell was broken now. She looked up at Theo. The interruption had sparked a change of mood. His face was stormy. He released her hand.

Kitty curtsied to him. 'Thank you, sir,' she murmured and gave him a glowing smile. Beside her, she heard Etienne draw in a sharp breath.

'It is this way,' he announced brusquely, indicating a curtained alcove near the top end of the vast hall.

CHAPTER TWENTY-SEVEN

Etienne held aside the curtain and Kitty passed through into a very small alcove. She looked around but there was no sign of Millie.

'My friend must have gone back to her mother,' she said in relief, 'and I must not linger, sir.'

'Oh but please, just give me a moment to explain.' Etienne's voice was husky, his large eyes burned fiercely in his pale face. 'It is so difficult to speak with you alone,' he continued, coming close to her. His eyes devoured her face. A little smile lifted the corners of his mouth. 'You are so beautiful, so charming,' he exclaimed, 'I cannot bear to wait any more. I must speak now.'

With a sinking heart, Kitty realized what was going to come next. Before she could move, her hands were seized and Etienne was covering them with kisses. She tried to pull away. His grip tightened.

'Please, Kitty, you must listen to me. I feel so much love for you, I beg of you, please marry me. I will do anything to be worthy of you.'

Kitty shook her head. 'Please, sir, let go of my hands.' She twisted again. This time he did release them but it was only to pull her into his arms.

'When I see you smiling at that man, my heart burns,' he announced in a throbbing tone. 'I want so much to protect you from him. You are so adorable, so innocent.' His eyes flashed and he gave a groan. 'It is too much—'

'No more!' Kitty spoke sharply. Her dismay had given way to anger now. She resented the way he had tricked her into coming into the alcove. Even more, she was furious at being crushed in such an iron grip and in such an uncomfortable position. She could feel his chest heaving against hers. The smell of vetyver filled her nostrils and added to her disgust.

It was obvious he had worked himself into a state of passion so she tried to speak calmly. 'I cannot return your sentiments, but even if I could, I deplore the method you have used – and the time of this declaration. I insist that you let me go, now.'

He groaned. 'Never! Not until you say yes, my beautiful Kitty.'

'I am not yours!' she protested furiously.

At this he leaned forward and planted his lips on hers. She uttered an inarticulate protest and struggled to break free. All at once she felt Etienne's arms wrenched away from her and she stepped back, wiping a hand across her mouth. She drew in a sobbing breath and looked up to see Theo, his face like thunder, holding a struggling Etienne by the arms. He looked ready to strangle the Frenchman.

Kitty looked from one to the other. She saw despair as well as anger on Etienne's face. It was the last straw. She gave a tiny sob. The sound seemed to recall Theo from his murderous intention. His expression turned to contempt. He pushed Etienne towards the curtain. 'Get out,' he grated, 'I will speak to you later.'

Etienne glanced towards Kitty. She turned her head away. He glared at Theo and fumbled his way through the curtain. Theo turned to Kitty. His face was as cold as ice. 'Has he hurt you?' His voice sounded almost indifferent.

She shook her head. It was impossible to speak. She swallowed hard and blinked. Suddenly her knees were trembling. She heard Theo mutter something under his breath and felt his hand grasp her elbow. He guided her to a chair and pushed her down on it.

'Come, Miss Towers, do not be distressed.' he said in an

impatient tone. He held out a large white handkerchief. Kitty clutched it thankfully and mopped her eyes, which would keep filling with tears. Theo waited for a few minutes.

'There is no need to cry,' he said at last. 'You are quite safe now.'

Kitty nodded her head and drew in a deep breath. 'H-How did you find me?'

'I heard him tell you your friend was here. But when I saw her with her mother, I realized that it was a trick. And at that moment Lady Caroline asked me to rescue you discreetly.'

'Oh. . . .' Kitty stared at him in consternation. 'Does everyone know I was in here alone with him?'

Theo raised his dark brows. 'Only Caroline – you know she has a talent for observing everything.' He inspected her. 'Considering how he manhandled you, you are still very neat. But if I may be so bold, he has disarranged your smart hairstyle.'

Kitty raised her hands but they were shaking too much for her to straighten her ringlets.

Theo frowned. 'We must make haste. Will you permit me?'

Kitty nodded and stood very still while he deftly adjusted the clasp. She felt his fingers brush her neck as he arranged her ringlets again. 'Thank you, you are very kind,' she said in a constricted voice. 'I think I am ready to go back into the ballroom now.'

'I will go first,' said Theo. 'When I leave, count to twenty, then come out and make your way back to Mrs Warrington. And I promise you, you will not have to speak to Monsieur de Saint-Aubin again.' He nodded abruptly, his face still a cold mask and slipped through the curtain.

Immediately, Kitty heard a strident female voice exclaim: 'Theodore! I have been looking everywhere for you.'

Stifling a gasp of horror, Kitty looked around but there was nowhere to hide. She gulped. If she was discovered there would be a terrible scandal. Then she heard Theo's voice.

'Lady Payne, Miss Payne.'

The woman's voice boomed out again, interrupting him. 'If

my eyes did not deceive me, you were dancing just now? With a young lady in a pink dress?'

There was a slight pause, then, 'Indeed, ma'am,' in a haughty tone.

'Oh . . . well . . . how splendid that you have recovered at long last. I am sure Letitia has a dance available for you.'

'Alas, ma'am, I fear I was too precipitate. My leg is still weak. That is why I sought shelter in the alcove – to rest it. But come, may I at least find you ladies something to drink? It is very hot, is it not?'

The voices faded. Kitty's heartbeat gradually slowed. She smoothed her dress down, counted to twenty and slipped through the curtain. She took a quick look around. There was no sign of Theo. Had anyone noticed her? How long had she been in there? A lively country dance was in full swing and the crowd was as dense as ever. She wove through the groups of onlookers until she reached Mrs Warrington. That lady was busily talking to a couple of other mothers. It was a few minutes before she noticed Kitty and even then, she just nodded at her and carried on with her conversation.

Kitty fanned herself, trying to look calm. He should have respected me, she thought angrily; how could he think I would submit to being forced into agreeing anything in such a way. She cringed inside as the memory of Etienne's embrace kept forcing itself into her mind. What would have happened if Theo had not arrived at that moment?

Kitty grew hot and cold as she remembered he had seen Etienne kissing her. And after that he had been so cold and impatient with her. There was no trace of the warm smiles and friendly conversation they had enjoyed during their first ever dance together, just before Etienne interrupted them.

As she looked back, Kitty realized how each time she had shown any pleasure in Theo's company, Etienne had stepped in to whisper his poisonous suspicions. She could see now that it was all due to jealousy. But he had succeeded in driving them apart.

When she considered the change in Theo's attitude after he

came into the alcove, she felt a dark shadow creep over her heart. Surely he could not believe she wanted Etienne to maul her like that. By this time, she was feeling so miserable that it was only pride that was keeping her upright. She longed to go home. But her sufferings were not yet over. Caroline appeared at her side.

'Well, darling, whatever will you do next?' she murmured, looking Kitty over with a critical eye. 'You are certainly setting my guests at each other's throats.' Her eyes moved towards a tall shape on the opposite side of the room. Kitty followed her gaze. To her horror, she saw it was Theo talking to Etienne. The exchange was very brief and obviously angry. Kitty watched both men nod sharply to each other and then Theo turned away. Etienne was glaring after him.

'You see?' Caroline glanced at her. 'Pistols, I expect. Theo likes pistols and he obviously issued the challenge.'

'A duel – oh, no,' gasped Kitty, 'what a stupid thing to do. I have to stop them.' She took a hasty step forward.

Caroline laid a hand on her arm. 'You will do no such thing. Let them settle the matter in their own way.'

'But what if one of them shoots the other?' Kitty looked at her in anguish.

'Oh, I doubt it.' She gave a brittle laugh. 'There is no need to go white, darling. I never heard that Theo actually aims at his opponent. He delopes.'

'What does that mean?'

'He fires into the air.'

Kitty shook her head in bewilderment. 'Why bother to issue a challenge in the first place?' Then she grew alarmed. 'But suppose Etienne wounds him?'

Caroline shrugged. 'I did warn you never to find yourself alone with him, darling. You will just have to wait and see what the outcome is.'

CHAPTER TWENTY-EIGHT

The first light of dawn showed the outline of the windows. Kitty raised her face from her pillow. She smoothed back her tousled hair.

'Crying will not solve anything,' she scolded herself angrily, scrubbing at her eyes with Theo's handkerchief. It felt damp. She held it to her cheek. 'It is all I will ever have of him now.' With a sigh, she sat up and thumped the pillow back into shape. The faint light was creeping into the room. A moment later, she slipped out of bed to pull the curtain back and stare out. Maybe even now Theo and Etienne were on their way to wherever it was that men went to fight a duel.

Kitty pressed the handkerchief to her mouth. Caroline had said he fought lots of duels, she thought, but he never aimed at his opponent. But what about Etienne? She remembered the look of despair on his face when she had rejected him. He might try to get rid of his rival. She screwed her eyes tight shut in anguish. What a shocking state of affairs.

Shivering, she turned away from the window at last and climbed back into bed. Her mind dwelt on that wonderful dance with Theo, and on the way he looked at her as he kissed her hand. At that moment, Kitty had felt sure he loved her. And then such a short time later, when he found her in Etienne's arms being kissed, even though it was against her will, he had been so cold, so abrupt, that she was sure his feelings towards her had changed to disgust.

Kitty dwelt for a while on Theo's blue eyes and then shivered as she remembered the sound of his deep voice, that special tone he used when he talked to her – until their last encounter in the alcove, that is. A life with no Theo in it stretched ahead of her. Kitty's heart seemed to shrivel at the idea. A tear dripped off her chin.

'Oh, merciful heavens!' Great-Aunt Picton collapsed against her sofa cushions with a moan. 'You did *what*?' Her voice was very faint, but Kitty could hear the anger in it. Lady Picton waved one white hand. 'My smelling salts.' Kitty hastened to find them from amongst the jumble of pots and pillboxes on the little table. She opened the bottle and pressed it into her aunt's hand. After a few sniffs, that lady opened one eye.

'Why did you refuse him? A fine young man like that, always so polite and attentive – and he is my best friend's grandson. I had settled with myself that I would leave my fortune to you so that between the pair of you, you could live in comfort. . . . Oh, I have no patience with you. Surely you like Etienne enough to consider his proposal?'

To her dismay, Kitty saw that tears were running down her aunt's cheeks. She knelt down by the sofa and took the old lady's hand. 'I am very sorry to grieve you like this, ma'am,' she began, 'but I do not feel able to trust Monsieur de Saint-Aubin. And I certainly cannot like him well enough to consider marriage with him.'

Lady Picton raised her head and directed a piercing stare at her. 'Who is it?' As colour flamed into Kitty's cheeks, she nodded grimly. 'It's Hethermere's boy, isn't it? Theodore Weston. You have fallen for a rake, foolish girl. You would do better to reconsider.'

'Oh, Aunt, truly I cannot – I do not trust him.' Her aunt was still glaring at her, so Kitty added, 'I think I must tell you the whole story.' The result, however, dismayed her even more. Aunt Picton became quite rigid with horror.

'Alone in an alcove with two of the most notorious rakes in town,' she exclaimed, 'and you think nobody noticed! It must be all over London by now – and as for this duel. . . .' She gave another moan and recruited her strength with a sniff from the vinaigrette.

'I am very sorry, ma'am—' began Kitty.

'Yes, well, it is no use to lament now. We must do what we can to stop tongues wagging. You will go about your affairs as usual.' She wagged a gnarled finger, 'No sign of consciousness about last night if anybody tries to hint at the matter.'

'It seems to me that I have caused you enough trouble, Aunt. Dear ma'am, I have made up my mind that the best thing is for me to go home as soon as possible. That way, you may be easy.'

'Go home? You will do no such thing! Good God, girl, after getting yourself into such a scrape, is that the best you can think of?' She cast a glance of scorn at Kitty. 'Have you learned nothing of society? You have to show the world that you have nothing to hide. You will oblige me by going to your room and dressing yourself ready for an outing in the park.'

Kitty stared mutinously at her aunt. It seemed a very foolish idea to her. And the last thing she wanted was to set eyes on anyone who had been involved in the painful scenes of the previous evening.

'Come, child,' her aunt's voice broke into these thoughts, 'you will do this to please me.'

Kitty duly presented herself to her aunt, dressed in the green cambric gown bought for her at the beginning of her stay. Her hair was carefully arranged into the topknot and ringlets that Great-Aunt Picton approved of. But nothing could disguise her pale cheeks and the dark smudges under her eyes.

'We will have to set your lack of colour down to tiredness after dancing the whole evening,' said Lady Picton, after trying in vain to disguise Kitty's wan appearance.

They set out on the short drive to Hyde Park. Kitty sat bolt upright in the carriage with her hands tightly clasped in her lap. She did not like to feel she was the subject of gossip. Her aunt was in a militant mood and kept a sharp lookout for any acquaintances. The coach stopped frequently, so they could exchange greetings with her many elderly friends. Kitty had only to nod and smile. She began to relax. So far, none of these persons had mentioned the ball and she was sure they were all too old to have been present at it.

She studied the throng of walkers, looking out for Amelia or Freddy, two friends she could talk to without fear of criticism. She was much encouraged when a couple of young ladies she knew exchanged bows with her as they walked along the path beside the carriageway. But she would not feel at ease until she heard that both Etienne and Theo had returned safely from the duel.

At the thought of Theo, her heart pounded. But it was no good, she thought numbly, he had shown her what his opinion of her was. Looking back, Kitty realized that they had never managed to be together for long without a quarrel, and yet, he had often shown such warmth when they talked together. She wanted so much to help him with his plans for his hospice. All such schemes had to be forgotten now. She felt the tears pricking the back of her eyes and blinked them away. Somehow she had to show a calm face to the world, today and every day until she could return home. Yet now the prospect of going back to her old life did not seem attractive any more. Kitty shook herself mentally.

'Whatever is the matter with the woman?'

Kitty roused from her thoughts to see her aunt staring at a couple of ladies in a barouche. Their carriage was stationary and the occupants were gazing at Kitty and nodding to each other.

'Do you know them, ma'am?' Kitty thought she had never seen two such plain women. What was more, their frilled and ruched pelisses and feathered bonnets drew attention to their own plain faces.

'Do you remember the conversation at Lady Deane's tea party, my love? There you see Lady Payne and her daughter. The one she plans to marry to your rake,' added the old lady viciously. 'If she has the slightest idea about last night, she will do her best to ruin you.'

174

'So that is Lady Payne. I overheard her asking about me – after I had danced with Mr Weston. I do not think she knows any more than that.'

'Hmm – enough to drive her wild with jealousy even so. Pretend not to see her, child.'

Satisfied at last that they had been seen by a good number of people, Aunt Picton directed her coachman to return to Grosvenor Square. Once she reached her armchair, the old lady fixed a sharp eye on Kitty.

'You are looking quite worn out, child – and no wonder. But that was a job we had to do. Now let us drink our tea and then we can both retire to enjoy a rest.'

Kitty was glad to obey. She needed time to school herself into a calmer state of mind. She would learn to live with the heartache. If only she did not feel so terribly weary. Putting Theo's handkerchief against her cheek, she lay down on the bed and closed her eyes. Tomorrow, she decided, she would set about persuading her aunt to let her go home. For the moment, however, she just needed to rest for a little while.

Eventually Kitty fell asleep. Nobody disturbed her and so it was not until the following morning, when the housemaid brought a cup of chocolate to her bedroom, that she received the note sent round by Amelia the previous evening.

CHAPTER TWENTY-NINE

'I see nothing for it but to take Amelia out of town for a few days,' Mrs Warrington informed Kitty. She sighed. 'She has been in a terrible state for the last two days. Really, when we arrived at that ball I was so proud of both you girls. You looked wonderful – and the young men were flocking to dance with you both.' She plucked aimlessly at her lace-edged handkerchief. 'Whatever went wrong?'

It was most unlike her to be sitting idly. Kitty could not remember ever seeing Mrs Warrington without some piece of stitchery in her hands. She said nothing, waiting to hear whether Mrs Warrington had picked up any gossip from the ball. But it soon became obvious that the poor lady's mind was totally taken up by her daughter's sudden collapse.

There was a short silence. Kitty felt the tension growing inside. First, her aunt, now Amelia's mother – so much explaining to do, so much misery to hide. Eventually, as poor Mrs Warrington just sat there, gazing rather blankly at the window, Kitty cleared her throat.

'May I see Millie? It is most unlike her to keep to her room.'

Mrs Warrington nodded. 'Do go up, Kitty. Maybe you can pluck her out of this silly state she has fallen into.'

Even as she spoke, a footman came in with a tray of refreshments. Mrs Warrington rubbed her forehead. 'Oh, Heavens, I had quite forgotten. . . .' She looked at Kitty, 'Make haste and bring Amelia down, if you please, Kitty. Lady Caroline will pay us a visit shortly.'

Alarmed, Kitty made her way up another flight of stairs. She had a fair idea of what had caused Millie to feel so unhappy. But it was unlikely she would reveal her feelings. She found Amelia seated on a chair by the window, twisting a damp handkerchief between her fingers. At the sight of Kitty she gave a sob.

'Oh, that will never do,' Kitty chided, smiling as she came up to the window. 'Do you know, Millie, it is most unfair that you can sit and cry and still look so pretty.' She pulled up another chair and sat facing her friend. Her own face twisted and she gave a gulp and said in a rather wobbly voice, 'I believe I said it before – we were better off at home.'

Amelia nodded. 'Things have become so complicated,' she whispered. 'I really do not know what to do with myself. I never felt so unhappy before in my life.' She scrubbed at her eyes and added, 'Mama is angry with me for allowing myself to be so cast down.'

'She is upset that we did not leave the ball in triumph.' Kitty hesitated, then said. 'I saw you in conversation with Mr Thatcham,' she prompted. 'You both looked extremely pale.'

Amelia looked at her for a long moment. 'What he said to me was very touching.' Her voice trembled and she had to try twice before she could carry on. 'I shall treasure his words all my life. I am only sorry I cannot return his regard.' She sniffed.

'He is a truly admirable gentleman,' agreed Kitty. 'but come, Millie, at least you were honest with him. And even if you did love him, you could never leave England to be a soldier's wife.'

'I shall never marry anyone!' Gentle Millie spoke with such force that Kitty's jaw fell open. She shut it hastily, remembering how Freddy had turned away in anger. It was something that Millie had at last shown what her true feelings were. In any case, Kitty was too heartsore herself to discuss the matter.

'The best thing we could do would be to go home, don't you agree?' Amelia said at last.

'That is what I want to do, but my aunt will not hear of it,' replied Kitty, 'I fear I have sadly disappointed her.'

Amelia looked a question. Kitty wearily explained what had happened. 'And until I know the outcome of this duel I can feel only a burning anxiety,' she ended, pressing her hand to her quivering lips. She sniffed. 'It is terrible to have provoked two men to fight – and perhaps kill each other – for something I did not want in the first place.'

They stared at each other. Kitty was the first to rouse. 'Well,' she said in a determined voice, 'I must get back to doing something useful with my life. This was never going to be more than a short holiday.'

'But, Kitty,' squeaked Amelia, round eyed, 'your mama expects you to find a husband before you return to Cheshire.'

'So does yours,' retorted Kitty. Slowly, Amelia shook her head. 'You know Mama is taking me out of town for a few days. She says I need a rest from this hectic lifestyle, but I suspect she is going to use the time to direct me towards whichever gentleman she considers right for me.' She pressed her lips very firmly together. 'It is not often that I go against my parents' wishes, but I cannot obey them in this matter.'

There was a tap at the door, followed by the entrance of a maid. 'If you please, Miss, Lady Caroline Bannister has arrived.'

'We shall have to go down,' insisted Kitty, pulling Amelia up and more or less dragging her to the door. 'it is better than moping in here.'

Caroline raised her brows at the sight of them. 'I did hope to see two bright young ladies, ready to assist me at the perfumier's.'

'We shall do our best,' said Kitty, firmly holding on to Amelia's arm and refusing to let her decline the outing.

Once the three of them were in the carriage, Kitty gave Caroline an imploring look. 'Is there any news?'

Caroline frowned. 'This is hardly the place to discuss such matters.' She looked towards the coachman. Reluctantly Kitty nodded. She was in such a fever to know how the duel had ended, she could barely respond to Caroline's flow of idle chat as the barouche took them to Bond Street. Her hands clasped tightly in her lap, she tried to smile and reply sensibly. It was no use to get angry with Caroline, after all, she had done what she could to avoid any scandal.

At last the coach stopped, the steps were let down and the three young ladies descended.

'Now then, darlings, I fully expect you to help me select the finest new perfumes and soaps. This is one of my very favourite shops.' Caroline led the way in to where the manager was already bowing, while an underling was rushing to set chairs for these fashionable clients. At any other time, Kitty would have enjoyed the experience. But today it was all she could do to affect an interest in the expensive scents and finely milled soaps brought out for Caroline to choose from.

'What about a walk to Hookham's Library?' suggested Caroline, as they left the perfumier's. 'We can talk as we walk, you know.' She unfurled her parasol and smiled at Kitty. 'You goose, you may breathe again now.'

'You mean—'

'Nobody was injured.'

'Oh, thank God. . . .' Kitty drew a shaky breath. The surge of relief was like a physical blow. She faltered.

'Of course,' Caroline went on, steering her in through the door of Hookham's Library, 'even if honour is satisfied, the two gentlemen are still at daggers drawn. According to William, Theo is completely unapproachable.'

Amelia, who was not really listening to this conversation, wandered over to the bookshelves.

'You should choose a few novels to take with you while you are in the country,' encouraged Kitty. She then turned back to Caroline. 'Well, you have relieved my mind of its worst fear. As for the rest—'

Caroline shook her head. 'What a pair you are! It reminds me of when I had to sort out all the childhood squabbles.' She moved towards the table displaying the most recently published novels. Having selected one to examine, she looked across at Kitty again. 'I accept that your great-aunt's connection with Etienne makes it hard for you not to be on good terms with him. But I did warn you.'

Kitty gave her a speaking look. 'I know.'

Caroline nodded. 'We just have to hope there is no gossip. That obnoxious Miss Harling would so love a juicy morsel like that.'

Kitty repressed a shudder. 'I am so afraid of causing my aunt embarrassment.'

'What about me, darling?' Caroline's voice was acid. 'However, I am doing my best for you both. Even Millie has caused havoc! Poor Greg! And – even worse – there is no doing anything with Freddy since the ball.' Her eyes were on Amelia as she spoke.

Kitty shrugged. 'It is a matter they have to decide for themselves. But would you object, Caro?'

Caroline laughed. 'I would be delighted. They have always been good friends and they are both home birds. Their parents had other ambitions, but they will soon accept it is the best – the *only* outcome for them.' She shook her head slightly. 'Time will tell. But would you believe, Kitty, Miss Harling was thrusting herself at Freddy at the ball. She is quite shamelessly determined to marry a title.'

CHAPTER THIRTY

At church on Sunday, Kitty strove to put all her troubles out of her mind. The familiar words of the service helped to subdue her problems and she came out of church feeling calmer. She walked beside her aunt as Lady Picton made her way slowly down the path from the church door. The old lady was happily exchanging greetings and gossip with a number of friends.

Standing nearby as she waited, Kitty looked about her, noticing the buds ready to burst on the shrubs. She gave a tiny sigh for the open fields of Cheshire and thought longingly of galloping across country with Millie and Freddy. She checked herself. That did not seem likely to happen ever again.

It had been the loneliest week of her life. Millie and her mother were still out of town. She knew from Caroline that Freddy had gone back home to Cheshire. There was no news of Theo and Greg and no sight of Etienne anywhere. This had caused Aunt Picton to grumble. She missed his lively conversation and kept lamenting that he could not visit her as he used to. Kitty suspected that her aunt still cherished hopes of making a match for her with the Frenchman.

That was never going to happen, however. Not only did she find Etienne untrustworthy, he was responsible for many of her quarrels with Theo. Kitty felt the now familiar ache in her heart. At the ball she could have sworn that Theo was in love with her. What had made him change so rapidly? Surely he understood that she had not wanted Etienne to propose to

181

her? He had fought a duel for her, but now he was showing by his absence that he did not want to see her again. The misery was like a physical burden. She stared fixedly at the treetops, trying to keep a polite expression on her face.

Suddenly, a loud voice almost in her ear made Kitty jump. She had heard those strident tones before. Reluctantly she turned to see the two ladies she least wanted to meet. Lady Payne was standing just behind her. Close up, she was even more overpowering with her shiny red cheeks and her ample figure squeezed into a straining velvet coat.

'. . . long time since we last saw you,' she was saying to Lady Picton, 'and so you have a young relative staying with you. How delightful,' she seized Kitty's hand and wrung it hard. 'Are you enjoying your visit to London, Miss Towers? Do you mean to stay long?' Her smile did not reach her eyes. 'I believe I saw you at Lady Caroline Bannister's ball last Tuesday? You were dancing with Theodore Weston.'

'Yes, ma'am,' said Kitty in a colourless voice. Beside her, Aunt Picton seemed to grow a couple of inches. Her gimlet gaze was fixed on the countess.

That lady gave Kitty another cold smile. 'We quite dote on him and all his family. You must know that Letitia' – she pulled her daughter forward – 'is absolutely a favourite with Lord and Lady Hethermere. In fact' – she leaned almost into Kitty's face as she continued in a rush – 'I should not be speaking of it just yet but we expect that dearest Letitia here will soon be announcing her engagement to Theodore.' Her prominent eyes were fixed on Kitty's as she spoke. She beamed a toothy smile at Lady Picton and nodded briskly, making the ostrich feathers on her bonnet flutter as if in agreement. 'It is the dearest wish of myself and of his papa.'

Letitia blushed and simpered but her little blue eyes were darting daggers. Kitty judged her to be well past eighteen or nineteen years old – the usual age for a debutante. Miss Payne looked like a snob and, if the looks she was aiming at Kitty were anything to go by, she was spiteful as well. But the worst thing, thought Kitty, was that she looked so empty-headed.

Would Miss Payne concern herself with the social ideas that Theo held to be so important?

Even if she had no interest there herself, she felt they would be a very ill-matched couple. Aware that both Letitia and her mother were examining her closely, she kept a fixed smile on her lips and inclined her head politely.

'I believe I have heard you express these wishes before,' Lady Picton commented drily. 'And this is your ... third season, is it not, Letitia?' She gave a short laugh, hastily disguised it as a cough and took her niece's arm. 'Come, Kitty, John coachman will not wish to keep his horses standing in this wind.'

'Well, child, how do you like Miss Payne?' Great-Aunt Picton watched Kitty pull down her mouth and chuckled. 'No, that does not surprise me. That girl has not one idea in her head. She just echoes her mother's opinions as she copies her dress. So they noticed you dancing with Theodore at the ball. They will not be pleased with that.' She laughed again. 'I trust I quelled them over their absurd fantasy that Letitia will ever become young Weston's wife. Hah!'

'But is it really so absurd, ma'am? If they are family friends, they have many opportunities to be together.'

Lady Picton was busy peering out of the carriage window at the shops, but at this she turned to fix a keen stare on Kitty. 'The whole town knows that young Weston avoids them like the plague. He certainly does not wish for the match. And by this time,' she added, turning back towards the shop windows, 'he is old enough to make his own decisions.'

It was now Lady Picton's great pleasure to enjoy a sedate ride along Bond Street after church each Sunday. She was alert for the latest fashions on display. It was useless for Kitty to protest that she already had a wardrobe full of pretty clothes. And if she tried to remind her aunt that spending money on fine dresses clashed with her principles, that lady just laughed at her.

'I get so much pleasure from all of this, my dear,' she replied each time, 'just indulge me, if you please.'

Today, Great-Aunt Picton wished to see the latest bonnets. 'This brighter weather has made me feel we must find you a really fetching hat for the spring,' she told Kitty, 'but something simple. I am still shuddering at the memory of Lady Payne's hideous red hat – so many feathers and ribbons. Oh dear!'

Kitty giggled. 'It did not set off her complexion to best advantage.' She thought of Letitia, also overdressed and with the same red, full cheeks as her mother. But that was not really important: what had angered Kitty was the resentful looks the other girl kept giving her.

She stifled a sigh. Behind the polite front she was just as miserable as she had been since Theo's sudden change of manner at the ball. Until she could go back to a busier way of life, where her time was occupied in caring for others, she would feel this pain just as keenly. Her aunt was trying to be kind, with offers of new bonnets and various events planned to keep Kitty going into society but whenever she was alone, she slipped into dreams of a handsome face, a pair of dazzling blue eyes and a bitter regret that she would not see him again.

There were plenty of young men eager to dance with her at parties or to accompany her when she walked in Hyde Park. None of them caused the slightest flutter in her heart. She knew there was no question of accepting any one of them as a husband. She had always believed that the foundation for any marriage was love between both partners. And now she had learned what it was to love, she preferred to spend her life alone rather than settle for anything less.

Throughout the long, lonely days since the ball, she responded with her normal good manners to all her aunt's remarks and plans. Kitty decided that it was easier than she had thought to hide a broken heart. So it was a shock the next day at the lunch table when Great-Aunt Picton suddenly said, 'Oh, I cannot endure this any longer. Watching you pick at your food in this way is making me nervous! Come now, child, I can see that this has gone deeper than I guessed. You have truly lost your heart to this rake of yours.'

'He is not a rake, ma'am,' protested Kitty, setting down her glass in rather a hurry, 'but – but I do not think I shall see him again.' She gave a little gasp and pressed her hand hard against her lips.

'No tears!' snapped her aunt. 'Are you telling me you have lost both your suitors? How careless of you!'

Kitty blinked at her, not sure whether this was an attempt to make her smile. 'Careless? It was not my intention to raise false hopes. Indeed, I wonder if Monsieur de Saint-Aubin thought he would be marrying a fortune. That may have fanned his ardour.'

Lady Picton considered this while she delicately sliced and ate a piece of cold chicken. She then took a sip of wine and pronounced, 'As I said, money is a necessity in our world. I think no worse of him for that.' She cast a shrewd glance at her niece. 'And it was quite clear that he admired you greatly. But it is all water under the bridge now. You have made up your mind it is Theo Weston or nobody – is that not so, miss?'

Kitty drew in a shaky breath. She nodded.

'Well, now we have established that, I know better what we need to do.' The old lady finished the wine in her glass and dabbed at her lips. 'We will start with that chipstraw bonnet, my love – the one with the rosebud trimming.'

Kitty frowned. Her tired mind could not follow her aunt's reasoning.

'You are going to be the prettiest and the smartest young lady in town.' Aunt Picton's eyes were shining. 'Not that there is any real competition from Letitia Payne, but gentlemen are always susceptible to pretty clothes, my dear. It will help to smooth the path, believe me.'

CHAPTER THIRTY-ONE

Kitty stood in front of the landscape and actually felt a flicker of interest. The sunbathed hillsides and open fields appealed to her.

'What a pity we are unable to visit Italy for ourselves,' she commented to Miss Walmseley, who was also inspecting this painting. 'I do so long to travel abroad and see what life is like in other countries.'

They moved slowly around the exhibition, admiring the sketches of peasant life as well as the pictures of more famous monuments in the major cities. A painting of the Grand Canal in Venice caught her attention. As she gazed at it she remembered the day in Hookham's Library when Theo had shown her the picture of Venice. She stifled a sigh. Theo had been out of town since the ball. It was plain he would not seek her out again.

This visit to the Royal Academy was a way of getting through another empty day. Her aunt would not hear of letting her return to Cheshire. Busy with schemes of her own, she had taken a reluctant Kitty shopping yet again. Now, Kitty was wearing a brand new chipstraw bonnet trimmed with roses and pink ribbon. She also carried a matching parasol.

It was all very smart but it did not make much sense when she felt so very unhappy and lonely. Here, Kitty checked herself. It was ungrateful to feel like this when her friends, the Walmseley sisters, were doing their best to interest her in this display of paintings and curiosities. At least, Amelia would be returning to town on the following day. They would be able to cheer each other up.

Although, if Millie was feeling half as heartsore as she was, that was going to be a very hard job, thought Kitty, moving away from the Venice picture at last. She looked around for her friends but instead saw to her horror that Letitia Payne was standing in front of the next picture. Her mother was also in the room but seated in an alcove and obviously resting her feet. Kitty turned her head away. She did not feel she could endure another encounter with them. They were always hostile if they spoke to her.

She made an excuse to Miss Walmseley and slipped out of the room without looking in Miss Payne's direction again. Rushing down the stairs to the entrance hall, she found Martha fidgeting near the main entrance.

'Martha, if we are very quick, I think we have just time to make a visit to your home. I have finished viewing the display sooner than I had planned.'

'Oh, miss, that would be wonderful. You are very kind to be thinking of us – Sam an' all – but you do look so pale, miss. Are you sure you can manage the walk?'

'Of course,' Kitty said bracingly. 'I am sure that we are going to see Sam up and about again . . . and I would not miss that for anything.'

'Oh, I do 'ope so – an' it's all down to you, miss.'

Martha was radiant on their return. Her little brother was nearly back to his usual bright self. She thanked Kitty and praised her knowledge of how to treat a fever.

'But it's not right for you to be coming down 'ere, miss. The people notice you and I do fear someone could rob you, 'specially today, with you wearing these smart new things. There are some real villains 'ere, you know.'

Kitty nodded. She was weary and would be glad to reach the peace of Grosvenor Square and a quiet evening with her aunt. She stepped carefully round the piles of wood chippings where an old man worked at mending chairs. The usual crowds of ragged children ran at her, hands held out as they shouted for pennies. She dodged through another pile of old rags and slimy rubbish, wrinkling her nose at the awful smell.

At last they reached the tiny passage that led them back into the alley where they had seen Etienne thrown out of a house. Kitty swallowed, she still felt sickened by that display of violence. They were just coming up to the very spot when a beggar stepped out in front of Kitty.

'Spare a penny fer ol' George,' he wheezed. He stank of spirits. Kitty shook her head and tried to walk past him. He moved to block her. She frowned and moved the other way. Still he would not let her through.

'Make way,' cried Martha, her shrill tone betraying her fear. 'Quickly, miss, never take no notice, just push by 'im.'

Kitty did, indeed, push herself forward. Old George laughed in her face as he blocked her again. 'You ain't goin' nowhere, missy.'

At this, Kitty turned back the way she had come and walked briskly down into the passage. Her heart was beating fast, but she thought she was dealing with a drunk and a few minutes later, he would have moved away.

'Miss!' She heard Martha's frantic scream and looked over her shoulder. She nearly froze with horror. The red-haired Irishman who had knocked Etienne down was just a few steps behind. His eyes were intent on her.

'Sure, there's no point in runnin',' he growled, reaching out his great fist to grab her.

Kitty leapt away and ran as fast as she could, back towards Martha's home. But the alleys were so crowded with people, animals and rubbish, that she could not go very fast. It was only a moment before she felt the Irishman's fingers touch her shoulders.

'No!' she screamed. She struggled and wrenched herself out of his grip. She ran on again. Behind her there was a heavy thumping and swearing as he followed. Again he grabbed at her shoulders. This time, he held on. Kitty was forced sideways. Still trying to escape, she struggled. She lost her balance and fell. Her head struck a stone. She saw a blinding flash of light, then sank into darkness.

Gradually Kitty became aware that she was lying on some kind of bench. If only it would stop shaking up and down. Her head was very sore and she was cramped. But worse than all of that, she felt terribly sick. Her eyes were too heavy to open. She tried to remember what had happened. The effort of thinking made her headache worse. She swallowed down another wave of nausea. Now she remembered running from the huge Irishman. She had fallen.

But what had happened after that? It was too difficult to understand anything further. She vaguely heard voices and felt herself being lifted then everything slipped away again.

The second time Kitty came round, she could feel she was lying on a more comfortable surface. There was some kind of cushion under her head. Someone had removed her bonnet. Even without opening her eyes she knew it had gone dark. But she was still being shaken up and down. She realized she must be in a coach and from the motion, it was travelling at speed. The constant jerking movement did nothing to help her throbbing head. She cautiously put up a hand to feel the sore place. Her fingers encountered a large lump. Even as she winced at her own touch, she realized her hair was matted with what must be blood.

'Do not touch it.'

At the sound of that accent, Kitty's eyes sprang open. With a mighty effort, she managed to say, 'Etienne! What? Why?'

There was no lantern inside the coach. The moon, darting in and out through the clouds, cast a fitful light, just enough for her to make out his shape on the seat facing her. He leaned forward. She caught the gleam of his eyes, very close to her face.

'I so deeply regret what they have done to you,' he said. 'I did not think that they would hurt you like this.'

'Do you mean they kidnapped me on your orders?' A very

unwelcome idea was forcing itself into Kitty's mind. 'Where are you taking me?' She quelled a rising fear, remembering the despair on his face when she had rejected his proposal. Surely he was not taking her to Gretna Green.

There was a long silence. Etienne gave a sigh. He shifted, sitting very upright now. Cautiously, Kitty put her feet to the floor and forced herself to sit up. Her head swam unpleasantly but she felt better able to confront him like this.

'Well?' she prompted. 'Where are we going?'

He looked at her. Eventually, he said hoarsely, 'Believe me, I would not do this if there were any other way. But I must have something to live on, you understand.'

Kitty stared at him. It did not make sense. She heard him heave a sigh.

There was such a long silence that she thought he would not speak again but then he leaned forward. His voice was almost pleading.

'When I could win at cards, I could survive. But' – he made an impatient gesture – 'one night I had a heavy run of bad luck. I kept trying to win my money back – until then, I had always been lucky, *parbleu*. But this time' – he grimaced – 'maybe they had fuzzed the cards, who knows... Anyway, by the end of the game I was in debt over my ears and since then, I am in the power of a man who demands payment through information.' He choked. 'I will never be free of him.'

Suddenly, a lot of things became clear. Kitty gave him a cold look. 'Do you mean you are passing information to the French, then?'

She saw Etienne's chin go up. 'So you think I would spy for Napoleon? My family lost everything at the Revolution but we would never – ever – work for that upstart. No, Kitty, it is nothing to do with that.' He beat his hand against the wooden panel of the door. Kitty thought that he ground his teeth.

The moon was shining more clearly now and by its light she could see how haggard he looked. For a few minutes they faced each other, Kitty struggling between feelings of horror and pity for his plight.

He shot her a glance. 'Behind the world of balls and concerts there are many battles being fought. Your English politicians cannot agree over their foreign policy. Lord Dalbeagh wants to end Wellington's campaign in the Peninsula so he may send the troops elsewhere. So, he makes me get information for him in order to force Wellington to return to England.'

Kitty was appalled. 'You mean – our own government is divided even as our soldiers fight the war? All those wounded men. . . . One politician working against another – in such a devious way?' She began to understand the meaning of some of Theo's remarks.

'Mr Thatcham's black eye. . . ?' she faltered.

He nodded. 'Oh, yes, that was me. And I had orders to do worse than that if necessary. But I did not succeed in getting what they wanted.'

'Did they punish you?' she faltered, remembering Etienne thrown down in the alley by the Irishman. She pressed a hand to her mouth, holding back the urge to scream.

'Of course!'

'So, what are you doing now?'

He shrugged. 'I am trying to decide. It seems to me that I have two choices.' He hit his fist against the door panel again. He eyed her speculatively. His gaze travelled over her so thoroughly that she grew hot with embarrassment. When he spoke again, his voice was husky. 'Either I can marry you and pay off my debts with the dowry your aunt will give you – and I would still marry you, beautiful, sweet Kitty, even if you do prefer another to me.' He leaned forward again, putting out a hand to touch her cheek, 'I would soon teach you to love me.'

Kitty struck his hand away. Quick as a flash, he seized her chin in a vice-like grip and forced her face up. He brought his own face close. His expression was fierce. 'I could make you marry me.'

'You can try,' she retorted. She stared at him defiantly. He scanned her face then suddenly let her go. She tried to hide her trembling by smoothing down her skirts. Anything to

191

keep her hands busy. She was horribly aware of his strength. She glanced across at him. He was still watching her intently.

He gave a bitter laugh. 'So! Then I have no choice. I must obtain the information that my master requires.'

She turned her head away, peering out of the window. She could make out steep-sided fields behind the trees that lined the road. The coach rattled on into the night. Kitty still had no idea where they were going. She thought of Great-Aunt Picton's alarm when she did not appear by tea-time.

'Where is Martha?' she asked eventually.

'Martha?'

'My maid. She was with me when they chased me.'

'Oh, a maid. How should I know?' His voice was contemptuous.

Kitty decided that at least Martha had not been taken prisoner. But would she run back to Grosvenor Square and raise the alarm? She felt a flicker of hope. Then she realized that nobody knew where she was.

CHAPTER THIRTY-TWO

Kitty shifted in her corner of the carriage. She was cold, tired and her headache was severe. The nausea had faded but she knew she was very weak. She spotted a light-coloured object on the floor of the carriage. After staring at it for a while, she picked it up. It was her new bonnet, squashed and stained with blood. She held on to it. Her eyes smarted with unshed tears. It was just another symbol of how she had ruined her day and with it, her aunt's peace of mind.

She closed her eyes again, struggling to think of some way of escaping. Perhaps there would be a chance when they stopped at an inn to change the horses. Meanwhile, if she pretended to be asleep, perhaps Etienne would leave her alone. Kitty could still feel the pressure of his fingers on her chin. He was in a dangerous mood.

At last the horses slowed and they came to a halt. Kitty opened her eyes slightly, hoping to see lights and people around. She was dismayed to find that they were still in darkness. She heard the driver climb down. The door opened and a bulky shape appeared, holding up a lantern. Kitty clutched at her throat as she recognized the red-haired Irishman.

He cast a glance at her but addressed himself to Etienne. 'This is the best place for the job.'

Etienne nodded. 'Get me some rope,' he ordered. While this was being done, he picked up the bundle that had served Kitty as a cushion. She realized it was his greatcoat. He pulled it on. The Irishman reappeared, holding out a piece of cord in his ham-like fist. Etienne took it.

'Hold her hands.'

'No! How dare you!' she panted, but it was useless to struggle. Between them, they soon tied her hands together.

'I cannot allow you to run off,' Etienne told her, 'you are my guarantee.'

She cast him a look of scorn.

Grim as he was, a smile lightened his face for an instant. 'Oh, those magnificent eyes,' he murmured.

She struggled but could not loosen the bonds. They lifted her bodily down from the coach. She found herself at the side of a road in the bottom of a valley. There were mighty trees arching up overhead. The road curved away before them. The Irishman led the horses a little further, until they had vanished round the next bend.

'O'Reilly, do not go too far,' warned Etienne. The only answer was a growl but the sound of wheels and horses' hoofs stopped. Etienne put an arm round Kitty's waist and half pushed, half lifted her into the verge, behind a large tree. Then he turned his back on her and began pulling something out of a small bag he had brought from the coach.

Kitty looked about her for any sign of life. There were no lights nor any houses. Behind the trees bordering the road she could make out thicker patches of woodland. It all seemed dark and deserted. There was nowhere she could run to. She clenched her teeth firmly to stop them chattering.

She turned to see Etienne holding a pistol. In the faint glimmer of starlight, his face was all hard lines and angles. This was a very different creature from the society darling she had known so far. What would her aunt think of him now? At the idea of her aunt, a wave of fear swept over Kitty. Perhaps she would never see Aunt Picton again. What exactly did Etienne plan to do with her?

As if he had read her thoughts, he turned to look at her. 'You must stay by me and whatever happens, keep silent. If you try to warn anyone, I will shoot to kill. You understand?'

Kitty nodded reluctantly. She was shivering and not just

194

from fear and weariness. Her city clothes were not thick enough for this cold open place. It was difficult to stand up for so long. Her head was heavy and sore. For what seemed an age they stood and waited. Then her ears picked up a faint sound. It came nearer and louder. It was definitely the sound of horses trotting.

Two horses, thought Kitty. She sensed Etienne move slightly. He held up a warning finger to her. He moved out into the centre of the path. The horses came nearer and slowed as they realized there was somebody in front of them.

'Who goes there?'

Surely, that was Greg's voice! Kitty felt a glimmer of hope. She opened her mouth to call for help but remembered Etienne's threat. The riders had slowed to a walking pace now.

'That is enough. Stop there. I have you covered.'

'Saint-Aubin? What the devil—?' That was Theo's deep voice. Kitty drew in a thankful breath. But would Etienne shoot to kill, as he had threatened? Her heart was pounding. She strugged again with the bonds but they were too tight to shift.

Etienne pointed his pistol at Greg. 'You are going to give me those letters you are carrying.'

'The hell I am! You have missed your bet.'

'I think not,' replied the Frenchman through clenched teeth. He reached out his free arm and pulled Kitty forward.

The two riders halted.

'You cur!' Theo's voice cut like a knife. He made as if to dismount.

'One more move and I will shoot her.'

'You cannot win,' protested Greg. 'There are two of us.'

'But I will shoot off her finger.'

They glanced at each other. 'What do you want?' asked Greg.

Etienne gave a bark of laughter. 'The letters.'

Kitty watched, appalled as, very slowly, Greg unbuckled a leather satchel fastened to the saddle in front of him. If she had not run away from Lady Payne at the art exhibition, if she

195

had not gone again into the Rookery, Greg would not have to lose the result of so much hard work. She shifted slightly.

'Be still!' ordered Etienne sharply. He kept his eyes on Greg. 'Now throw the bag down in front of me,' ordered Etienne.

Greg flung it towards him. Etienne went down on one knee to pick it up. As he reached for it, Kitty flung herself upon him, knocking him off balance. He rolled sideways and the gun went off. He shouted.

It felt as if a hot wire had gone through her shoulder. Kitty screamed in agony and dropped like a stone.

The last thing she heard was Theo's voice in a frantic roar: 'No!'

When Theo made out the figure on the road ahead of them, he was not unduly surprised. The whole business of getting these letters had been highly dangerous from first to last. Undoubtedly, some politicians would try anything up to the last minute to stop Wellington from continuing the campaign in Portugal. That was why he was accompanying Greg on his way down to Portsmouth to board the naval frigate for the return journey to Lisbon. This was also why they were travelling under cover of darkness. They knew the roads well, after all it was in the area of Greg's family home.

Theo discreetly pulled the pistol out of his belt. He would wait to see what the fellow demanded before shooting the villain. Beside him, Greg was swearing under his breath. They slowed their horses to a walk. At Etienne's challenge, Theo's hand moved ready to whip out his gun. Damn it, why had he deloped at the duel last week? Even if he had given the Frenchman a small wound, it would have saved them this unpleasant incident now.

Then, to Theo's horror, he saw Etienne drag Kitty forward. She had her hands tied. A black rage rushed through him. 'You cur!' he exclaimed, in the act of dismounting to help her.

But the villain was threatening to maim her if they did not obey his order. Theo sat taut as a wire, fists clenched hard, trying to see if Kitty had been harmed. Beside him, Greg slowly unbuckled the dispatch case and flung it down in the road. They watched Etienne pounce on it. At the same moment, Kitty flung herself against the Frenchman. He was caught off balance and fell. At that second his pistol went off.

Theo heard the Frenchman shout. He heard and felt Kitty scream. Even as her cry of agony echoed round the little valley, Theo was leaping from his saddle. 'No!' He was not aware he was shouting something. He rushed forward. Three strides brought him to Kitty's side. Etienne was struggling to his feet. Unthinking, Theo aimed a couple of punches, sending the Frenchman flying into the bushes at the side of the road. Then he spun round to kneel over Kitty.

She was lying in a heap, face down. He gently turned her over. His hand came away soaked with blood.

'Oh no,' he groaned, 'oh God—' He examined her more carefully, untying her hands as he did so. Then he spotted a growing dark stain on the right shoulder of her dress. Without hesitating, he ripped the bodice of her robe open to lay bare the wound. Gently, he felt the damaged flesh. It seemed too high to have penetrated the lung. Theo pressed his hand over the hole but the blood was still flowing through his fingers. He ripped a piece of her petticoat to make a pad.

'Greg! Brandy, man. Quick!'

Greg had dismounted. He held out his pocket flask. Theo tipped some brandy on the open wound, then bound it up as best he could. His hands were not quite steady.

'Oh, Kitty, my darling,' he whispered, looking at her still face in the moonlight. He wiped his bloodstained hands on the grass of the verge and began to chafe her cold hands.

From the bend in the road came a small sound. A shadow moved. Greg raised his own pistol.

'Come out,' he said in a firm voice. 'I have you covered.'

For answer there was a click and a half-hearted report. The blunderbuss had misfired. There was no effect other than the sound of horses neighing in alarm and pulling against the brakes of a carriage. They heard a clatter as the unseen person threw the weapon down. Then heavy footsteps, running away. Greg darted to the corner and saw the shape of a big man disappearing down the road. He discovered the coach and searched it for more men or weapons. Then he turned his attention to Etienne, who was lying just where Theo's punch had knocked him.

When he returned, Theo had wrapped Kitty in his great-coat and was attempting to get a little brandy into her mouth, by repeatedly dipping his handkerchief into the flask and then squeezing the couple of drops inside her lips.

'She is alive – nasty wound, but too high to have touched her lung,' said Theo, still concentrating on his task. 'She is as cold as ice, though. Give me your coat, old man.' He wrapped her in the second driving coat and huddled her in his arms. He looked up at Greg in appeal. 'Got to get her to shelter quickly. She has gone into shock.'

CHAPTER THIRTY-THREE

They carefully lifted Kitty into the coach. Theo would not leave her and it fell to Greg to bundle the dazed Etienne on to the outside box seat, next to himself. He attached their two horses at the back of the carriage and set off towards the nearest shelter.

Inside the coach, Theo cradled Kitty in his arms. She lay limp as a toy, her uninjured arm sliding down to dangle as the coach swayed. Theo muttered a curse. This jolting could open the wound again and she was too weak to lose any more blood. He held her close, checking again to see if she was any warmer.

How ironic that it had taken such an event for him to get her in his arms. Why the deuce had he been so slow in wooing her? He heaved a sigh. He knew the answer to that. It involved giving in to emotions that he had tried to avoid for so many years. His jaw clenched. If you felt deeply about someone you got hurt when you lost them. That was a lesson he had learnt early in life. It was easier to live on the surface and keep dealings with other people free of any deep ties.

He looked down at the still form in his arms. Somehow, she had slipped through all his defences. And it was just as he had expected. He was racked by anguish that just when he realized he could not live without her, it was perhaps already too late and he had lost her. Why had he let his temper get the better of him at Caroline's ball? After dancing with her he had been on the point of admitting how much he loved her when that damned Frenchman interrupted them. Then when he found her in Saint-Aubin's arms, being kissed, he felt betrayed. Somehow he had held his temper in check but only by keeping his distance from her.

He examined her face. It was such a perfect oval. Her eyes were closed but even without their glory he could never tire of gazing at her lovely features.

'For the Lord's sake, hurry, Greg, will you?' he muttered. 'Find a house quickly.' He felt her face and hands again. Still icy. He smoothed back her curls and gently rubbed at her cheeks. There was blood smeared everywhere. He had even got it around her mouth – must have been when he gave her the brandy.

The coach jogged along, the horses were weary and the night was growing old. He felt the coach turn at a sharp angle. There was the sound of wheels crunching on gravel.

'Just turning into the drive,' Greg called down. 'Nearly there, old fellow.'

Theo did not reply. He was cradling his precious burden. She should have shown some sign of life by now. There was a pricking in his eyes. His heart seemed to contract. He could not bear to lose her. He bent his head and kissed her cold forehead, her cheeks and then, drawn irresistibly, her lips. He kept his kiss very gentle, remembering with a pang how she had kissed him back on the one occasion he had managed to kiss her properly.

He ran his finger over those lips that had attracted him from the first time he ever saw her. Suddenly, his eyes sharpened. Her eyelids were fluttering. She blinked up at him. He could see her returning from far away.

'Theo. . . ?' Her voice was a thread of sound.

'Do not talk, Kitty. You are very weak.'

'I-I thought. . . .' She gave a little sigh. Her hand reached up towards his face but fell back and dangled helplessly once more. Her eyes closed again.

The coach stopped.

*

There was a tall figure standing against the window. The sunlight behind the person made it hard for Kitty to see who was there. She blinked, frowning slightly at the effort and closed her eyes again. Her shoulder hurt and she could not turn her head. She was aware of a hand on her brow, a deep voice whispering her name. It seemed to her that someone planted a kiss on her forehead, then she sank back into sleep.

She was roused from her dreams by a stabbing pain in her shoulder that went on and on. Her head was sweating, someone was wiping her face with a wet cloth but the pain was too much to bear. She wanted to tell them to stop but she could not get the words out. Exhausted, she slipped away into a faint.

The next time Kitty awoke, she saw Martha, seated by the bed.

'Oh, miss, thanks be to 'Eaven!' whispered Martha. 'We were that frightened for yer. . . .' She wiped her eyes.

Kitty stared round at the unfamiliar room. 'Where am I?' It was an effort to get the words out.

'I will tell you all about things, miss, but first, you must 'ave summat to eat. Doctor says so,' she added firmly, as Kitty frowned in distaste.

As she was feeding Kitty a weak broth, Martha smiled at last. 'Oh, miss, when they chased after you in St Giles, I never thought to see you again. That big feller, 'e took you away wrapped in a cloth. I couldn't do nothing. I followed 'im for a bit but the other man chased me off. I ran 'ome to Lady Picton. She was in such a taking as never was! The whole household was up all night.'

'When was this?' Kitty felt too weak to make much sense of the impressions lurking in her mind.

'Why, 'tis nigh on a week now. We received a message from them two gentlemen, Mr Thatcham and Mr Weston like, to say you were 'ere. . . .'

'Where?'

'This 'ouse belongs to Mr Thatcham's grandmother. I dunno rightly where it is. I come in a carriage,' explained Martha,

201

her eyes round with awe. 'Them two gentlemen were looking after you – well, the one as is sweet on you, Mr Weston like, 'e was in such a state, miss. What with 'im being wounded in the war, 'e was afraid you would get a fever from the bullet.' She scraped the last of the soup on to the spoon and put it to Kitty's lips. ' 'E kept fussing the doctor to do everything to be sure you was going to get better.'

Kitty put up a hand to her bandaged shoulder. 'It is certainly very sore. I can remember most things now.' Etienne's face, grim and desperate, the confrontation with Theo and Greg and her determination not to let those precious letters fall into the wrong hands. She shut her eyes, overcome by horror at the whole tragic story. Tears would force themselves through her tightly closed eyelids. After a while, she opened her eyes again and found Martha still waiting patiently.

'You are too weak yet. Time to rest again,' said the maid. 'Doctor said to give you this.' She held out a glass half full of a dark potion.

Kitty felt she had too many sorrows to ever sleep again but somehow everything was fading away. The laudanum soon did its work, but it was a troubled slumber and she woke little refreshed. She felt stronger, however, and more anxious to get the full story of her adventure.

Over the next week as she gained strength, Kitty learnt from Martha that there were just two elderly servants left in the house while Lady Deane was in London. Theo had nursed her until Martha had arrived, after which the two young men had departed in haste, nobody seemed to know where.

'Doctor says that Mr Weston saved you from bleeding to death – poured brandy on the wound, 'e did,' said Martha with relish.

'Oh!' Kitty put up her good hand to feel the poor shoulder. 'But that means he must have pulled my dress down. . . .' She bit her lip.

'Ripped it open,' nodded Martha with a giggle. Then she shook her head. 'Your best jaconet muslin – but it's no good for nothin' now, it's all stained and torn. His clothes were in a mess an' all. Covered in blood, 'e was. We did what we could to smarten 'im up. Well, I mean to say, 'e saved your life.'

Kitty stared out of the window at the puffy white clouds racing across a pale-blue sky. Her lips tingled at the memory of Theo's kiss. She could still hear his voice urging her to hang on. But if he really loved her, surely he would still be here. She waved away the dish of fruit that Martha was offering her.

It occurred to Kitty that Martha was looking extremely cheerful. Her usually pale face was rosy and her grey eyes were sparkling.

'Are you going to tell me now why you look as if you had lost a penny and then found a shilling?' she asked, while the maid was carefully brushing her hair. 'Mind my bruise,' added Kitty hastily.

'Yes, miss. 'Tis not near so bad as it was and your hair is clean and free of tangles now.'

'Thank you. But I am still waiting for your story. . . .'

'Well, I'm not s'posed to say anything yet. An' it fair beats me how you can tell, miss. But I do feel as if my worries are over.' She brushed soothingly for a while.

'Well?'

'Mr Weston made me tell 'im about where you got kidnapped. Then he asked me about my father, bein' in the army an' all. And I told him about little Sam an' how you saved 'im' – she wiped her sleeve across her eyes – 'an' he said – he will soon be married an' he'll need more staff. He reckons he can find a cottage for me an' my family an' the boys can help in the stables. So you see, miss.' Her voice cracked. She gave a sobbing little laugh.

Kitty felt her limbs slowly turn to stone. Her tongue stuck to the roof of her mouth. Theo was going to be married. Countess Payne had somehow succeeded in organizing the match of her dreams for her plain and spiteful daughter. Kitty found her fingers had curved into claws and hastily straightened them. She realized that Martha was waiting for some reply and made a supreme effort.

'How wonderful for you, Martha. You will all benefit from such a change.'

'Do you want to rest now?' asked Martha, eyeing her anxiously. 'You do look white again, miss.'

It was not a rest. When Martha had gone, Kitty remained frozen, staring unseeing at the wall. So nothing had changed. Theo did not want to marry her – or he did not want it enough. Perhaps he was angry at her refusal to listen to his advice. By persisting in her visits to the St Giles Rookery, she had put herself in danger and nearly caused the ruin of Greg's mission. In short, she had only herself to blame. This awful feeling of misery was so much more painful than the gunshot wound. And it would never leave her.

CHAPTER THIRTY-FOUR

It was getting dark when Theo walked into White's Club. He had left Nimrod to the care of his groom and now, arrayed correctly in a dark-blue jacket, dove grey breeches and a fresh cravat, he was ready for a good dinner and a chance to find out the news. He made his way upstairs to the dining-room.

While tucking into a hearty meal, he glanced around the room. There was nobody he particularly knew in there at present. That suited him well. After the adventures of the past couple of weeks, he was glad just to have time to recover this evening. He was rounding off his dinner with some cheese when a familiar voice caught his attention. Looking up, he saw Lord William Bannister, entering the room with a group of friends.

When he noticed Theo, he excused himself and came over. His good-natured face beamed a greeting. 'Where have you sprung from? Where is Greg?'

Theo shook hands warmly. 'Greg is on HMS *Endymion*, on his way back to Lisbon.' He rolled his eyes. 'And thank God for that.'

William laughed. 'Was he such a difficult charge to care for?'

Theo poured some wine for them both. 'William, you know you blurt everything out without thinking. But – yes, it was hard. I am heartily thankful he is now away from all those who did their damnedest to sabotage his mission.' He shook his head and looked at his friend with feeling.

'Discreet or not, I must hear about all this,' exclaimed William. 'However, I am engaged with Huntington and his party. Will you wait for me later?'

Theo nodded. 'You will find me downstairs. I intend to see what is in the newspapers.'

It was considerably later that William appeared in the library. 'What, still hard at work?' he exclaimed. 'How glad I am that I never went for a soldier.' He settled himself at the little table and accepted the glass of port that Theo offered him. 'Have you discovered what you wanted to know?'

Theo pushed aside the clutter of newspapers and slipped a notebook into his pocket. 'There is precious little mention of Wellington's campaign. But yes, now I am up to date on the political news.'

William sipped his port. 'But not up to date on the latest gossip in town.'

Theo's brows snapped down. 'Do you mean I figure in that?' When his friend nodded, Theo groaned. 'Tell me the worst. . . .'

William shook his head. 'You never heard such faradiddles. It was noticed that you and Saint-Aubin did not part on good terms at our ball – then you both vanish. That started a frenzy of rumours.'

Theo stared very hard at him from under lowered brows. William stared back. 'Oh no! Swear to you I never said a word about the duel.'

Theo nodded. 'Very well. But there is more, I can see.'

William cast a glance around. They were in a quiet corner of the large room and the noise of other conversations provided some cover. However, he leaned closer and dropped his voice. 'Greg's absence has also been remarked on. But what really spiced up the rumours was when Kitty also mysteriously disappeared – vanished from an Art exhibition at the Royal Academy and never reached home. Everyone is agog to know which one of you she has run off with.' He laughed as Theo dug both hands into his hair and raked his fingers through it.

'Oh Lord!' Theo groaned. 'Just when we needed to pass without being noticed.'

'Well, you cannot expect creatures like that Harling girl to let such juicy items go without comment. She was the one who started the elopement story.' He grinned sympathetically at Theo, who was staring at him, lost for words. 'Caroline has done what she can to stop the excitement. She gave it out that Kitty became ill and has gone out of town until she is well again.'

At the mention of Kitty, Theo found his tongue. 'What is the latest news of her?'

William gave him a speculative glance. 'She is back with her aunt, I believe. Think Caroline went to visit today.'

Theo nodded. He frowned as he turned his wineglass between his long fingers. His cousin, Tom Bingham, had warned him earlier that evening that there must be no admission of any spying or incidents, that Kitty's wound must be kept secret. The Prime Minister, who supported Wellington, did not want any hint of the matter to reach Lord Dalbeagh. The longer they could keep him uncertain, the more time there would be to get the funds ready to send out to Wellington.

But it seemed there was going to be a lot of disagreeable gossip to live down. He felt certain that Kitty would react rather badly to that. She was so forthright. He must see her. He wanted to see her. At the very idea, his expression lightened. He looked up to find William watching him with a twinkle in his eyes.

'This is going to be hard,' Theo said, 'good job you warned me.'

William savoured his port before saying, 'Oh, you will manage. I shall enjoy watching you. For once you will have to try being pleasant to one and all – although that might make them suspicious,' he added with a laugh.

'I wish I could share your amusement,' snapped Theo.

'You will not have to suffer for long, old man. Once Saint-Aubin gets back and starts charming the ladies again, I dare say they will be so busy with him they will forget all about this little mystery.'

Theo shook his head. 'He is not coming back. After what he did. . . .' He pointed a warning finger at William. 'Just see you do keep this to yourself.' He quickly gave an account of Etienne's activities. 'We handed him over to Intelligence at Horseguards for interrogation. My cousin informs me that he sang like a bird in exchange for a passport to leave the country.'

William thumped the table. 'Devil take it, he was a French spy—'

'No, just penniless. He was being blackmailed.'

They sat in silence for a while, thinking over the events of the past weeks. When he came to consider Kitty's situation, Theo found himself strangely uncertain. How would she react to finding herself the subject of malicious speculation, especially when she could not give the true reason for her injury and her absence from town? His lips curved into a smile. One thing he felt sure of – she would want to fight her own battle.

'So, with Saint-Aubin gone for good and Greg on his way to Portugal, that leaves only you.' William was watching him curiously. 'Do not try to palm me off with some tale or other. I have known you too long, old man! Trust me, I know the signs. You have fallen for her in a big way.'

Theo shook his head. 'You are going too fast. You should not expect Kitty to accept an offer from me as a way out of her difficulties. She is more likely to insist on outfacing the scandalmongers on her own.'

Nevertheless, the following morning, Theo took great pains with his appearance before setting off to Lady Picton's huge house in Grosvenor Square. He gave the impression of an elegant young man out for a stroll. But under his casual front, his heart was beating so fast he felt breathless. He needed all his self-control when Lady Picton's butler informed him that her ladyship was not receiving visitors.

'It is a very urgent matter,' stated Theo. 'If her ladyship is indisposed, I would be more than happy to explain it to her niece.'

Broome stared into the middle distance and announced, 'I regret that Miss Kitty is not able to receive visitors at present, sir.'

Theo glared at him in mounting frustration. If only Kitty were not the subject of scandalous gossip, he would push past and find the ladies for himself. But as it was, the last thing she needed was for him to create more gossip with a tale of men chasing her even into her home.

He directed a thunderous glare at Broome, who continued to stand impassively in the doorway. Biting back a curse, Theo turned on his heel. He struggled with a suddenly raging temper as he strode across the square. But by the time he rounded the corner into Bond Street, he had remembered his cousin's warning and managed to school his face into a bland mask.

Etienne de Saint-Aubin was not the only agent working for Lord Dalbeagh and his cronies. Theo knew he must appear to follow his usual pursuits and act normally. He would certainly be under suspicion because of his friendship with Greg. How much easier it would all be, thought Theo grimly, if he could just be certain that Kitty was getting better.

He grimaced, remembering when the doctor had removed that damned bullet. She had suffered terribly and he had felt powerless to help, even though he did the practical things like sponging her head and holding her still for the doctor to extract the lead ball. Then Martha had arrived and he and Greg set off again to get down to Portsmouth. Indeed, they were in such haste to reach Portsmouth before Greg's boat set sail that they could not wait to see how Kitty recovered. The last time he had seen her, she was still unconscious, her face as white as the sheets on her bed.

'Why, Theo Weston! What an age since we saw you in town. But you are alone. . . ?'

Theo looked up and found himself face to face with Miss

Harling and her companion. Rousing from his thoughts, he touched his hat. 'Good day to you, ma'am.' He made to carry on along the street but Miss Harling put out a hand to stop him.

'It is also a long time since we have seen Miss Towers. We are wondering what has befallen her.'

Theo looked down his nose. 'I could not possibly say.'

'But you have just come from Grosvenor Square,' purred Miss Harling, her eyes alight with malice. 'There does appear to be some mystery about her disappearance.'

'If you say so,' snapped Theo. 'It is no concern of mine, but you will no doubt discover the truth from herself. Pray excuse me, ma'am, I have an urgent appointment.' He crossed the street and plunged into the alleyway. Damn all gossips! If Kitty knew anything about this, she would insist on keeping him at a distance, just to prove her independence. Theo sensed he needed an urgent outlet for his unruly temper. With a curse, he turned about and made for Jackson's Boxing Saloon.

CHAPTER THIRTY-FIVE

'Do you not need a sling to hold your arm still?' asked Amelia. She and Kitty were pacing slowly round Grosvenor Square in the afternoon sunshine.

'My arm is quite comfortable so long as I move it gently,' replied Kitty. 'You do not expect me to come out looking a figure of fun, do you? And besides, we must not let anyone know that it is a gunshot wound. I have sprained my arm falling from a carriage – and had a chill as well.'

'Certainly, anyone would believe that – you look so thin and pale, Kitty. But I would say it comes more from a lack of spirits than from physical ill health.' Amelia looked at her carefully.

'It has been a difficult time,' began Kitty, knowing she could not explain that her heart was broken and life seemed to stretch ahead like a dreary desert. 'My aunt is still recovering from the worry over my disappearance and from the shock of Etienne's behaviour. He was a great favourite of hers.' She paused, swallowing back the tide of anger at how Etienne had used her aunt to get close to herself.

They paced on for a while. At length Kitty was able to control her voice enough to continue, 'She has received a letter from him to tell her he has gone to look for his sister. As she lives in Moscow, that is a way of saying that he will not be reappearing in London – for which I am heartily thankful.'

'So am I,' agreed Amelia, 'His behaviour has been so very shocking. It must be very painful to realize how you were deceived in him.' She glanced at Kitty. 'I cannot imagine how you must have felt when you came round in the coach and discovered that he had kidnapped you. It is wonderful you were rescued so quickly.'

They had reached a bench and both sat down. Kitty raised her head to look at the young leaves just unfurling on the branches. 'I find I am not so tired any more,' she said, 'tomorrow perhaps we could walk as far as Hookham's Library.'

When there was no reply to this, she leaned forward and looked curiously at her friend. 'Millie. . . ?'

Amelia stared at her out of wide, anxious eyes. 'I— if you wish it.'

'Why is there a problem?'

Amelia fidgeted with her reticule. 'Well, perhaps it is time to tell you the whole story. You see, Kitty, when you left the exhibition at the Royal Academy, Miss Walmseley understood you were feeling unwell. But you did not return home . . . and when there was no sign of you by the next day some of the more spiteful young ladies began setting it about that you had run off.' She eyed Kitty's face of disbelief and went on in a rush: 'It was unfortunate that three young men of our circle all disappeared at exactly that same time. So. . . .'

'Oh, what a silly tale!' Kitty went quite pink with anger. 'How can people be so foolish?' She shook her head. 'So, I am a figure of fun?' She jumped up, needing to move about. Amelia joined her as they set off around the square once more.

'I am afraid that it is more serious than that. Even though it is all untrue, some people may consider you to be compromised.'

'What?' Kitty almost shouted.

'Oh, do not allow it to upset you so. I wish I had not told you; no doubt it will all die down shortly.'

'You are saying society has condemned me through ill-informed gossip. So I am compromised! I must either hide away or be married to save my reputation! Hah!' Kitty almost choked with rage. This was the last straw. After being

212

kidnapped, fighting to save vital military secrets and being shot, she was to be condemned as a girl of no moral principles. They had almost reached the house before she could control her feelings enough to speak again.

'I am not going to be blamed for something I did not do,' she stated in a tight voice. 'And I can guess who is behind these foolish tales about me.' She glanced at Amelia, who was watching her with an expression of mingled alarm and admiration. 'Do you think we could go for a drive in the park tomorrow?'

'But of course. It is wonderful to have your company once more,' said Amelia.

It was past midnight and Kitty was still pacing her bedroom. After such unkind news, she found it impossible to subdue the anger she felt. As she had thought, society lived on gossip and shallow ideas. Why, if a quarter of what she had heard was to be believed, a great many ladies had dark secrets to conceal. It seemed that the only unforgivable sin was to do something that could not be hidden.

Kitty frowned. She would go about her usual daily activities and ignore those people who chose to condemn her. Indeed, it was her duty to act in such a way. She had worked it out for herself that Greg's business was too secret to be mentioned. Amelia had said that she looked pale and thin – well, that could be set down to a chill.

She paced across the room again, head down. In addition to all this, she had to bear the never-ending unhappiness of knowing she had lost Theo. Perhaps it would not seem so bad if he were marrying a girl she could respect and admire. But Letitia Payne was the very worst wife he could have.

Kitty rubbed her lips. She drew a trembling breath. Theo's face came to mind, the way those bright blue eyes had smiled at her at the ball. If only he had not turned so cold afterwards.

Her memory of the shooting was hazy but she could remember how Theo had cradled her in his arms and encouraged her to hang on. He had kissed her as well. She could remember that perfectly well. And now he was avoiding her. They could only be strangers from now on. A tear slid down her cheek.

CHAPTER THIRTY-SIX

Kitty surveyed her appearance in the mirror. Somehow, her eyes appeared rather larger than they used to. Perhaps her face was indeed thinner, as Amelia had said. It was definitely still pale. Otherwise, thanks to Martha's help, she was looking fashionable with her hair swept up and little tendrils carefully arranged around her cheeks and behind her ears. Martha clasped the pearl necklet round Kitty's throat.

'There, miss, you do look fine.' She smiled at Kitty in the mirror. Kitty considered the smart dress of sprigged muslin. The soft pink material gave her a little colour and set off her chestnut hair beautifully. She put her chin up.

'This time I am using my appearance as a weapon,' she said.

She shook her head when Martha offered her the sling. 'My shoulder is better now. In any case, I shall not need to move my arm very much.'

'Where is your sling?' In the drawing-room Great-Aunt Picton inspected Kitty.

'I really do not need it any more,' said Kitty, trying to smile at the old lady. 'Besides, it would ruin the appearance of this lovely dress Miss Dilworth has made.'

Lady Picton nodded. 'It is charming, I agree. That light pink is exactly the right colour for you. But I do think, my dear, that you have grown thinner, even since you returned to me. Are you sure you feel well enough for this outing?'

'Indeed, ma'am. With such a close friend as Amelia, I can

be at ease – and you may be sure she will look after me.' Kitty made a little business of pulling on her pelisse and adjusting her bonnet. It is time I showed my face again or people will be thinking I have left Town. Now, where did I put my parasol? Oh, there it is.' She went over to the side table near the door to pick it up.

Lady Picton still sounded anxious. 'Very well, dear child. But do not stay out too long. I could wish you looked more robust. What your dear mother would say if she could see you, I dread to think.'

Every step downstairs and out to the waiting carriage was more difficult than the last one. Several times, Kitty was tempted to give up. However, she kept reminding herself that she had nothing to be ashamed of. If people were going to point at her or ignore her, she would simply pretend not to see them. Amelia would not abandon her.

At that thought, she suddenly realized that Millie might well be as heartsore as she was herself. They had not discussed anything but Kitty's adventures and recovery so far. She promised herself to see what she could do to cheer Millie up. She managed a smile for Broome, holding the door open for her. Then she halted in surprise. Freddy was waiting on the step. He laughed and offered his arm. Kitty took it gladly.

'How splendid,' she said warmly. 'I had no idea you were back.' As he helped her into the barouche she felt relief to know that she now had another friend to support her in this first outing. However much other people might shun her, she knew that Freddy and Amelia would remain loyal.

Freddy jumped in and took the seat opposite Kitty and Amelia. He smiled at Kitty, then his eyes turned to Amelia. Kitty saw the tender look they exchanged. Her eyes sharpened on them both.

'I do believe,' she said slowly, 'that you have something to tell me.'

They both looked embarrassed but then Freddy grinned. 'How quick you are, Kitty. Yes, we have settled it between us.'

He reached for Amelia's hand as he spoke.

'At last!' said Kitty, 'I almost despaired of ever seeing you reach this point. Oh, Millie, how wonderful.' She embraced them both, laughing with pleasure.

'Knew as soon as I reached home,' said Freddy. 'Shouldn't have left her. Told m'mother and set off back again.'

Kitty turned to Amelia. 'You said nothing of this when we were talking yesterday – you were your usual calm and composed self.'

Amelia blushed. 'This only happened last night.'

They were in such a state of happy excitement that they had nearly completed a full turn of Hyde Park before they stopped discussing the glad news and paused to look about them. Suddenly, Kitty's pleasure drained away. She was delighted for her two dear friends but their happiness only served to emphasize the stark contrast with her own situation. Where was Theo? Not that it mattered to her, she reminded herself yet again. He had accepted marriage with another. She would not demean herself by clinging to her belief that he loved her. It was over.

As if to rub salt in the wound, their carriage slowed down in the press of traffic alongside the barouche belonging to Lady Payne. Letitia noticed Kitty and whispered something to her mother. Both ladies stared for a moment, then turned their heads away. Kitty told herself she was being sensitive but she felt the snub keenly.

Just then Freddy raised his quizzing glass. 'Hate to say it, Kitty' he said, 'but you are looking dashed peaky.'

'I think it is time to leave the park,' agreed Amelia.

Kitty did not have the strength to argue. She sat in silence, absorbed in her own thoughts. She was not going to be deterred by snubs but they did hurt. When the coach stopped she looked up and realized that they were not outside her aunt's house but in Cavendish Square, in front of Caroline's mansion. Before she could ask why, the other two were hurrying her down from the barouche, in through the door and across the entrance hall to the morning-room.

Caroline rose to greet them. 'Hello, Kitty. I am so glad you are well enough to join us at last. And of course,' she added with a laugh, 'you have heard our good news. We are all so happy.'

'Yes indeed. Just look at the difference in both of them. No more moping and not able to admit why.' With a valiant effort, Kitty smiled. 'I think Freddy and Millie are the only ones who feel any surprise.' She saw how Millie was glowing. While delighted for her friend, it made Kitty realize just how difficult the coming weeks and months were going to be for her.

Through the open door they heard the sound of voices in the entrance hall.

'Ah, that will be William.' Caroline moved towards the sound. She held out a hand to Kitty. 'Come with me, if you please.'

Mystified, Kitty followed her out of the room. She looked behind her but the other two made no move to follow.

Caroline pulled the door shut. She gave Kitty a conspiratorial smile. 'Well, they finally managed it. I could not be more pleased for them. But what about you, darling?' She guided Kitty over to an ornate mirror and turned her to look into it. 'I can see you are pining. You should not be so pale.'

Kitty stared back at Caroline's reflection. She drew a deep breath. 'Do you not know you are talking to a social outcast?' She could not keep the anger out of her voice. She clutched her reticule, feeling lonely and hurt.

Caroline gently turned her round and gave her a hard look. 'Oh, don't be ridiculous, Kitty. That is all fustian, dreamed up by a couple of jealous cats. Besides, when did you ever care about gossip?'

Kitty blinked hard. 'You are right. It is just that. . . .' She heaved a sigh, biting back the urge to mention Theo. 'Dear Caro, always sorting out our problems, just like when we were naughty children.'

'Sometimes,' remarked Caroline with asperity, 'I wonder what has changed.'

Kitty was saved from replying by the arrival of William. He beamed at them both. 'Good news, eh?' he remarked to Kitty, nodding towards the morning-room. He gave a wicked smile. 'We will allow them a few minutes' peace. I shall be in the library. I will rejoin you all shortly.' He disappeared into his book-room.

Caroline slipped an arm through Kitty's and walked with her towards the back of the vast house.

'We shall have to set about arranging a splendid ball for the new young couple, just as soon as my mother can reach us.' She chattered on, leading Kitty through the ballroom and along another wide passage.

Puzzled, Kitty walked with her. She supposed they were simply giving Freddy and Amelia a little time to themselves. At the entrance to the conservatory Caroline stopped. She withdrew her arm.

'You walk around in here for a little while, darling. I have just remembered something. I need to consult William about our visit to the opera tomorrow. I will not be long.'

What was going on? Kitty, still feeling miserable and sad, wondered if she was being deliberately left out of some family consultation. She could not possibly be bothered to look at the plants. She sighed. It was beginning to sink in that she would not be as close to Millie in the future. She put her hand against the trunk of a large potted palm. It's rough texture felt appropriate for her current state of mind.

Giving herself a mental shake, she took a few steps forward towards where the late afternoon sunshine shone through some delicate ferns.

It was at that point that she realized she was not alone.

CHAPTER THIRTY-SEVEN

A tall figure moved towards her.

Kitty caught her breath in a gasp. 'W-what are you doing here?'

Theo halted, as if turned to stone. His eyes were fixed on her. His own face was pale and set.

Kitty felt the blood drain away from her cheeks. Suddenly Theo was right in front of her. He put out his arms to clasp her round the waist. She murmured a protest and tried feebly to push him away.

'You look as if you might faint,' he protested, continuing to hold her gently against him.

'It was only the shock. I did not know you were in London.' Now she was in his arms she could not resist the pleasure of remaining there. Just this one last time, just for a moment, she was going to enjoy the strength of his tall, muscular body. Her head whirled and she rested it against his broad shoulder. It felt good to be so close to him, breathing in that smell of fresh linen and a hint of lemon cologne, together with the scent of Theo himself. She shut her eyes. It was a smell she would always remember, familiar from the time after she was wounded and he had held her in his arms in the carriage.

It reminded her of something she had to say to him. 'I wanted to thank you,' she mumbled into his coat front, 'for saving my life. Martha told me how you—'

He dropped his arms. 'Please do not thank me,' he interrupted, in a deep growl. 'Can you imagine how it felt to see you in the hands of that villain, to see you act so bravely and so foolishly. Oh Kitty!'

She took a step back. The potted palm was right behind her. She put an unsteady hand out to lean on it. Theo made as if to come close, but Kitty held up her other hand. He stilled, his eyes searching her face.

'Kitty—'

'Please,' she breathed, 'do not make this any harder than it already is.' Resolutely, she drew in a deep breath and raised her head to look directly at him. 'Just hear me out. You warned me about going into the Rookery. I was headstrong and I paid the price. And I bitterly regret bringing Mr Thatcham's mission so close to ruin. As for my injury' – she put up her good hand to rub the poor shoulder and blushed a little as she went on – 'it was your prompt actions that saved me from bleeding to death. I shall always be grateful to you. And you nursed me when you did not really have the time to stay.'

He was watching her with a twisted smile on his lips.

She cleared her throat and went on, 'So – so now I want to wish you every happiness in your future – life.' The last word came out in a whisper. She just could not say the word *marriage*. A tear slipped down her cheek and she turned her head away hastily.

Theo bent his head to study her face. His eyebrows met in a puzzled frown. Kitty stole a sideways glance at him from under her lashes. She wanted to imprint his features on her mind before she left him. She was finding it a torment to be in the same room, knowing that soon he was going to marry Letitia Payne, of all people.

She put up a hand to stifle the sob that would come out. The next instant, Theo's arms slipped round her. Struggle as she would, she could not break free. He turned her gently towards him. 'What is going on here?' he asked, coaxing her face against his shoulder. 'Hey, there is no reason to be so upset.'

Kitty felt him press his handkerchief into her hand. She

221

choked back her tears angrily. How could she make such a fool of herself? The trouble was, his voice and his actions told her he cared about her. That must be why he wanted to see her one last time as well. She gulped, sniffed back the tears and raised her head.

'I am sorry,' she said in a decidedly husky voice. 'It must be because I am still not quite well.' She edged back. Please just forget it. And now, sir, I will bid you farewell—'

'Oh no! Not after all the work I have had to get to see you. I must speak to you. Kitty, wait!' he exclaimed, as she continued to back away from him, shaking her head.

'You stubborn little—' He strode past her and held out both arms to block the way.

'Please, sir, let me pass.' She did not look up at his face. Those blue eyes would overcome her resolution.

Theo gave a strangled exclamation. 'If this is your idea of being independent.'

At that, she did glance up. He was looking furious now. How could he be so domineering? It seemed that they were going to finish on another quarrel! Her heart was thumping uncomfortably. She swallowed hard and gave him a stern look. 'You know there is no other way. Not when you are going to be married to Miss Payne.'

Theo froze. His dark brows snapped down. 'Who told you that?'

'Well, you told Martha you would soon be married and – and I knew how much Lady Payne was trying to. . . .' She faltered to a stop.

Theo was grinning, his shoulders shaking. 'So that is why you are evading me. Miss Towers, I fear you have been listening to gossip again.'

Kitty stood rooted to the spot, her eyes fixed painfully on his. There was a lump in her chest that made it almost impossible to breathe.

Theo's gaze changed, became more intense. 'I thought' – he took a step towards her – 'that if we met in the conservatory' – his arms went round her and she was unable to resist – 'it would remind you of what you and I do in conservatories.' His hand feathered along her neck and gently tilted her chin up. He bent his head down towards her face. 'And I am afraid,' he murmured, 'that I cannot wait any longer to do it again.'

The next moment his lips met hers. Kitty surrendered to the growing passion in his kiss. Her good arm slid up around Theo's neck. The other hand clutched at his jacket. Theo gave a little groan of pleasure. He dug a hand into her hair, urging her closer still. When he finally broke the kiss, Kitty blinked at him, dazed and panting. Her legs were trembling and she clung to him for support. He kept one arm firmly round her waist, with the other hand he traced her lips. A satisfied smile came over his face.

Slowly, realization dawned. Kitty gave a horrified exclamation. 'But your bride. . . !' She scrambled back, out of his embrace.

Theo raised his dark brows. The dimple showed in his cheek. His blue eyes glinted at her. 'Just listen to me, Kitty, please. When I first met you – in that stable in the snow, I was running away from my father and his plan to marry me to Miss Payne. Yes, I know I was rude and surly. I was still furious at his plotting and I was feeling wary of all females.' He moved closer and this time, she stayed put. He reached out and grasped her hands. 'but I still noticed that you were pretty – and spirited.' He slipped an arm round her shoulders again. 'I even told Nimrod – and he agreed with me.'

At this Kitty gave a gurgle of laughter. Theo cut it short with a swift kiss. He gave her one of his considering looks. 'So can you feel easy at receiving my advances now?'

Kitty shook her head.

His expression became more serious but his eyes still sparkled at her. 'Why not?' His voice was a low rumble and sent a tremor down her spine.

She retreated a couple of steps. 'Because society has decided I am compromised. There is no way I will give in to such pressure.'

Theo slanted her a look. 'You really must stop listening to gossip. How am I to be saved from Miss Payne's ambitions if you abandon me now?'

Kitty could not help laughing. Her heart seemed to swell with happiness. All the pain and loneliness of the last weeks melted away. She took a step towards Theo and caught her breath at the tenderness in his expression. He opened his arms to her and this time, she stepped into them.

He breathed in deeply. 'Mmm, roses.' He dropped a kiss on the top of her head. 'I love your curls,' he murmured, 'In fact, I love everything about you. You are a darling. I can think of nothing else but you. Marry me, Kitty, please.'

'You are not going to object to my work for the poor?'

His arms tightened around her. 'No indeed, how should I ? But no more going into the Rookery. There are plenty of other ways to help. You have not yet seen my hospice.'

'Well, with that inducement. . . .' She laughed at him and reached up her hand to stroke his lean cheek. 'Theo, I love you so much it hurts. I have been so unhappy. And now – I feel wonderful.'

There was a tinge of colour along Theo's cheekbones. 'I shall endeavour to make you feel even more wonderful very soon. But now, I think we had better go and put our friends out of their suspense.'

Kitty clutched his lapels. 'Yes, in a minute, but while we are here – in a conservatory – do you think we could have one more kiss?'